Tanya Ravenswater is
Jacques and the short
Fairy Tales for Grown-
award-winning poet. B
she now lives in Cheshire, UK.

Peninsula

Tanya Ravenswater

Tanya Ravenswater

Dalzell Press

First published in 2020 by Dalzell Press

Dalzell Press
54 Abbey Street
Bangor, N. Ireland BT20 4JB

ISBN 978-1-8380871-1-1

Cover painting © Jon Clayton

Supported by the National Lottery though the Arts
Council of Northern Ireland

LOTTERY FUNDED

For all my family.

To the people and places who give space to the soul.

Summer Shore, County Down

Her arm coaxing, welcoming
to her shoulder
of rock,
her
high
proud
forehead,
winkled, kelped,
brows ablaze with lichen,
hair dressed with barley, vetches,
crown afire with stonecrop diamonds.

Flexing backbone
her
embryo bays
and
humming pods
her
shingled womb.

Chapter One

Northern Ireland, June 2008.

Gillian

This time no one knows I'm here. This time will be different. Closer in some ways to how things once were. Me and this land. Enduring connection; bridge never broken.

'Whatever happens,' Dad used to tell me, his voice thick with emotion, 'whenever we've gone, you'll still have this place to come back to, won't you? You'll always belong to it and it to you. It'll remind you of who you are and of a few of the things that shaped you earlier on.'

In my mind's eye, first a map, basic as an X-ray, of that crooked forefinger, knuckle bare to the Irish Sea, the lough's palm protected behind it. Then the flesh of the place arriving, stirring the senses. On the outer front of the peninsula, exposed wind-brushed coast. Sandy bays. Jagged rock, diving cormorants. Numbingly cold, clear water. On the lough side, sheltered shallows simmering with life. Beached purple-brown jellyfish, ragged undersides up. Flat fish slipping under your feet. Birds calling incessantly. Scatterings of terns, oyster-catchers, redshanks, landing and feeding, then lifting again. Dried seaweed banked up against ochre-lichened rocks. Cushions of sea pinks. Bladder campion. Glasswort and sea purslane on the foreshore. I'd looked first for a cottage on the east side of the peninsula. I thought it might suit my purpose better somehow – the intense colours, choppy waves and sharp light. But I'd left the booking late. When I discovered there was a converted barn available on the lough side, I told myself I could easily cut across and travel down the other coast every day if I wanted to.

A few miles from Stewartsford, along the lough-side road, I take a left turn behind a spluttering tractor and follow it slowly down the narrow lane, looking for the second turning on the right. It's June, the hawthorn in dusty blossom, hedgerows overrun with rangy grasses, cow parsley lace and stitchwort stars. Everything feels drowsy, exhaling slow, warm breaths. At a skewed sign pointing to 'Lough-side Cottages', I steer down a narrow pot-holed track, shaded by over-arching ash trees. The ditches either side are deep, making the track like a kind of small causeway, leading from the road to a gravelled yard fronting a terrace of three white-washed stone cottages.

There's a silver Golf already parked outside the end cottage on the left. Mine is the cottage in the middle. Straight away, I feel irritated – for a moment it seems as if I'm being forced into something. But I tell myself that the presence of a stranger doesn't have to change anything. I'll be able to stay disconnected and fixed on my own plans. As I pull up, a man emerges from the door of my cottage. He lifts his long arm like an outsized windscreen wiper, waves in broad sweeps, then strides towards me, followed by a limping old sheepdog. It only has three legs. I assume the man must be the owner, Derek McEvoy, waiting to give me the keys. I open my window.

'Gillian Watson?' He's probably in his mid-fifties, wears kneed loose-fitting jeans and a blue and white checked shirt with rolled-up sleeves. His steep forehead is set in furrows, his weathered shiny scalp bald as a chestnut. We shake hands through the car window. He smells of machine oil. His palms are sand-paper rough, his grip almost too tight, but genuinely welcoming. I should get out of the car really, but I want to avoid getting caught up in prolonged conversation.

'Yes. Sorry. I'm a bit late. The ferry was delayed at Liverpool. I couldn't get hold of you on the phone.'

'Not to worry, Gillian! Derek McEvoy – pleased to meet you. Did you have a good crossing?'

'Not bad. I hope you've not been waiting too long?'

'Not at all. Just making sure everything's ready for you. The door's open. I've put the keys on the table. There's fresh milk in the fridge and some vegetables by the sink to keep you going. Want me to show you round and explain about the heating? There's full instructions in there, but I usually . . .'

'No, but thanks anyway. I'll be okay with the instructions. I probably won't have the heat on if the weather stays like this. Do you want the cheque now?'

'Och, no. Sure it'll do some time later on.' He looks uncomfortable, shuffles his feet on the gravel, grimaces slightly. I'm rushing him. He has his own unspoken rules of hospitality, including a sense of appropriateness about the timely receipt of a cheque. 'I just hope you'll be happy with the place. Where is it you're from over here again?'

'Used to live near Saintwood. I've still got two sisters there.'

'I thought that's what you'd said. Can't remember whether I'd mentioned it on the phone, but the man renting the cottage on the other side is over from England, like yourself. He lives near Manchester. You'll have something in common.'

'Yes, I suppose we will.' He's only being friendly, but I resent the implication that I'm expected to be sociable.

'It's the first time he's been here, from what I can gather. He's just taken himself off down the shore for a walk.' Derek pauses. He glances towards the drive and back at me again. 'Could be ex-army . . . or maybe *police*,' he then adds more quietly, in a confiding tone. It's a bit of a generalisation, but it's something that I both like and can find a bit wearing about a lot of Northern

12

Irish people. They're naturally curious and want to know all about you. It can feel intrusive, although usually it's less about prying than about the need for a new story and a real conversation. 'Could be wrong, like, but he looks the type. Big, well-built, strong-looking fella. Smart haircut, dark navy outdoor jacket. 'You can often tell, can't you?'

'You could be right.'

'So. What do *you* do for a living, Gillian?' he continues, barely pausing for breath. 'If you don't mind me asking?'

I don't want to get drawn in, but still feel guilty about being so aloof. 'I'm an artist. I work with stained glass.'

'Church windows and that kind of thing you mean?'

'Well, yes, I've done bits and pieces of restoration work. But mostly I do commissions for people – decorative windows and framed pieces for their own homes. Inspired by landscapes, particularly.'

'Plenty of ideas around here then! Is that what you've always done?' He's getting his story. In spite of my reticence, he's luring me out, wily as a snake-charmer.

'No. I went to art college in London originally.'

'Oh?'

'I designed wrapping paper and greeting cards. I only got into glass a couple of years ago.

My mother and father died. And I . . .' I never cry properly. It isn't a grief that flows. It's a stiff sharp mix of sadness and anger that stings your eyes and gives you the sensation of trying to swallow something sticking in your throat. 'My husband and I got divorced. I moved to Liverpool and set up my own studio.'

'Good on you.' Derek shuffles again on the gravel, looks at his feet and goes quiet for a moment. He then points over to the dog lying on the yard, nose and front paws arrowed towards me. 'Would you look at *that* now? You're already part of the flock.'

'She moves fast, doesn't she?' I'm grateful for the distraction. 'Especially considering she only has three legs. '

'She's a good wee dog. Very loyal. So . . . you've booked for two weeks, haven't you? Same as your neighbour.'

'Is that right? Well, I'll not keep you back, Derek.' I know it's too brusque, but I want to stop talking and get into the cottage. And I don't feel like thinking about the man next door.

'Well, if you're sure that there's nothing more I can do, Gillian. I'm always round the yard every morning anyhow. Or just follow that track on up to the farmhouse. You're always welcome to join us for a cup of tea. Bye for now, then.'

The cool stone-floor and emptiness of the kitchen makes me feel calmer. Derek's cardboard box of carrots, leeks and soily potatoes is on the work top beside the sink. There are jam jars full of wildflowers on the dining table and on the mantelpiece – dead nettles, forget-me-nots, buttercups. I pull off my shoes and socks and go upstairs to look at the bedroom and bathroom, both with views out across the farmyard and the surrounding gently undulating fields. The sandstone walls have been left exposed in places. I run my hand over the renovated old wooden beams.

I won't relax properly until I've unpacked the car. I dash to and from the boot with my head down, determined not to meet anyone. My bags need to go straight upstairs, my clothes into the wardrobe and drawers. I arrange my toiletries in the bathroom, then downstairs, I hang up my jacket and waterproof on the hooks by the door and set my maps and field guides in neat piles on the coffee table. I've become more neurotic since Mum and Dad died, trying to pretend perhaps that I can impose some order on life. Finally, I make tea in the glazed brown pot and sit at the kitchen table. A clock ticks softly on the wall behind me and I let my thoughts drift.

I'm used to my own company. Apart from brief meetings with customers to discuss details of commissions and payments, the occasional drink with a friend or exchange with another artist, I'm mostly alone. I have fleeting feelings of isolation, but as soon as I become absorbed in working on a piece of glass, everything else recedes into the far distance. While creatively demanding and technically exacting, it's a complete, emotionally simplified world that suits what my ex-husband Matt used to refer to as my 'obsessive, nit-picking personality'.

With his freckled skin and thick, fair eyelashes, Matt reminded me, I often joked, of a 'sunny bullock'. We met at a party in Manchester, after I'd moved up from London to start my second design job. He was smartly dressed, sociable, and worked in insurance. It's hard to believe that we were actually married for 15 years. We never really spent that much time under the same roof. After the first frantic years of our marriage, when we did our best to prioritise our relationship, we lapsed back into pursuing virtually independent lives. When Matt got a new job and worked increasingly away from Manchester, we stopped making time for holidays together and developed our own circles of friends. We each kept in contact with our families, also usually separately.

I still wonder how it might have been different if we'd had children. We did try for a few years before Matt suggested we should have some investigations. I was told that I had a degree of polycystic ovary disease. It wasn't impossible for me to get pregnant, but it could reduce my chances. The tests also revealed however, that Matt had a very low sperm count. He immediately pronounced that it was his 'fault' and fixated on the result as a mark of personal weakness – no matter how much I tried to persuade him that it didn't mean he was any less of a man. From then on, he often suggested that I would've been better off marrying someone else. Even though it had been his idea for us to have the investigations, he said that he found the thought of any kind of assisted conception 'humiliating'. It didn't appeal to me either. We didn't discuss the issue directly after that, but it hung heavily in the atmosphere between us.

We finally parted after my parents died. There was nothing particularly acrimonious about it. I'd obviously fallen out of love with him, he said. He'd never been 'deep enough' for me, he thought. He suggested that we separate, that I have the house and that he would move permanently down to London.

I didn't really blame Matt. I still don't. He needed someone more like himself and an ordinary, consistent boost to his self-esteem. A lot of it was my fault, or at least to do with my lack of motivation for working on our relationship. After Mum and Dad died, I lost my appetite for living. I was apathetic. Numb with grief. Nothing else seemed to matter that much. Nothing, but the mind-blowing loss of those crucial, steady people I'd loved all my life. My connection with Matt, which by this stage had become quite tenuous, seemed so insignificant and shallow in comparison. His attempts to comfort me, however well-intentioned, barely touched the surface of my distress.

'*My* parents are here, aren't they?' he'd kept telling me. 'They love you too, you know. They'd be happy to spend more time with you.'

'I know. It isn't any comment on them, but I'm not looking for substitutes! It isn't the same. No one can ever be the same as . . .'

'Though at least you still have your *sisters,* don't you? You can always visit *them!*'

'I know, Matt.' Matt didn't quite understand the way that I had come to feel about Claire and Laura either. He'd tried. He was able to see some of it, he said, but he thought that I should just try and forget the details, gloss over the difficulties. I only saw them occasionally, after all. It wasn't worth getting 'embroiled', as he put it.

When I'm not working, I find myself starting to fix on painful details of the past. It's as if they become the centre of a wheel. My mind quickly forms a circle of spokes, and turns round and round them. My stomach churns with the relentless movement. I'm determined not to let the thoughts get to me this time. I need to be outside and put myself in front of the things that have always kept me sane. Take my sketchbook, go down to the sea, do some drawings, collect some ideas.

I lock the cottage, drive back down the lane and return to the lough-side road. On the right, there's a small car park. I can stop there and get down onto the shore.

Chapter Two

Gillian

For a relatively quiet part of the world, this stretch of the lough-side road has always been fast and has had more than its fair share of accidents. It's narrow with blind bends. Risk-taking bikers and boy racers – 'morons and maniacs', as Dad used to call them – overtaking, pushing their speed, taking chances. I keep the windows down, air blowing through the car, so that I stay alert. It's a relief when I'm safely parked off the road.

It's nearly 4 p.m. Low water. I put on my sunglasses and take my sketchbook down to the edge of the shore, looking for a flat rock to sit on. There doesn't seem to be anyone else around. The brilliant summer light has softened now. The expanse of uncovered beach gleams like a wet pan of slowly drying cement, half-submerged shells and stones standing proud in the level of muddy sand. I make myself breathe slowly, taking in the unmistakeable, complex scent of the lough.

A peal of Dad's laughter rings through my mind, together with an image of him with a thick cheese and onion sandwich in his hand, made from the heels of a white loaf. Quickly followed by a memory of Mum, swimming far out at high tide, in her bubbled yellow 1970s bathing cap, while I lie on my stomach on the tartan picnic rug and Claire and Laura crouch down near the water's edge, filling their shared plastic red bucket with shells and stones. There were frictions between the three of us even in childhood. I was the youngest, a fact which always made me 'Mummy and Daddy's favourite baby girl', according to Claire and Laura. They resented any attention I got, especially Claire, who was the eldest. I had 'got away with' so much more than she had, Claire would keep telling me. She saw herself as the wise, hardened pioneer, the one to first brave the world, who had to make the sacrifices and soldier on, in order to test the ground.

Laura was less domineering, more thoughtful, but constantly aware of being in the middle, and having, as she saw it, neither the privileges of an eldest or a youngest child. It was inevitable that she would be dressed in the hand-me-downs. She had a fear of being passed over, which made her inclined to be on edge and quickly defensive.

I felt that they were each relieved in their own way to see me leave Northern Ireland at eighteen. They were already working by then – Claire had a job in the Civil Service, Laura was training to be a nurse in Belfast. They were openly sceptical about my plans to go to art college, something which Mum and Dad had always encouraged. 'You have to be *very* good to succeed in a career in art! I hope you're doing the right thing, Gillian,' Laura would say, in a way that seemed to suggest that I might not be quite good enough.

'Och well, you can always give it a wee go, can't you?' was Claire's attitude. 'If it doesn't work out, you can come back. Sure, we'll not see you stuck!'

When I got a job related to my course, I sensed that Claire and Laura couldn't bring themselves to be wholeheartedly happy for me. They began to insinuate that my departure from Northern Ireland implied a choice to deliberately turn away from my birthplace and our family.

It wasn't something that either of them could bring themselves to articulate in a straightforward way, more a brimming set of assumptions that leaked out every time we met. Assumptions they had in common, which strengthened their bond. As time went on, they began to share other things too: well-appointed homes, hard-working, dependable Northern Irish men, children with meticulously groomed hands, clothes and manners.

I gave up suggesting that they could visit me. Every time I mentioned the idea, they would come up with reasons why they couldn't, why it just wasn't 'practical'. If I wanted to stay connected with my roots, it was taken for granted that I would have to be the one doing the travelling. When I came over to visit, Claire and Laura liked to manage the organisation of my trip between them as far as possible.

'Laura and I can probably sort out most of your evening meals between us,' Claire would typically tell me on the phone, weeks before I was due to arrive. 'It'll take some of the strain off Mum's shoulders.'

I came to dread those meals – claustrophobic contrasts to days spent outdoors with Mum and Dad or by myself, walking on the peninsula, in the Mournes or up on the Antrim coast. Claire and Laura would take turns to hold court, making a show of their dutiful generosity, of taking me into the bosom of their apparently perfectly ordered families. Big Robbie, Claire's placid, bank manager husband, would chew methodically on his steak, hardly uttering a word. Laura's Tony would use his slick conversational skills as a leading County Down estate agent to keep me talking about the price of greeting cards and property, about anything and actually, nothing at all.

Afterwards, as I helped Claire and Laura clear up in the kitchen, they would make a point of asking, in forced tones of sympathy, about my life. They seemed to enjoy highlighting difficulties, feeding on my vulnerabilities. They said that they couldn't imagine living the way I did, hardly seeing my husband, in a 'wee city flat' without a garden, 'so cut off from everybody'. Inevitably, one of their favourite topics became our fertility problems.

'You need to get on and do something

about it, Gillian! They might suggest you try donor insemination or adoption. Get a further consultation, as soon as! *Drag* Matt in there, if you have to!' Claire liked to give the impression that nothing fazed her, that she was *au fait* with every imaginable issue related to coupledom and family life.

'But neither of us really. . .' I would start to try and explain.

'Och, for crying out *loud*, Gillian! What's this *about?* Sort yourselves out, will you? We can't help you any more with this one! This time you'll have to deal with it yourself! You'll have to be strong for your husband and for the sake of your future family! That's what you *want*, isn't it?'

'I . . . I don't know, Claire. I mean, I'm just not completely sure if . . .'

'Well, yes. There we are. That's you all over, isn't it, Gillian? Always putting things off, dithering. Going to pieces on us!'

'No, Claire. That's not right. I'm not like that. I never *was*.'

When Mum died of cancer, and then when Dad went soon afterwards with a heart attack, things got worse between Claire, Laura and me. Grief could have brought us closer, but it didn't. The recriminations and festering resentments just intensified. Claire and Laura took it upon themselves to deal with all the practicalities, quickly dismissing any suggestions that I tried to make, telling me that everything was already 'well under control'.

'There's not much you can *do*, Gillian,' they told me in the weeks before Mum died. I had come over and arranged to take a week off work to be with her. I just wanted to sit with her and hold her hand. 'Why don't you just go *back?* Don't worry, we've got it covered. And it's best not to try and call the house, we think. They're both too exhausted to talk to you. The nurses and doctors are always coming and going. Call *us* in the evening instead. Sure, we can pass on any messages.'

At times they would 'forget' to give me information, which made it impossible for me to respond to situations in the way that I would have wanted to. When Dad was admitted to hospital, they downplayed the seriousness of it, told me too late that I needed to come. He was dead by the time I arrived.

Even in the days before the funeral, while Dad was still lying in the funeral parlour, waiting to be buried, Claire and Laura wasted no time in starting to discuss who was entitled to take what from Mum and Dad's house.

'There's no point in you having anything *big*, Gillian,' Claire told me, briskly. 'Maybe you could have some of their silver cutlery, or a light wee picture or something?'

She and Laura had already haggled between them over who should take Mum and Dad's dressing table, their dining table and chairs, their china cabinet and its contents. Robbie should have Dad's lawn mower, Claire said. Laura agreed, on the condition that her children could have Grandad's fishing bag and rods. Tony would have his father-in-law's tools.

'No, I don't need anything,' I told them. 'You two have it all. It doesn't matter. Mum and Dad aren't here. I can't think about anything else now.' I felt beyond speech, feeling or fight.

'Don't be cutting off your nose to spite your face now, Gillian!' Laura told me.

'You could regret it someday. You might need, like, a wee memento,' Claire added.

'No, it's alright. I've got some photos. I've got the *mementoes* in here.' I pointed to my head. 'No *thing's* ever going to bring them back, is it?'

I force myself back to the present, to the here-and-now of sitting by the lough. I open my sketchbook and start to draw and think in glass. Verticals, horizons, borders, curving edges. Translations of the landscape into more simplified shapes, separate and juxtaposed panes. The transparent. The opaque. Flecks, bubbles, ripples, waves of texture. Colours, contrasts, vivid and subtle. I want it all to take me over, so that I can think of nothing else. I continue to sketch quickly. I jot down single words, ideas; I forget about the time.

After a while, I notice the figure of a man in the distance, making his way round the curve of the foreshore, on the grassy edge above the rocks, where our family used to picnic. He cuts across the beach and strides out in my direction. He's wearing sunglasses, a dark jacket that appears to be zipped up in spite of the weather, binoculars, a backpack and walking boots. He has short hair and is possibly in his late forties. My first thought is that he must be the man renting the cottage next to me. He seems to fit Derek McEvoy's description. I look back down at my paper, not wanting him to think that I'm staring. When I next look up, he's standing about fifty yards out, still as a bollard, with his back to me, facing the sea.

As I'm about to continue working, out of the corner of my eye I become aware of something moving, fluttering against the length of wall to the left of me, between the road and the shore. It's a herring gull. Bright yellow beak with a red spot, white body, pale grey back, black-tipped wings. I think it must be injured. It flaps one of its wings intermittently, then stays still and makes a strange sound in its throat.

I should go over and have a look at it, but I can't. I hate the thought of leaving a creature to suffer, but wild birds in distress, flapping like that, unnerve me. If Dad had been here, he would have gone over to investigate. Dad was able to put a bird out of its misery if he had to. All I can do is to try and ignore it, tell myself that the best thing is not to disturb or frighten it, just to leave it alone. I try to concentrate on my drawing instead.

The next time I look up, the man is crouching in front of the place where I saw the bird. I can hardly believe it. I never heard him, had no idea that he'd walked past me, up the beach. When he stands up and steps back, the gull is lying motionless against the wall, in front of him. He lifts it up by its tail feathers. Unmistakeably dead, its body swings limp and loose from his hand as he walks back with it, across the beach, towards the grass edge. I watch him, carrying the bird up into the grass, then crouching again and putting it in a place that I can't quite see. There are deep pockets and holes in the grass up there, where we used to bury banana skins and apple cores after picnics.

Although I keep telling myself that he's only acted out of compassion for the creature, which is what I should have done myself, I can't help feeling uneasy at the speed and efficiency of his style of killing. This man I know nothing about really, who might be staying beside me, and might be ex-army or police. Or who knows what else? I know I'm probably being paranoid, but as quickly as I can, before he turns round, I gather up my pencils and sketchbook and make my way back over the rocks, straight to my car.

Chapter Three

David

It seems like a long time since he killed a bird with his bare hands like that. His father, who'd worked on farms, taught him how to do it when he was a boy. He also showed him how to kill those miserable diseased rabbits, tortured and maimed by myxomatosis. The first couple of times he'd been made to watch, though from then on, David had been expected, when necessary, to do it by himself.

He'd only been eleven the first time. His dad praised him to the skies afterwards for being so brave and decisive. For proving that he was already a man. David's fear and initial squeamishness had mixed together with the idea that he'd done something his dad approved of, that'd made a father proud. A man had to be prepared to do unpleasant jobs sometimes. To confront things, not run away. You couldn't just leave an animal or a bird to suffer. You had to grit your teeth, tell yourself it was the kindest, the right thing to do. After a while David found that he could kill more easily. It never felt good, but he could do it if he had to.

He wipes his hands on the grass. The dead gull is well out of sight, in a deep hole, covered with handfuls of dry grass and dock leaves, under

28

the wild mustard. When he turns round to look back across the beach, the woman who was sitting on the shore has gone. It looked as if she was drawing. He then sees her up in the car park, getting into a red Fiesta. He'd noticed her earlier, but had been so preoccupied with his own thoughts and then with dealing with the bird, that he'd momentarily forgotten. Perhaps he should have acknowledged her and made a point of explaining what he was doing. He hopes that he didn't frighten or shock her; that she understood.

He walks back down onto the beach. The lenses of his sunglasses seem cloudier, as if smeared with something. He takes them off, unzips his jacket, polishes them against the black fleece underneath, does his jacket up again before heading towards the car park. He could go further along the shore – it would be safer, more pleasant – but it'll be quicker if he walks back along the road instead.

As David reaches the road, he sees a buzzard circling inland, high up above the tops of some straggling pine trees. He stops to take a look through his binoculars. As it moves closer overhead, he studies the pale undersides of its wings. You get a lot more buzzards now than you used to. There are certainly a lot more in Cheshire, flying close to the motorways and larger roads.

He's always been excited by birds of prey – something to do with their commanding pres-ence, unquestionable handsomeness. You can't help admiring their single-mindedness. You can never be inside the mind of a bird, but from what you know and observe, they seem so completely at one with their preying natures, so totally accepting of who they are. They target, they kill, they consume, without turmoil or remorse, without doubt. Continually repeat the cycle. They live and die, carrying nothing on their consciences.

He carries on walking along the lough-side road. It's almost 6 p.m., getting a little cooler, but still a beautiful summer evening. He probably won't do much for the rest of the night. He has some cans in the fridge. He might just go into town and get some fish and chips, then come straight back to the cottage, watch television and have a few beers to take the edge off. Leave doing anything else until tomorrow.

McEvoy's cottage is the kind of place he was after. Clean, all mod cons, but not too fussy. Quiet and private. Close enough to Stewartsford to easily get a takeaway and go to the off-licence. McEvoy seems helpful and friendly, not pushing too hard for personal information. No more than you would expect – a farmer's life can be solitary and you can hardly blame the man for wanting a bit of conversation.

McEvoy had mentioned that there would be a woman renting the cottage next door for the same two weeks. She's originally from Northern Ireland, now living near Liverpool. David hopes that she's the type to keep herself to herself. He's not usually averse to a woman's company on holiday, but it can complicate things and he doesn't need any more complications. He needs to be alone, think things through, do what he has to do.

It's been quite a while since he's had a holiday from work. It's just how it is in the CID. Often working day and night to follow things through to their conclusion. Getting hooked on the adrenaline. Completely consumed by the process of tracking down the people, the information, the truth. It takes time to unwind. You never really do.

The last time he went on holiday, it was a cheap package to Corfu. The time before that, it was Ibiza. In his forties, he felt in some ways as if he were reverting to how he'd been in his younger days when he joined the police. Choosing beach resorts with plenty of night life, heaving with twenty-somethings. Not at all his kind of places really, the crowd far too young. But it was a way of escaping. Sometimes he just needed to try his best to forget and merge in.

In Corfu, he'd hired a scooter during the day, drunk heavily in the clubs in the evenings. He'd carelessly chatted up the women, had someone different lying beside him virtually every morning. He hadn't felt good about it afterwards. He'd pitied them for the way they'd come after him, allowing themselves to be so quickly and clumsily seduced. When he was sober, he didn't like the thought of women offering themselves too easily. But he'd tried not to dwell on it. The women involved seemed to take it lightly enough – they hadn't thought anything, apparently, of moving on to other men in front of him the following night in the same clubs. He'd tried to convince himself that it was a mutual thing – they'd probably used him just as much as he'd used them.

The last time he'd gone on holiday with someone else had been five years ago, when he had gone to Spain with Sophie. They'd broken up not long after that. After only two years together. He'd been drinking when he first met her too. He hadn't meant to get involved with Sophie any more than with the other women he'd had casual relationships with. But he'd found her over-whelmingly physically attractive. Addictive. Eve-rything about her had seemed luxurious, the gloss of her long hair, the smoothness of her skin, the way she came with all her perfumes and flimsy dresses and teetering heels. The feminine fuss, however trivial and stereotypical, that comple-mented his own roughness and minimalism. His lust had allowed him to overlook their lack of in-tellectual connection. It had made him forget, for a while, his plans to live a detached, solitary life. He'd felt uneasy even as they were getting mar-ried. But he wanted to hold on to her; he couldn't resist. Until two years later, when he had to con-front the truth – that lust couldn't compensate for a lack of love and understanding; that it wasn't long before he'd felt more lonely living with Sophie than he'd ever done without her.

David crosses the lough-side road. It takes him five minutes to walk to the lane leading to the cottages. At the end of the lane, on the yard, he notices another car, parked next to his own. It's a red Fiesta, like the one he saw the woman getting into down at the shore. The woman who was drawing, who probably saw him killing the gull. The thought makes him feel uncomfortable, but he continues on down the lane.

Inside the cottage, he throws off his boots and coat, makes a cup of coffee and sits down at the kitchen table to look at his map of the peninsula. His finger traces the roads, quickly skims the east coast, lingers along the line of the lough-side road.

He used to have a colleague in the police with a passion for orienteering, who collected and obsessed over maps, the way some people do over books. At work, most of the maps were on screen, of course, but if the guy ever got the chance to handle a 'proper one', as he put it, this eccentric side of him came out. He wouldn't have a cup of tea, a biscuit, or even a sneeze, near that map. He would squirm when a map was marked, rolled or incorrectly folded. Almost as if it were sacred.

A map's a strange thing. Just a flat, neutral piece of paper really. A guide. Apparently objective, but often so much more. Pointing beyond itself, to things out there, experiences past and present. A reminder of happiness and triumphs. Of tragedy, a state of peace or a bloodied history. A source of comfort or torment.

He folds the map up quickly, gets up from the kitchen table and pushes it down, deep into the pocket of his backpack. Looking at it has made him feel more on edge again. Some of his restlessness shifted when he was down by the shore, and particularly after he killed the bird, but it has come back. He could do with a can of beer, but he won't drink and drive. He'll have to go into Stewartsford for fish and chips sooner rather than later.

David gets ready to go out again and lifts his car keys. He's on the point of leaving when he hears a knock on the cottage door. He's not in the mood for being sociable. It's the woman renting the cottage next door. The same woman he saw on the beach. She's probably around forty - certainly a bit younger than himself - lightly built, striking rather than pretty, with wide cheekbones, brownish black hair, green eyes and a very pale skin - what some people would probably call a typical 'Irish complexion'. She wears jeans and a turquoise T-shirt under a grey cardigan, hardly any make-up. David notices and remembers details. He always did, not just because he was trained to. Even if sometimes he might prefer to forget.

Gillian

It's definitely the man I saw on the shore. He's taken off his outer jacket. Close up, without his sunglasses, I notice that his eyes are greyish blue. The colour of a 'sniper's eyes', I remember Dad saying. They're lined and shadowed underneath, but overall, his face is handsome. His nose is long, well-defined, his lips flat and neat. There's a slight hint of red in his dark, grey-flecked hair and stubble. He's an attractive-looking man, but I want to try to ignore the thought.

'Hello! How can I help?' he asks immediately, standing in the doorway, looking me straight in the eyes for a moment, then intermittently shifting his glance away. He has a mild Northern English accent, with an element of something else that I can't quite pinpoint. He has the ring of his car keys round his finger and jangles them in his hand. He's obviously about to go out.

I'm uncomfortable about knocking on his door. I think that I must have tripped a switch when I was boiling the kettle this time to make a coffee. The cooker and microwave aren't coming on. I've searched everywhere for the fuse box, but I can't find it. I'm cursing myself now for not accepting Derek's guided tour. I'm reluctant to bother him at the farm unless I really have to.

'I'm very sorry to bother you, but you don't happen to know where the *fuse box* is in your cottage, do you? I think I've just tripped a switch and . . . Oh, sorry! I'm Gillian Watson. I'm renting the cottage next door.'

'I'm David.' He smiles slightly, keeps jangling his keys, seems edgy. 'Mine is in the cupboard with the ironing board and the vac. I'm happy to help you look if you want.'

My mind keeps darting back to the thought of him killing the bird. I'm still not sure whether I should accept his help, but I did ask for it.

'Well, if you don't mind . . . I need my cooker working.'

I lead the way back to my cottage, show him inside first, leave the front door open behind us.

'There you are!' he says at once. As he points it out, I see there's a door, hardly noticeable, near the bottom of the stairs. He opens it to reveal the fuse box inside, flicks one of the switches. I instantly feel stupid, can't believe I didn't see it before. I don't like the feeling of being a 'little woman' asking for a big man's help. I hope he doesn't see me like that. I hope he doesn't think I'm using it as an excuse to chat him up.

'Oh, I am sorry. I feel really stupid now.' I stay close to the front door.

He turns back towards me. Stuffs his hands into his pockets. For a moment, he looks more boyish, shy. 'No problem. Anything else I can do, you know where I am.'

'I do. But don't worry, I won't bother you again,' I say, emphatically. *I won't bother you and you won't bother me*, I mean. I still feel obliged to search for a few words of conversation, to compensate him for having to come in. 'Enjoying your holiday so far?'

'Yes, thanks, I am. How about you?'

'Yes. The cottage is great. This *is* one of the most beautiful places in the world, but I am biased, I suppose.'

'Biased?'

'Yes. I spent a lot of my childhood on this peninsula.'

'So, you're over visiting family?'

'No. Not this time. This time I'm just having a break, gathering some ideas for work. I'm a glass artist. I work from my own sketches.'

'I saw you earlier, down on the shore, didn't I? Don't know if you saw me?'

'Yes, I did.' I'm not sure where he's leading, so I let him talk.

'So you must have seen me killing the gull?'

'Not actually killing it. But I saw you taking it over to the grass afterwards.'

'Hope that didn't upset you?' His voice is serious. He looks at me, then shifts his gaze, tugs on the skin between his nose and his upper lip.

'Well, no. I mean I thought that the bird must have been pretty badly injured and that you *had* to do it. I don't like any sort of killing, but . . .'

'Yes, it was in a really bad way. Its wing was torn, it was all soaked with blood underneath. Its leg was ... Sorry, should spare you the details. I couldn't leave it like that. I don't like killing either. I'll only do it if I have to.'

'I know what you mean. I'm a coward myself when it comes to things like that. I really *can't*. I once left a frog half dead on the road. I just couldn't finish him off. He was obviously suffering, but I couldn't do anything. Makes me feel ashamed sometimes, when I think about it.'

'You shouldn't blame yourself. He would have died fairly quickly anyway, wouldn't he? We're all different. You did what you could, didn't you?'

'I did *nothing*.'

'Sometimes nothing *is* the best that we can do though, isn't it?'

He looks up at me this time. There's a force behind his question, that makes me suddenly feel that it matters to him how I answer it.

'Yes. You're right,' I tell him. 'We can't always be in control of everything, not even ourselves. We can't always be totally responsible or do exactly the right thing. Even if we want to.'

'No. Although . . .' He looks lost in thought for a moment, rubs his forehead hard, repeatedly, stares down at his walking boots. Then his mood seems to lighten again. 'Look. I'm driving into town to get some fish and chips. Can I get you anything? You wouldn't have to cook.'

'No. I'm fine. But thanks for the offer. I'll need to get some shopping anyway. I should let you go now.'

'No problem. I haven't got that much organised. The main line up being some of those tall, slim but curvaceous containers in my fridge!'

His words and the way he says them strike me as familiar somehow. I wonder if I can hear a slight Northern Irish intonation. But then I remember Derek McEvoy saying he thought it was the man's first visit.

'See you around then, Gillian.'

Yes, thanks, David. Have a good holiday, won't you?'

'I'll do my best.'

Chapter Four

David

The bike's upside down. A lad in a leather jacket and jeans – probably only eighteen – is lying crumpled up, among the brambles, on the side of the road. There's blood everywhere. Another young lad, probably the driver of the van, is kneeling on the ground, in shock, whimpering, hugging himself like a child. People are slamming car doors, gathering round. What'll we do?' and 'Move him! Onto his back!' and 'Shit! He wasn't even wearing a helmet!' and 'No, leave him be – don't make things worse!'

David delegates – the call for ambulance and police, management of the traffic, care of the van driver. At the same time, he's examining the motorcyclist. He's unconscious. Airway. Breathing. Circulation. The lad isn't breathing. He can't get a bloody pulse. C.P.R. No barriers. Just his mouth, sealing the lad's mouth. Taste of blood. Hand over hand heel, pressing down on ribcage. Metallic taste of blood.

Gillian

After two full days by the lough, today I crossed to the east side of the peninsula. My cheeks sting from sun, sand and wind. Inside I feel like a freshly restored stained glass window, dull milling thoughts replaced with vibrant images. Outdoors, in wild places, I've always felt more real, more solid somehow. In a wood, on a beach, life seems pared down, just as it is.

It's almost seven in the evening. On the way back to the cottage on the lough-side road, there's a build-up of traffic. Ahead, on what seems to be the opposite side of the road, I can see the flashing lights of a stationary ambulance. It doesn't surprise me. There have been so many serious accidents on this road. But I still feel a cold flash run through me. In some ways, I think I'm quite a strong person psychologically, but the thought that I'd have to help in an accident makes me panicky. In such moments, I have to admit that Laura could be right – perhaps I am 'completely hopeless, when it comes to practicalities'.

The line of traffic eventually gets moving. I try to stay focused on the road, but as I approach the ambulance, I can't help wondering what's happening inside it. While I understand the need for privacy, there's something almost inhumane about the opaque, dispassionate windows of ambulances. The lights are still flashing, the doors are closed. I catch a glimpse of an overturned motorbike on the verge. There are uniformed policemen and other people beside the bike and in the field next to the road. Then, as I pass the ambulance, I notice a silver VW Golf parked behind a police car and a van. My immediate thought is that it belongs to David, my holiday neighbour. For a second it crosses my mind that perhaps I should stop, but I keep going. We're strangers. There's no reason for me to get involved. I would probably be more of a hindrance than a help anyway.

Back at the cottage, I notice that David's car isn't there. It still doesn't mean that the Golf at the accident was his, but the uncertainty unsettles me. I can't shrug the feeling off. I was planning a long soak in the bath, but I have a quick shower instead, put my dressing gown on over a long shirt and come downstairs. I'm not really hungry, but I have a slice of toast and sit in front of the TV with a glass of wine.

I'm still picturing the lough-side road, the closed doors of the ambulance, the flashing lights, the Golf on the verge. For some reason that I can't completely understand, I keep thinking about David, who I really know nothing about. I'm visualising him in tones of black and white, on a stretcher inside that ambulance behind the opaque windows and intransigent doors. Lifeless as a recumbent wax figure. His skin white-grey, the pricks of his stubble, short, dark, extinguished candle wicks.

The image links in my mind with thoughts of my Dad. I didn't want to see him when he was dead, though now I wish I had. I only keep trying to imagine how he might have looked, irrevocably drained of life and colour. A once vigorous green pane – I always associate him with the green of his shirts – that I can never restore, except in windows of my imagination.

Just before 8.30 p.m., I hear a car pulling up on the gravel outside. It's not completely dark and the curtains are still not drawn. It's David's car. He gets out slowly, slams his door. He then stays standing in front of it, resting his head on his arms on the car roof. I feel a wave of relief wash over me. Before I can think about it, I'm turning on the outside light, then standing there in the open doorway in my dressing gown.

'Hello again,' he says, turning his head, nodding. He's wearing a short-sleeved, khaki T-shirt and dark, combat-style trousers. The shirt is darker in patches, I assume of sweat, under his arms and down the front of his chest. 'Everything okay, Gillian?' He sounds tired, but surprisingly calm for someone who has been involved in an accident.

'I was just . . . I was going to ask you the same question, actually. Only, I thought I saw your car on the lough road. There'd obviously been an accident. I wasn't sure if you were involved, if it was *you* in the ambulance. I just hoped you were alright. Not my business really, but . . . '

'Appreciate the concern.' He makes a small salute with one hand. 'I'm fine. I got there just after it happened, so I had to stay and help out. Motorcyclist lost control by the sound of it.'

'Yes. I saw the bike in the undergrowth. Although the doors of the ambulance were closed by the time I arrived. So, was the cyclist badly injured?' I'm suddenly aware that the front of my dressing gown is gaping open, gather the lapels together and retie the belt. I hope he didn't notice.

'Afraid so. Had to resuscitate him, but he came round. I'll have to phone the hospital later on, to find out how he's doing. So, did you have a good day?' He turns to face me squarely, wiping his hairline with the side of his hand, one arm still resting on the car roof.

'Yes, thanks. I've done a lot of drawings. How about you? I mean, apart from tonight, of course. Actually, probably a stupid question at the moment. Hardly the kind of situation that makes you think 'happy holiday', is it?' I add, lamely. I'm beginning to feel awkward now, wishing I hadn't stumbled out to talk to him.

'That's true. Although I am fairly adept at keeping life in separate compartments. Some people call it hard-hearted, some, a survival mechanism.'

'I wish I was more like that, not so highly-strung. I admire people who can switch on in emergencies and switch off afterwards. Worrying all the time about things doesn't help you or anyone else, does it?' I hadn't meant to start talking so personally. I begin to feel more vulnerable and at the same time, driven to carry on the conversation.

'Maybe not. Although if you compartmentalise, some people can think you actually don't *care*. Anyway, yes, the holiday is going fine, thanks. Sorry, you're in your dressing gown. I'm sure you don't want to be hanging around outside.'

'You're welcome to come in. I've got wine or whiskey. Or I could make you a cup of tea? We could talk more about the accident if you want – I'd probably need to, if it were me.' I know in fact that I probably wouldn't talk. Even if I needed to.

'I'm not so sure you would,' he replies, smiling. 'If I was honest, I'd say . . . You strike me as a pretty independent person. I'd say you'd have a wee whiskey on your own, talk yourself down and head off to bed. If you don't mind me saying. Probably far too direct there. Still too much adrenaline on board.'

'No, actually you're right,' I admit. I'm unnerved, disarmed. Just talking off the top of my head. Because I feel unsure, a degree of attraction, guilt? 'I'm prepared to give you the benefit. And I'd feel guilty if I didn't invite you in, after what you'd been through.'

'So, it's just pure selfishness really?' he returns, laughing.

'It could well be. If that makes it easier for you to come in for a drink?"

'Go on, then. But just one.'

David

Hard-hearted. It was what Sophie called him. Whatever way he'd played it, he was wrong. She wanted to play house, the perfect romantic couple, in suburban Manchester. She wanted the dream, the beautiful life. He'd worked hard to give it to her. He tried to shield her from the ugly side of things, the raw side of himself especially, the harrowing details of things he'd had to see and do. He wanted to spare and protect her, but she said she wanted to know her husband 'properly'. She wanted him to confide in her. On the occasions when he'd allowed himself to start to unravel, she couldn't cope, she didn't want to hear. He was 'a cold one'; he was 'freaking her out'. His mind held darker, more chilling places and experiences than she could possibly have anticipated. Sophie hadn't heard the half of it.

He takes his boots off, leaves them on the mat outside and follows Gillian into the cottage. She leaves him to help himself to a drink while she goes upstairs to put on her jeans. She makes a joke about making herself 'more decent'. He'd sensed she felt a bit uneasy, standing in front of him in her dressing gown.

'Okay if I wash my hands?' he shouts after her, up the stairs.

'Help yourself! There's some anti-bac handwash by the kitchen sink.'

His hands are filthy with dirt and dried blood, his arms covered with scratches from the brambles by the road. He smiles to himself when she mentions the anti-bac soap. The scratches sting as he wets and lathers up his arms. He's never been particularly worried about bacteria. He feels unclean most of the time, but it isn't a problem that can be solved by any amount of anti-bac soap.

He pours himself a small glass of her red wine and sits on the edge of one of the two small sofas facing each other, near the fireplace. He likes the way McEvoy, or more than likely McEvoy's wife, has left the jars of wildflowers around. There's one on his fireplace as well, filled with purple dead-nettles. It makes him think of his mother. He tries not to think about her most of the time, but such small details can trigger potent memories, beyond his conscious control. They couldn't afford fancy flowers at home, so she would pick little wild posies just like that and arrange them in old glasses, jam jars and milk jugs. He also notices the way the guides and maps are stacked in neat piles on the coffee table, the cushions on the sofas are arranged upright, the way Gillian has everything hung on hooks, in its place. That reminds him of Sophie. Sometimes it seemed that it was all she thought about, all she was. Sophie would have had him plumped up and on a hook too if she could.

'You're very neat! Not a squashed cushion or a used tea bag in sight,' he tells Gillian as she reaches the bottom of the stairs. 'You should see my place. Slovenly in comparison.' He hopes she can take the joke. Sophie couldn't stand him making fun of her tidiness. She couldn't bear much humour, let alone analysis.

'One of my many annoying traits!' Gillian comes back, laughing as she pours herself a drink and sits down on the other sofa. 'You're far too observant, you know.'

'Very true. Believe me, I really wish I wasn't. Although, you're probably fairly observant yourself. Being an artist.'

'Yes, I suppose I am. Takes one to know one – an observant person to know an observant person, I mean. Unless you're an artist as well and I don't think you . . . '

'Not a single artistic bone, I'm afraid.'

'Let me guess. You're a doctor?'

'No. I wouldn't have the patience for that.'

'A lawyer?'

'Hell, no.'

'A teacher?'

'Never. Not even for my sins.'

'A fireman?'

'That's better. I've extinguished plenty of fires in my time. And I've a rare talent for putting a dampener on things. Yes, go on, let me be a fireman.'

'Fair enough.' She laughs again, plays along with his game, doesn't push him for any more information about what he does. 'I hope you're feeling okay after the accident?'

'Really, I'm fine. I'm sure I did what I could. I just need a wash. Then you can anti-bac your sofa!'

'I certainly will.' She smiles again. Her skin is good, lifts into fine creases when she laughs. There's a space between her two upper front teeth, something he's always found attractive. 'So, what have you been doing with your holiday? Any ideas for me?'

'Walking, bit of fishing, reading, eating, drinking. Drinking, eating. Did I mention drinking? And enjoying not being near Manchester.'

'Yes, Derek McEvoy mentioned that's where you're from,' Gillian says. 'You can't keep too many secrets round here, I'm afraid!'

'You're right there. I've been around quite a bit, as they say, but that's where I live.'

You can't keep too many secrets round here. No lies. But he knows he's not telling the whole truth. It's the way he's decided to manage things. At moments like this he wonders how it would be, to just let go and talk. If only it were that simple. He's usually a good judge of character. Gillian seems like an intelligent and trustworthy sort of person. But he doesn't really know her well enough yet to be completely sure.

Gillian

The fact that David doesn't immediately volunteer much personal information, especially about his career, makes me think that Derek McEvoy could well be right about him being 'ex-army or police'. You still have to watch what you say and who you speak to in this part of the world. You don't want to put yourself or someone else in danger. I don't want to probe, even if it feels he knows more about me than I do about him. It isn't my business and it probably suits both of us if we keep our relationship superficial.

'So you said you were having some work time alone, without your family?' he asks. 'Are you not likely to bump into them anyway?'

'It's possible, but unlikely, believe it or not. Everyone works during the week and at weekends, my sisters don't really *do* outdoors. They used to when we were younger. We at least had that in common in those days. But now they spend any spare time they have feathering their nests, shopping, at each other's houses. So I might see them, I might not. They wouldn't thank me for not telling them I'm here. Anyway, I'm sure you don't want to hear about my family disputes. You probably have your own share?'

'Not anymore. My older brother's in The States. We're in touch occasionally, but we never really got on. Both my parents are dead some time ago. I'm divorced, no kids.'

'Same.' I'm not quite sure what to say next. It feels a bit awkward to stop at this point. It could seem as if I'd engineered the conversation. Or that we'd accidentally on purpose arrived in a clearing of *so it seems we're both single.* Although I know I didn't plan it and I don't think he did either.

'I must really stink!' he says quickly, returning to his joking tack, setting down his glass, lifting his arms, then pulling out the front of his T shirt.

'Well, I didn't like to tell you, but . . .' I reciprocate, wrinkling up my nose.

'I must get a shower. And I should phone to find out what's happened to that lad in hospital. Thanks for the drink. I hope the rest of your holiday is productive on the artistic front. No doubt we'll meet again in passing, but I promise not to make a nuisance of myself!'

I go to bed not long after David has left. I'm glad I asked him to come in. At the same time, I'm still attached to the idea of a solitary working holiday. Now that we've spoken and that I've asked him in for a drink, I know I'm going to feel more obliged to talk to him, even if he doesn't expect me to, out of basic courtesy. I won't be able to ignore him the way I intended. To distract myself, I try to think about my plans for tomorrow. As long as I'm out, I won't have to worry about being sociable.

As I drift off to sleep, I call to mind a part of the coast, further along the lough side, close to an old pub. It's like a kind of creek. The narrow inlet of water moves in silently. You can sneak over the side of the pub wall, get down among the sedges and make your way round a curve, first over boggy cushions of grass, then over stones and shingle, through clumps of sea asters and scurvy grass. After the bend, you have a broader view, out to the edge of low rocks covered with bladder wrack, where the inlet is a wider channel, a sheltered, hidden paradise for sea birds. I can see the place already in glass, the smooth, flexing body of the water like the dark body of an eel, cutting through swathes of grass, rock and weed.

Chapter Five

Gillian

It's half past twelve. I drive into the car park near the pub. There are a few other cars, but I'm fairly sure the owners are having lunch inside and there'll be no one down by the shore. It isn't very good for swimming and I imagine a lot of people find the strong hum of fermenting weed off-putting. You quickly forget about it, or at least get used to it, once you're out there. This was one of the places our family visited on days out. We'd scramble over the wall and find our own quiet spot. We always seemed to be the only ones about, as far as I could tell, although there are plenty of places a person could hide if they really wanted to. Any other time I've been here as an adult, I've been on my own.

As I land in the wet grass below the wall, there's no one in sight. I decide to take a walk round the shore first before I start drawing. The place has its own kind of insulated silence, punctuated by occasional calls of birds. Though close, the road seems very far away. The moist, plant-infused heat feels almost tropical. I move quickly and lightly over the boggy area so that I don't sink in, and slow down when I reach the shingled, firmer ground.

I see scenes, in pieces, compositions of separate panes, bounded and joined by black lines. In flux. Dismantling, reassembling. Endless possibilities for renderings in glass. As I reach the bend, I look forward to the wider, bigger view. This time however, what I see beyond the bend makes me step back immediately.

Sitting on a rock at the edge of the bladder wrack with his back to me, his hands on his knees, looking towards the channel, is a figure I recognise at once. It's Tony, my sister Laura's husband. He's in his shirt sleeves, tie loose around his neck. He's wearing his work trousers rolled up and is angling skimming stones into the water. I'm not supposed to be there. I have to suppress my impulse to call him. Even more so when I look further up the shore.

It's definitely not Laura. There's a young woman, sitting in the grass. Actually, she looks more girl than woman – I'm guessing she could be eighteen or so. The front of her yellow dress is unbuttoned to the waist. She's leaning forward, one leg bent up, putting on her knickers.

'You're just a wee boy really, aren't you, Tony?' she says, in a sing-song voice. 'If people could see you now. They wouldn't know you, would they?'

Tony laughs. A loose kind of laugh I don't associate with Tony, my hit-the-ground-running, slick, estate agent brother-in-law. 'Too right, Kelly.

Too right. And it's all your fault, isn't it? You're the naughty wee girl who led me astray.'

She puts her head back, opens her mouth wide. Her laugh is unrestrained, earthy, guttural. They're totally absorbed in their own world.

I move backwards, as quietly as I can before they notice me. I hurry towards the wall, scramble over and run back to my car, my heart racing, stomach churning. I can't believe what I've just seen. It seems surreal. Especially there, in *my* place, that beautiful unspoilt haven of sea birds. Tony. Sitting on the weed, throwing stones among the rises of the mullet. Tony. With his trousers rolled up, in a place you'd least expect to find him, a place where I wasn't supposed to be. Tony, carrying on with a girl who looks young enough to be his daughter. The little shit! The same man who had made a show of always doing the right thing by Laura. Insisting on expensive anniversary presents and family meals to celebrate, talking about renewing their wedding vows while condescending to comment on my failing marriage. 'Long-term commitment isn't for everyone, Gillian. But sure, plenty more fish in the sea, aren't there? You're still a good-looking woman for your age. You'll be fine.'

Tony, you stupid slithering hypocrite. Why did I have to witness your mess?

David

'Don't I *know* you?' the woman at the check-out in Tesco's in Stewartsford asks David.

'I'm pretty sure you don't. Count yourself lucky – believe me,' he adds, to soften the effect.

She's probably in her sixties, a weary looking sixty, obviously a smoker, judging by the stains on her fingers and the deep pursing lines round her lips. David's mother and father were heavy smokers. They always used to light up as soon as they'd finished their dinner, over the remains of their meat fat, cabbage and potatoes. He smoked for a while himself when he was in his late teens and twenties, but the thought of his parents exhaling, leaving their spent matches in that fatty gravy, can still make him gag sometimes.

'Och no, sorry. You're from across the water, aren't you?' the woman replies, opening a plastic carrier. 'I just thought you looked a wee bit familiar, you know. Something about your eyes. Is the shopping all okay in one bag? I'll put your eggs and tomatoes on the top so they don't get squashed.'

'Perfect. Nothing worse than squashed tomatoes, is there?' There are any number of things, actually, but what the hell? She's a friendly person and there's no harm in a bit of small talk.

'You're right there, son. Have you got a wee card? Cash, is it? That's great now. Over on your holidays, then?' she carries on, passing him his change.

'Certainly am. Thanks very much now. Bye, love.'

He lifts the bag of shopping and shifts briskly away from the check-out, before the next question, which is likely to be something along the lines of, 'So where are you staying?' or 'So, where are you from in England?' He wants to keep the information-giving to a minimum.

Driving back to the cottage, on the road out of town, he passes a squat grey church hall with grim metal grills over the windows, hemmed in by a chest-height pebble-dashed wall. Behind the wall there's one of those basic wooden boards where they paste different posters with biblical texts, written in bold black or fluorescent marker pen.

He hasn't time to read the full text, only to take in the New Testament reference, *1 Corinthians 13.* As he reaches the lough-side road, without any deliberate effort, words start running through his head. *When I was a child, I spake as a child, I understood as a child, I thought as a child. But when I became a man, I put away childish things. For now we see through a glass, darkly ... but then, face to face ... now I know in part ... but then shall I know even as also I am known.* He wants the words to stop. But he keeps hearing them, over and over again. *For now we see through a glass, darkly ... but then shall I know ... even as also I am known.*

57

Of course, he knew it was a risk to come here. A risk in many different ways. But he wanted peace, so badly. He wanted to lay the past to rest, once and for all. To be able to forget the bad, remember the good. To reconnect with the indisputable beauty of the landscape. He had to come back.

He needs to get moving now, fast. It'll be good to drive over to the east side of the peninsula and push himself to walk along the shore.

It feels like a different world, on the other side of the peninsula. David goes down the concrete steps with the rusted tubular hand-rail, onto the concrete path which leads from the littered, less inviting stretch of shore below the car park, past a walled play area, to the beginning of a long, curving sandy beach. On the headland, at the far end of the beach, there's a caravan site. It reminds him of a densely barnacled rock. To his right, the beach is bordered with low sand banks and rough grass. Huddles of people are sitting on rugs, talking and picnicking there, while children scuttle and jig about with balls and buckets, shrieking, hurdling over the waves. There aren't many walkers, only a few, mostly with dogs. He walks into the blast of the wind, keeps his head down, zips his jacket to the neck, pulls the baffle up over his mouth and nose.

The place has changed very little really in forty years. They'd gone there often back in the 1970s, he and Sammy and Skinny Kev, in the years when The Troubles had really started kicking off. The three of them had messed about on the sand, just like those kids. A bit crazy after they'd shared a couple of cheap cans of lager, a few cigarettes and a box of chocolates Kev had lifted from the shop while David and Sammy kept the girl at the till talking. They sheltered behind the wall of the play area, teased the little kids on the slide and swings, throwing chocolates at them, putting on strange voices, then ducking down again, behind the wall. They'd come on the bus to begin with, but Kev was six years older than David and Sammy, and as soon as he'd passed his test at seventeen, he loved to drive them around in his scrap-heap of an ancient Mini.

Despite the age gap, Kev didn't look much older than they did, so it was sort of strange, seeing him behind the wheel and using the pumps at the petrol station. He was all skin and bone, Kev, with huge hands and feet. *Skinny malink, melodeon legs, big banana feet, went to the doctors and couldn't get a seat,* they'd chanted when they were kids. He burnt and peeled easily if he took his top off in the sun, like a bright pink, cooked shrimp. And he had a shrimp's spurting way of moving about too, a jerky, nervy energy. He had a spiky, cheeky haircut, short on top, longer at the back of his neck and he squinted all the time, whether the light was bright or not.

Sammy was much slower, mentally and physically. He was kind, round and biddable as a fat lumbering Labrador, and would do anything for you. He also had a habit of drifting off into a dream-world of his own. Kev and David would often knock on his head, asking 'Anyone in there?' Sammy would just nod and grin from ear to ear, as the meaning of the words took time to dawn on him.

David and Sammy and Skinny Kev. Sammy and Kev, long gone. A past life in another era, but still as real as this one. *But when I became a man, I put away childish things. For now we see, through a glass, darkly . . .*

When he was only fourteen, David had been made to stay with his Uncle Keith and his Auntie June near Manchester – they had moved from Northern Ireland many years previously to live there. David's dad had died suddenly. He'd been swallowing baking soda and custard and Milk of Magnesia for years, to try and ease his stomach ulcers. But then one had bled in a major way and he didn't make it. The shock of his dad's sudden death made David's mother even worse with her nerves than she had been before. At only thirty-four, she was taken to the psychiatric hospital – what they used to call 'the loony bin' at school. His move to Manchester was only supposed to be a temporary thing, but when his mother succeeded in taking her own life in hospital, his aunt and uncle adopted him.

His older brother, Mark, a builder, had em- igrated as soon as he'd served his apprenticeship, and had kept in touch now and then with the family by phone. He and Mark had always been very different. Having things mattered less to David. He was shyer, more of an introvert, less competitive. His mum and dad had missed Mark, David knew, though they'd put a brave face on it. 'Your brother's always had his head screwed on, Davie,' his Dad would often say. 'Knows how to look after himself. No looking back for him, once he's made up his mind to do something. He's his own man.' The words had made David feel like he'd never quite measure up. He'd missed Mark too in his own way. At the same time, it eased something in him, no longer having to live in his brother's shadow.

When their parents died, Mark came back for the funerals and shouldered the coffins with his younger brother and the other men. From then on, he would send David the odd short letter or postcard, asking him for news, but mainly telling him how well life was treating him and his new wife in the States.

Auntie June and Uncle Keith had had no children of their own. They were strong Christians, older than David's parents and much better off. At the same time, they tried to practice what they preached and were dedicated to their own undertaking business. Before he'd gone to stay with them, David could only imagine that they lived constantly under a heavy, gloomy cloud, but discovered that the truth was quite the opposite. Believing themselves blessed to be doing such privileged God-given duties, Auntie June and Uncle Keith always appeared to be grateful and positive about their work. They wanted to do their best for David and made sure he got into a good school. At home, he'd failed his Eleven Plus and had ended up going to the local secondary, when really he was clever enough to go to the grammar. In Manchester, he could make a fresh start with his education and achieve his potential, Auntie June and Uncle Keith had said. In spite of the sadnesses in his past – and he should never feel that he had to forget it – he was God's gift to them, they'd kept repeating. He was the son they'd always wanted and had never been able to have. They'd encouraged him when he'd shown an interest in getting into the police, helped him get fixed up in his own flat, and took a genuine pride in his success.

Auntie June, with her cotton hankies sprigged with embroidered violets, ironed in neat, flat triangles, her old-fashioned tweed suits and blouses smelling of moth balls, her thick brown stockings and sensible low-heeled brogues. Uncle Keith, spraying minty Gold Spot on his tongue, his sleeked hair black and white, his head the shape of a badger's, his thick neck and square shoulders in dark suits, immaculate shirts, his mirror-shiny shoes. Auntie June and Uncle Keith, with their matching leatherbound Holy Bibles on their bedside cabinets, their spare toilet rolls in the bathroom hidden discretely under the crocheted flounces of lady dolls' skirts. Auntie June and Uncle Keith long gone.

Gillian

I'm sure it's David coming towards me along the beach. I thought I'd walk as far as the caravans. It looks as if he's on his way back.

'Fancy meeting you here,' I shout to him as he's about to pass. He's obviously lost in his own thoughts, blown along by the wind.

'Oh hi, Gillian.' He comes over, undoes the baffle on his jacket to speak to me. 'Bit windy, isn't it? But a good day for a walk. Taking some photos for your work?' He points to the camera round my neck.

'Yes. I probably will. The light's good. And I'm not really in the mood for concentrating on drawing this afternoon.' I hadn't meant to go into that. But I'm really churned up after seeing Tony. My eyes feel gritty and I'm annoyed by the way the wind is whipping my hair all over the place. 'Everything okay?' David asks quietly. He could easily have said something funny or dismissive and walked on. He isn't obliged to take me seriously.

'Oh yes, I'm fine,' I begin automatically, then stop. I keep thinking of Tony's face, his smug smiles and condescending tones. Stupid selfish git. Tony cheating in broad daylight with a girl probably half his age, on the shore, in *my* special place. Little Boy Blue Tony, with his trousers rolled up, looking carefree, skimming stones. Why should I lie for you?

'Well, to be honest . . . I don't actually feel so good. Something happened to me this morning that I'd just like to be able to forget, but I can't. I mean, it's not a *crime* as such. More of a family situation that I shouldn't even have become aware of because no one knows I'm here . . . that I was *there.* And now I'm left with this horrible knowledge.'

David keeps nodding, stays silent.

'Sorry, I really hadn't meant to say all that,' I continue. 'It isn't your problem and I'm not even giving you enough information to make sense of what I'm talking about. It's only . . . if you weren't supposed to be there, but you witnessed something . . . I'm not sure what to do.'

'Perhaps it comes down to a personal choice,' David offers tentatively. He doesn't make eye contact as he speaks, which reinforces my impression that he seems to be talking to himself as much as to me. 'Perhaps it's about what difference it would make, if you were to tell? Something about weighing up the costs or the harm to yourself, and to others. The consequences of the particular choice. What you know to be right. What *you* could live with?' He lifts up his head and looks at me now, directly.

'Yes,' I say, wondering what to say next. 'Yes. You're right.'

'Just heavy words probably. That's me – master conversation-stopper.'

'No, really. Thanks. What you said is very relevant. Even without knowing the exact facts, you've obviously got the benefit of your own experience.'

'Well, I don't know if I'd use the word *benefit,* but yes, perhaps so.' He keeps on nodding after he finishes speaking.

'I must let you get on with your walk. I think I've off-loaded enough now, haven't I?' I say. 'Bet you didn't expect all that baggage to be dumped on you on the beach?'

'Don't worry about it. I always expect baggage. And when it's not my own, well . . . As I said, I can compartmentalise. I'm the original hard bastard. Tough as old boots.'

'I'm sure that's not true.' In spite of his apparent confidence, he's pretty self-denigrating at times. 'Oh, by the way, did you find out about the motorcyclist? Is he going to pull through?' I've carried an image of that upturned motorbike in my head since the accident.

'From what I can gather he's doing well. He's out of intensive care, they said.'

'No small thanks to you.'

'We do what we can, don't we? Most of the time? Hope you get some good photos.'

'Thanks. See you again, David.'

I carry on along the beach, taking photos: distant figures of a dog and owner looking out to sea; a lone windsurfer, red sail vertical; various shots of the headland covered with caravans. Mum and Dad always used to complain about caravan parks, 'eye sores' encroaching on the coast, 'dumping grounds' with fag ends, broken glass, trails of damp toilet paper, bins crammed with beer cans and fluttering nappy sacks. Still, from a distance, the conglomeration of pastel shapes gets me thinking in glass again, seeing the possibilities for an abstract composition.

David

When he gets back to the cottage later, David goes straight to the fridge and takes out a six-pack of beer. He sets it on the coffee table, twists a can free from the plastic and throws himself down on the sofa without taking off his jacket or his boots. He doesn't turn on the TV, just sits there with the can in his hand, staring at it between swigs. He finishes it in less than five minutes, then cracks open another.

He could feel the place working on him as he walked out there. The effect all the more intense no doubt, because of the contrast with the cityscape where he has spent so much of his working life with his head down. The raw truthfulness of the countryside is getting into him. Making him look up, breathe, begin to loosen his grip. Connecting him to the past, with feelings and things of childhood, with his child self. Held, still breathing, at times so deeply buried within his adult self. The child breathing again brings good and bad. Pleasure and pain. Breathing heals and opens wounds. Fragments of his conversation with Gillian on the beach keep coming back.

And now I'm left with this horrible knowledge. I'm not sure what to do, she'd said. *Perhaps it's about what difference it would make if you were to tell. Something about weighing up the costs,* he'd answered, in all his infinite bloody wisdom, like a pompous smart-arse. She thought what he'd said was helpful and relevant. She could have just been saying it, but she'd looked at him as if she really meant it. *I always expect baggage. And when it's not my own, well . . . As I said, I can compartmentalise.* His fraudulent smoothness. *I'm the original hard bastard. Tough as old boots.* He cringes at the memory of his own words. Cracks open another can.

Occasionally, in spite of all the traumatic things he's dealt with, David still gets random flashbacks, images from incidents at work. The unnerving eyes and unflinching expression of a man or a woman he'd interviewed, knowing long before he had the proof that they had dispassionately murdered spouses, or strangers. The heart-rending sight of an elderly victim of serious assault, fragile skin torn and deeply bruised, body and mind irreparably maimed. The haunted look of a woman who'd been gang-raped, leaving him feeling that every question, however necessary in the investigation, was adding to her suffering and sense of violation. All part of the disturbing, violent territory of his job, which over the years he's had to learn to live with, but which he's still never become completely inured to.

An image from the accident on the lough-side road suddenly returns now to his mind. He remembers the motorcyclist crumpled up in the brambles. Blood everywhere. The lad's body as thin as skinny Kev's, in black leathers, his foot at an angle, in a huge clod of a biker's boot, making his narrow ankle look even narrower. *I'm the original hard bastard, tough as old boots.* He gets another flash of that foot, the narrow ankle, and again that hefty zipped black boot, like a close-up now.

Then, unbidden, from the more distant past, flashes of Sammy and Kev's faces, close. Their hushed, quaking, urgent voices. 'C'mon! Quick, get a move on! We can't get caught!' The sound of swishing grass, the three of them running back, along the edge of the field.

Chapter Six

Gillian

'*Gillian?!* What are *you* doing here?'

It's half past eleven in the morning. Only a short drive from the cottage, on the west side of the lough, there's a wildlife reserve fronted by a newly renovated visitors' centre. The café has windows ceiling to floor on one side, and overlooks a small lake with a shrubby central island, bustling with a variety of ducks, geese and other birds. For some time, I've been thinking of capturing that view, in shades of turquoise and green glass, with angular pieces – whites, browns and blacks – to suggest the scattered, choppy movement of the ducks. I've decided to have a coffee and spend some time drawing and turning over ideas.

I can't believe it. It's Laura. She's spotted me from her place in the queue at the till and is on her way over.

'Laura! I thought you'd be at work!' I say, as evenly as I can. 'Didn't expect to see you.'

'Well, obviously not! What do you think you're doing, sneaking over and not telling us? Or did *Claire* know you were coming?' Typical of Laura, anticipating she would be the one left out. Automatically piqued and on the defence. It's Christmas since we last saw each other. She's put on weight, dyed her short hair a darker shade of brown and is wearing a tomato red coat, but still she looks haggard and brittle. She stands over me, arms crossed, blinking fast. 'So. Where are you *staying?*'

'I'm renting a holiday cottage. It's just a short working break, which is why I didn't mention it. I didn't tell Claire either. I wasn't meaning to offend anybody.'

'Right,' Laura simply states. 'Well, I suppose you're entitled to do what you want.'

'Och, c'mon, Laura. Sit down. Want me to get you a coffee?'

'Och yes, I'm sure a *coffee*'ll solve it all!' she answers ironically, one of her eyes twitching with tiredness. 'But I wouldn't want to be getting in the way of your work, now, would I?'

'It's fine, honestly. Look, I'm sorry, Laura. I feel really bad now. Can I get you something to eat?'

When I come back with coffee and sandwiches, Laura is still in her coat, tightly belted, her hands in her pockets.

'Drawing the ducks?' she asks, staring expressionlessly at my sketches.

"Yes. I've been thinking about doing the scene in glass for quite a while. Maybe triangular browns and whites for the wings. Planes of water and grass. Quite an abstract piece, I think.'

'Right,' she acknowledges, devoid of enthusiasm. 'Well, I'm sure you'll work it all out,

Gillian. You're the one with the talent, aren't you? Is it for someone in particular?'

'No, not as yet. I might sell it I suppose, or just keep it for myself. Is this your day off?'

'I've just finished a set of nights. I couldn't get to sleep, so I thought I'd have a bit of a drive and a coffee. Used to come here when the girls were small, but I haven't been for ages. I did ask Tony if he fancied meeting for a bite of lunch, but he's too busy at work so . . .'

'That's a shame.' *That's a sham.* I'm almost on the point of saying the words out loud. I hadn't expected to be in this position, facing Laura, so soon after seeing Tony with the girl. I haven't quite decided what to do. My instinct is to say nothing, especially now, when we've met so unexpectedly and she's obviously annoyed with me.

'Yes. Tony and I don't get much chance to catch up with each other these days. Especially with me doing a lot of nights,' she admits, in a resigned tone. 'But I suppose we're no different from most other couples with kids at this stage of our lives. It's all about the family, both of you doing your best to add to the pot. Your relationship has to be put on hold. Tony provides well for his family. He works his socks off.'

'So do you, Laura,' I say quickly, emphatically. I try to distract myself from thoughts and images of sham Tony. Laura's stock phrases, which usually infuriate me, seem poignantly ironic today. In spite of everything

71

that's happened between us, the thought that I know something about her life that she doesn't know herself – especially a part so tied to her own sense of self-esteem – gives me an uneasy sense of power and sympathy. The way she warms her hands around her coffee; the chinking of her wedding, engagement and eternity rings against the mug; her enduring ritual of slicing her sandwiches into precise squares; even the fact that she's wearing Mum's antique watch: it all makes me feel more sorry. Knowing about Tony would break her. I can't tell her. But how can I not?

'So, still a vegetarian?' she asks, nodding in the direction of my sandwich. She repeats the same question virtually every time we meet. 'And you used to *love* Mum's Irish Stew, didn't you?' With the same implication – that my decision to be a vegetarian represented so much more than a personal choice. In Claire and Laura's minds, the fact that I stopped having Mum's Irish Stew amounted to me rejecting her, the rest of the family and a fundamental part of Northern Irish culture. It went together with other things too, including how I'd gradually lost some of my accent – further evidence, apparently, of my disowning not only them, but my Northern Irish roots too.

'Yes, I did. Mum was a great cook. It wasn't anything personal. I just came to feel strongly about not eating meat. Sure, we've been through this so many times, Laura. Some people change, don't they?'

My observation immediately seems cruelly apt. I'm starting to feel at sea, churning with the unwanted power, compassion and guilt. I'm still easily riled by Laura's predictability, her refusal to give up the niggling petty questions and small retaliations that prevent us from relating to each other as the women we are now. Can't we do something different? *You'll make sure you three girls stay in touch and look after each other when we've gone, won't you?* I keep hearing in my head in Dad's voice, remembering Mum widening her eyes and nodding at each of us in turn. They often knew us better than we knew ourselves, but they still hung on to the hope that our future didn't need to necessarily follow on from the way we'd related to each other in the past.

'That's true. Although don't you think sometimes, Gillian, that maybe it was something that you got into, without really meaning to? Just because you wanted to be *different?* A bit of a rebel, kicking back? I mean, you went all sort of *alternative* then, when you went to art college, didn't you? You dyed your hair that wacky colour of blue, you had those little punky studs in your eyebrows and round your ear. Maybe the vegetarian thing was part of a phase that you could just let go of now?'

'No, Laura. I don't think so. No, it wasn't just a *phase*. It was a choice, that's still important to me. I know you never really got it. But we're *all* different, aren't we?'

I'm struggling to stay in control now. Knowing I have the means to really hurt Laura makes things worse. I don't want to just lash out. But her total inflexibility is getting to me, the way she refuses to allow that my view of the world and my feelings are as valid as her own. It seems as if we're bound to keep going round in the same, ever decreasing circles, unless one of us decides to give something up.

'There's no need to be so snippy now, Gillian!' Laura comes back. 'I was only saying, sometimes we need to be able to let ourselves off a hook, don't we?'

'You're right.' The terrible irony in her words again. 'So, what are you doing for the rest of the day, Laura? We could go for a bit of a walk round the lake if you want?'

'I can't, Gillian. I haven't got time. I've too much to do at home. And shopping to get. I'm doing a bit of beef for tea. Tony loves his roast beef and gravy. I'm not working tonight, so it's only fair. I mean, if you wanted to come and eat with us, I could do you a baked potato and cheese, or something. I'm sure Tony'd be fine about it. Even though it's short notice.'

'No. It's not fair on you. But thanks, Laura. Maybe another time?' I can't stand the thought of sitting down to tea with Tony tonight, watching him tuck into his beef and gravy, pointing pretentiously at his mouth corners with his

74

serviette, all the time asking myself how long I can continue to keep quiet about his deceit.

'But then I might be on nights again, so . . .' Laura starts. *So, if you can't come when I want you to come, then you can't come at all,* I finish for her, in my head.

'Don't worry, Laura. I came unannounced, so I don't expect to be entertained. Only if it really suits you.'

'So, do you want *me* to let Claire know you're over, or are you going to phone her yourself? I can't pretend I haven't seen you, can I? It wouldn't be fair. Claire'd never forgive me.'

'I'll get in touch with her, but if it's putting you in an awkward position in the meantime, then I don't mind you saying.'

'Och thanks, Gillian. I know you probably think I'm bossing you about, but I just hate that sort of thing. It gets me really worked up, you know.'

I do know that's how Laura is, has always been. She likes things to be clean and simple mentally, even if it means she avoids putting herself in other people's shoes. Her mind is full of streets she'll only allow herself to travel so far along. She prefers the routine, the boring even, to the complicated or the uncertain. I envy her that in a way, although I also want to expect more of her.

'Give us a buzz anyway, won't you, Gillian? I'll let you get back to work. Bye for now.'

She's less hostile as she leaves, having spoken her mind, some of her anger channelled no doubt into her remarks about my continuing vegetarian 'phase'. Her main project now will be the preparation of Tony's roast beef.

I'm left thinking about when I should phone Claire. And about Tony too, what I didn't say, whether I should say anything. I'm wondering if he's spending another lunchtime with the same girl, the two of them tucked away somewhere, by the shore. If he's hearing her indulgent, tender voice, teasing him about being just 'a wee boy'.

David

On the other side of the peninsula the tide is on its way out again, leaving the broad beds of rock saturated and glistening, the deep pools brimming over. He found an old shrimp net in the cottage in a bucket in the under-stairs cupboard and carries it now against his shoulder as he makes his way out across the slippery weeds and crunching barnacles. As he crouches down over a ragged pool, close to the sea's edge, David thinks about Kev and Sammy again, how they used to go shrimping, the three of them hunkered down in bare feet, soles sore from treading on barnacles and blades of rock.

Kev's net was the best, the mesh the finest, the cane tightly bound where the net fitted into it at the top. Sammy only had a margarine tub, punctured with knife slit holes – that didn't let the water drain through properly. David's net was too shallow, really – he tended to lose the shrimps before he could nip and trap them in his fingers. It wasn't long before they decided it was best for Kev to wait with his net for the catch, while David and Sammy took it in turns to drive the shrimps up, out of their dens in the weed.

David quickly became good at it, sneaking slowly through the waving fringes, gently working them out, then keeping the net edging behind, making it a part of their habitat. He had a feel for the best places to look, the small underwater caves and crannies below ledges where he imagined a shrimp would be most at home. 'Good man! Good man!' Kev would be telling him. 'That's it! Just keep sneaking along! He thinks you're dancing with him! Keep him in the mood!'

Sammy, on the other hand, much to their frustration, was clumsy and loud when he got excited. 'Och no! We've lost him now, Sammy!' they'd yell at him, and 'He was a really big one! They can hear you coming. They're not stupid, you know. Unlike some people!' Sammy would keep saying sorry and rub hard at his forehead and his eyes. Sammy often rubbed his eyes. In spite of his size and the way he kept going off into a dream, Sammy was as soft as brown banana. He hated himself if he ever let them down. David would cry too, but only occasionally, at home, in bed, when he was sure no one would know. David would always cry on his own. David and Sammy and Kev. Sammy and Kev, long gone.

David lowers the head of the net into the water now. Looks down into the depths of the pool. There's a faded dead starfish upside down, on the bottom. They feel strange in your hands, soft bodies under sandpapery skin, rough as a man's face, a day after shaving. The pool's floor is covered with fine stones, a few larger ones on top. Its steep sides are softened with feathery brown weeds, bright green frills of sea lettuce, pinkish coral-coloured backgrounds showing through. It has always made him think of silky underwear and the soft hidden parts of women. Then he feels his mind sinking down into the water together with the head of the net. The weed gives way, the edge of the net slowly sweeps along, nudging out the shrimps.

You get lots of tiny shrimps, only just visible, like watery ghosts, or eye floaters, falling and propelling erratically across your vision. Then, larger ones, bolder, less trusting than the babies, though still naïve – the cocky teenagers of Shrimp World, stronger in colour and movement. If you work a bit harder, slipping the net into the crevices, patiently probing the depths, you'll flush out the bigger ones, what they used to call the 'Kingpins'. Some of them are females, laden with eggs. Others wily males, with all the wisdom of experience. They're the hardest to catch. They'll be lurking somewhere behind the others, watching from the depths of the weed. And even if you think you're in just the right position and you're sure you've got them, they can suddenly disappear right at the last minute, leaving you feeling a fool, nipping an empty corner of net.

David follows the shrimps lightly to the end of the pool, before sharply lifting the net clear of the water. He hears the distinctive sound of their bodies, flicking against mesh, the whispering of the nylon web draining. He holds the shrimps trapped, squeezes them hard in the corner of the net. Their sharp spines prick his fingers, their bodies become less resisting, giving up, lying limp and finally, still.

Later that evening back at the cottage, after a couple of beers, David fills a pan with water from the kettle, adds some salt and brings it back to the boil. He peels the lid off the lunch-box where he put the shrimps and tips them in, watches as they rise and roll and turn that fluorescent shade of pink, that makes him think of flamingos. He remembers his mother's cheeks, flushed with the steam, her pleasure as she cooked his catch. He butters some slices of white bread on a white plate just as she did, drains the shrimps and puts them on a saucer. 'That's all you could ask for, now, isn't it, David?' she'd 've said. 'Some fresh shrimps and bread with plenty of butter.' 'With a squeeze of lemon and a good shake of salt,' his Dad would've added in.

He peels the shrimps. The tiny crescents of meat barely cover the circle in the centre of the saucer. But they taste fresh and sweet. He rubs his eyes.

Gillian

'So. You're over without telling us!' are Claire's first bitter words when I speak to her on the phone, just after 6 p.m., back at the cottage. 'Laura said you were on a *working break?* I don't know why you didn't tell us, Gillian. Laura and I could've taken it in turns to have you round. I mean, I'm working all week and I've done my planning already.'

'I know. I'm sorry, Claire, it was just that –'

'Sure, you're hardly ever here, Gillian. You'd think that when you were, you'd really *want* to see your family. I mean, have we done something to offend you, or something? Something you're not telling us? Och, for pity's sake Gillian, what's this all *about?*' Claire can easily work herself up to the point of hysteria, drawing on a full reservoir of resentment, effortlessly entering into the role of the wounded and wronged one.

'It isn't *about* anything, Claire. I just wanted to concentrate on work, keep things simple. If you wanted to, you could come over here for a coffee, or we could . . .'

'A bit late for that now, isn't it? Robbie and I are both up to our eyes this week! If we'd had some warning, we might've been able to fit you in.'

'Really, Claire. It's fine. You don't have to do anything, honestly.'

'You'll have to leave it with me, Gillian. Bye for now,' Claire ends, brusquely. It all has very little to do with her wanting to spend time with me and much more to do with her own need to stay in control.

It's after midnight when I get to bed. I feel restless after what happened with Laura and Claire, and at the same time annoyed with myself for letting it bother me so much. I can't stop thinking about Tony either. His infidelity shouldn't have really surprised me. I've never really trusted him and always knew he was stupid. Although there's something especially sickening about the idea of him messing around with such a young woman.

I try to relax before I go to sleep. I imagine Claire and Laura's faces first, side by side, each face made up of stained-glass panes. I outline each head in dark black and repeatedly go over and over the lines, making them heavier and thicker. Finally, I work on an outer, even more solid, frame. Now they occupy space in my mind, but I'm in charge of it. I can lighten or darken their colours, shrink them down, hold them fixed, enclosed, boxed in. I can choose to lay aside the frame and move on to another one when I want. I then do the same for Tony and the girl on the shore, finally shrinking the scene to a tiny square, fading it out, then replacing it with a vibrant image of a summer sea, which fills in the whole screen inside my head, in jewel colours of blue and green. Eventually I feel myself drifting off.

I wake with a start, not knowing immediately why. It's twenty-five past five in the morning. Then I hear banging, that seems to be coming from next door. It comes in bursts, at first, like quiet, repeated knocking, then louder, as if a hand is slamming against the other side of the wall, behind the head of my bed. Occasionally I've been aware of creaking floorboards and the faint babble of a radio before, but nothing much else until now.

When Matt and I had our place in Manchester, we lived next door to a couple who always seemed to be 'at it, like humping rabbits', as Matt put it, at all times of the night and early morning. Perhaps David has brought a woman back with him, but as far as I can hear, there's no woman's voice, no give-away sound of bed springs.

'*No! No!*' I hear, suddenly, shouted loudly. It must be David, but it doesn't sound quite like him. The voice isn't as deep. It seems broken, more like a teenager's.

'Don't! No! You can't *do* that!' I can make out, clearly. 'No! *Please!* Stop!' Perhaps David's just having a bad dream. Matt used to say I often called out in my sleep. Occasionally, I'll still wake up shouting.

Then I hear crying. Jagged, high-pitched at first, deepening into more full-bodied sobbing, which gradually gets louder and eventually builds into tormented yelling.

'*No! Stop it*, you filthy bastard! Fucking bastard!'

I just can't lie in bed any longer, listening. I put on my dressing gown and go downstairs. It's already a bright morning, light reaching through the unlined curtains.

I don't know what to do with myself. My head is full of dark thoughts. I'm sure I'm getting it all out of proportion. But I can't help wondering what's happening. How would I feel if I found out later that David had been attacked, or worse, and I hadn't done anything?

I slip on my shoes, still not knowing what to do. If there *is* someone in there, I'd be putting myself at risk at well. It could be a burglar, picking on a holiday cottage – a calculating local, or an opportunist. But it could also be someone with a different kind of motive. They could be armed. I feel hot, cold, then sick, my heart racing. *I think he could be ex-army or maybe police,* I remember, in Derek McEvoy's voice.

Something else comes back to me too, from the 1970s when I was a child. In a nasal, Northern Irish radio voice, turned down low. Dad often had the radio on at mealtimes, especially for the six o'clock evening news. As we ate our shepherd's pie and vegetables and our dishes of set custard with dollops of stewed apple, terrible things were announced. As we girls argued and kicked each other under the table, in the background there were reports of bombings and shootings. Rioting, beatings, booby traps, tarring-and-feathering. Things that were happening close to us, which we needed somehow to keep at a distance, even when Dad turned up the volume and told us to be quiet.

A police officer was shot dead last night in his home. No one has yet claimed responsibility. We heard the same kind of phrases many times. 'Can you just imagine it?' Dad would comment sometimes, mainly to Mum, setting down his knife and fork, screwing up his eyes as if there was something bitter in his mouth. 'You're lying in your bed one night. Then there's a knock at the front door. Masked men with guns outside. They're asking to have a quiet word with the man of the house. And the next thing the poor woman knows, they're heading upstairs. She hears the husband yelling. They're giving him a kicking. Or holding a gun to his head, shooting him at point blank range.'

We girls would listen, shake our heads, say how awful it was and try our best to be mature and appropriate. We had no real understanding of how that would be, couldn't connect to it with imagination, let alone with feeling. We were only children, taking on board what we could manage, believing what our parents would keep repeating

– that we were lucky to live in one of the peaceful areas of Northern Ireland where there was much less chance of such things happening. As we grew older, we realised, of course, that terrible things happen everywhere. Brutal, grotesque killings occur in remote farmhouses, irrespective of beautiful landscapes. Atrocities are committed on country roads, in quiet towns. It hasn't been until more recently that I've found myself thinking about how horrific some of those incidents really were.

I think he could be ex-army or maybe police . . . might be wrong, of course, but you often know, don't you? I wonder if I should call Derek McEvoy and ask for his advice. I'm on the point of lifting the phone when I hear a door slamming and brisk footsteps on the gravel outside. Through the crack in the curtains, I see David, zipping his coat as he walks. He gets into his car quickly, starts the engine and drives off immediately, without fastening his seat belt. I feel a sense of relief. Whatever was going on, David appears at least physically unharmed.

Chapter Seven

David

He'd stayed up late, watched an old Clint Eastwood film into the early hours, worked his way through another four cans, felt himself nodding off. Sometimes the beer would have the desired effect and knock him out, though often after the initial drowsiness it would make him feel more unpleasantly alert and vulnerable to preying negative thoughts. Afterwards when he took himself up to bed, he lay thinking about his mother and father, about shrimping and Sammy and Kev, voices echoing around his head, sounds of gulls calling and water breaking. Eventually he fell into a restless wakeful sleep, carried along on wave after wave of vivid dreams. The grand finale, a variation of that recurring dream he'd had, for so long, about the same terrible thing.

He wakes in a sweat, kneeling up on his pillows, hands in tight fists, head pressed against the wall behind his bed, disoriented at first, not quite knowing if he's really awake or still dreaming. *'Fucking bastard!'*

He's whispering now, but recalls himself yelling, with 'Don't!' and 'Stop!' and 'No!'. He remembers sobbing, outward distress weak, when compared to the strength of the unquantifiable agony inside. As the dream starts to recede, he struggles to claw it back and pin it down. He wants to recoil from the pain and at the same time wants to make himself feel it even more keenly, to fix the haunting images in his mind.

The pain is the truth. The truth was, is, about suffering. Power. Punishment. His. Theirs. Hers. And especially *His* – the one with the power to give and take, to protect or destroy. Punishment deserved and undeserved, for acts omitted and committed. And also that punishment never given, still owing.

Suddenly remembering where he is, he hopes that Gillian didn't hear him next door and that his words were contained in the sound-proofed dream world, for so many years the only safe place where those words could be addressed to whom they concerned, even if they didn't have any real effect. Most of what was seen and said and done in that dream had actually happened, but David's voiced protest was a fiction, a sad fantasy constructed over time by his mind for the sake of its own preservation.

He gets out of bed and goes to the bath-room, suddenly aware his bladder is uncomforta-bly full. Back in the bedroom, he pulls on yester-day's clothes and trainers without socks, snaps on his watch, sweeps up car keys, wallet and walking jacket and leaves the cottage, slamming the door behind him.

It's already bright outside, but the cool, still damp air of the summer morning gives him some relief. His heart is racing, head pounding, mouth dry. He imagines his breath must be foul from the beer and lack of breakfast, but he has to get going. He throws himself into the driving seat, reverses quickly to turn, then makes his way down the drive, opening the windows, turning on the radio.

There's an old heavy metal track playing— AC/DC, 'Highway to Hell'. He's hardly in the mood for humour, but the timing of the lyrics and the crazy electric drama of it strikes him as darkly funny. He brings up the volume. Dependable AC/DC. Always ready to encourage you to move on and throw caution to the wind. Always prepared to stay with you, in the depths of your own shit. *And aren't you the wee poet who knows it?* In skinny Kev's sharp, cheeky voice.

Instead of heading for the shore, he turns inland. The twisting narrow roads here hardly lend themselves to high speed, but there's virtually no one on them so early in the day and he's used to driving fast, having to trust his reflexes, his own limits. He presses up to the bends, tries to concentrate on just driving, steering anticlockwise, clockwise, eyes trained on the details of the road ahead, checking his mirrors. There's no real escape from the truth of the dreams, but he feels less heavy somehow when he's accelerating, as if some of the weight lifts, temporarily. As if he's a skimming stone, set in fast motion.

He's always lived inland. In Manchester

and when he was a child with his parents, in Northern Ireland. His family had a simple, two-bedroomed house in Bryansbridge, just a handful of houses really, to the west of the lough, within easy cycling distance of Stewartsford. You knew that the sea was never far away, but you got used to being surrounded by fields and trees, fences and hedgerows, a landscape that protected and enclosed you. The countryside had a cosy, sheltered feel. But it could also seem isolated, claustrophobic and bloody oppressive, depending on what was happening at the time. In a country with an already relatively small and concentrated community, the towns and villages could be even more intense, both for the better and the worse. They could harbour extreme loyalties, a devotion to a staunch pride in their own. They could be wells of acrimony, tension and bitterness, microcosms mirroring wider, learned attitudes of mistrust and blinkered defensiveness, with inflexible laws, rulers, judges, enforcers. Sometimes all rolled into one. As it had been for him, for them, with Him – because He was the one. The man they called Santie.

The sexy, up-you feeling, the cocky AC/DC kickback that he wanted to convince himself was everything he knew, if even for a moment, has gone. His abstract thoughts, the *learned attitudes* and *defensiveness* and *wider community* – his bloody feeble attempts at sociology – give way to something much more basic, wordless, raw. He feels the pain getting strong again, the lump coming back to his throat, his eyes smarting. No longer able to concentrate on driving, he slews off the road, where the grass verge broadens in front of a rusted field gate. He switches off the ignition and sits with his eyes closed, his jaw clamped, hands sweating, gripping the steering wheel.

Often, when you try to remember a familiar face, because you've seen it from so many angles, forming different expressions, you struggle to visualise. But it was different when it came to Santie. While his features must, in reality, have altered with time, they remained fixed in David's mind, where the man was eternally in his prime, somewhere in his forties. Santie's face had a sinister, tenacious magic. It felt sometimes as if it had incorporated itself carefully but surely into the depths of your brain, like a crab sinking into sand. At other times, it was more as if the image had forcefully drilled itself down and inwards, with a pointed intention to never let you forget.

In some ways Santie's face might have been described as unremarkable, ordinary even. A big, round fleshy face. To go with a half-bald, spud-like head between heavy, ruddy-lobed ears, attached to a neck and body as strong as a bull's, with a proud bass-drum of a belly. His mouth was wide, his nose comparatively small, shiny and smooth, contrasting with the open-pored, pocked roughness of his cheeks.

It wasn't often that you got a chance to see

Santie's eyes. They were usually shaded behind rectangular, metal-rimmed photo-chromic lenses. But if you did get a glimpse, there was something about those eyes that meant you couldn't completely read them or even precisely name their shifting, murky colours. That might have given you a clue to the less open and jolly Santie, his trickier side.

Santie did his best for the community. A lot of people looked up to him, David's father had often emphasised. The way he spoke on such occasions made David think of the way his dad talked about God. Soberly, self-consciously. As if an omnipresent omnipotent was monitoring his every move, his every word. As if he was bound to give praise and train his family to do the same. There was a forced reverence in his dad's voice, a nervousness behind his enthusiasm. He spoke differently when he was talking about things he really knew about and believed in, the things he loved and understood - birds, tending animals, growing and lifting vegetables. His tone was warm, his vocabulary less considered and he was quite happy for you to take it or leave it and not have to be standing to attention listening.

David's mother agreed with his father about Santie. Quietly, keeping her head down, not making eye contact, with, 'And you'll do well to stay on the right side of him, Davie, if you know what's good for you. He's a very powerful person. And he knows a lot of hard men high up. He helps them, they help him. He'd not stand for any messing around.'

Santie's parents, like David's, hadn't had much, but the man had worked hard to make something of himself. He'd done well, but he'd never forgotten how it was to struggle and go without. Where he saw a deserving cause, he wasn't slow to put his hand in his pocket. *The Lord giveth and the Lord taketh away.* So it was with Santie. *Hallowed be thy name.* It had taken a lot of determination and work for him to establish himself as a businessman with three thriving shops to his credit.

For as long as David could remember, Santie was Santie. The name said so much more about him than the name his parents had given him, which seemed almost irrelevant. Skinny Kev sometimes joked that Santie had been 'Santie' since the beginning of time, even if it took a while for his true identity to be acknowledged. It was a nickname the man himself knew about and proudly owned, although he wouldn't have accepted some of the interpretations and associations it would go on to gather in the minds of others.

Santie's first shop was a general hardware store, which sold a mixture of house and garden supplies, as well as a selection of children's toys. Other shops in the town sold similar things and had the same smell of linseed oil and hessian, but Santie's was seen as a bit of a 'cut above' in terms of the quality of the goods and the carefully planned style of the displays. There was none of the happy-go-lucky chaos or the scuffed make-do-and-mend style that characterised other places. Santie's counters and floors were always clean and uncluttered, invoice books lined up, pencils sharpened, the tills spotless. The china tea sets had been tastefully arranged and dusted, the glassware sparkled. There were perfect fans of kitchen knives, neatly coiled ropes, superior ranges of tools with smooth handles and pristine heads and blades. The ranges of quality paints, solvents, potting composts and fertilisers were constantly well-stocked.

Around Christmas in the shop, beside the till next to the toys, there was a stout wooden barrel, decorated with red crepe paper and gold tinsel, covered with a small circular green tablecloth. On the side of the barrel was a notice, hand-written in capital letters, in black marker pen, which said, 'Santie's Gifts. Please do not touch without His permission'. Beside it there was a high-backed upholstered armchair, with a red velvet cushion.

On selected afternoons, having delegated the general tasks of running his shop to his trusted, stolid assistants, Santie would sit waiting in the chair ready to receive children whose parents brought them to visit. He would be wearing his Santie suit, complete with its red velvety cape, hat and gloves trimmed with white fur, as well as a woolly white full beard, hooked over his ears. The tunic under the cape was tightly belted, always with the same thick leather strap which matched shiny black, military-style laced ankle boots.

David had only been about four when he'd had his first visit, but he still remembered it. He'd been half-excited, half-scared when his parents had held his hands and took him into the shop. He'd started to feel sick as they got close to the chair. There was a pale, serious younger man dressed in an elf's hat and tunic wearing a round badge, which said 'Santie's Helper'. Santie himself, bigger and older, with glasses and a beard, seemed frightening. He wasn't the fairy-land kind of Santie David had expected. This Santie was just too much like a strange man peering at him, who made him feel shy and worried, as if he might need to go to the toilet at any minute. He'd stopped and tried to pull his parents back.

'Och c'mon, Davie,' his Mum had whispered. "You'll be fine! There's nothing to be frightened about. You want your present, don't you now? Sorry, Santie. I think he's just feeling a wee bit shy.'

He could tell his dad wasn't pleased with him, especially when Santie lifted his hand and cheerfully waved at them. 'Catch yourself on, David!' his dad hissed, and then, more loudly, for Santie's benefit, 'You'll not be getting anything if you're a bad boy. I'm right, aren't I, Santie?'

David had suddenly felt alone, humiliated and betrayed.

'Och don't be too hard on him this time, Daddy!' Santie had suggested, gently. 'It's only his first visit! Are you going to come and have a wee seat on Santie's knee?'

It'd felt like he'd no choice.

'Of course he is! Let's be having you now, David!' his dad replied, pulling him towards Santie.

On Santie's knee, David had felt too high up and wobbly, but he'd kept his hands on his own legs. He didn't like the smell of Santie's unfamiliar, grown-up body and breath, the way he could feel Santie's legs through his trousers. His stomach had felt empty, and made loud gurgling noises, which seemed much too private a thing to be overheard by a stranger.

'Ho! Ho! Ho!' Santie had said loudly, resting a heavy gloved hand on David's shoulder. 'So, David. Can you tell Santie what boys and girls have to do in Santie's town, to make sure they get their presents?'

David had tried hard to think about what Santie wanted him to say.

'Be very *good?*' he'd decided on quickly.

'That's it, David! So, do you think *you've* been good enough since last Christmas to be on Santie's List?'

David had nodded, trying not to think about how many times his dad had told him he was an 'eejit'.

'I *think* so,' he'd said quietly, not daring to look up at Santie, in case the man would know what he was thinking.

'What do *you* think, Mummy?' Santie had asked next.

'Och, yes!' his mum had answered, smiling. 'He does his best!'

Santie had paused for a while, stroking his beard thoughtfully. 'Well, I think, if David promises to be good and comes back to see me next year, then he deserves to choose himself a gift from Santie's bran tub!' He'd set David down from his knee, lifted the cover off the barrel and told David to close his eyes and put his hand into the sawdust.

David lifted out a large flat parcel in thin shiny paper covered with elves and Santa faces. Inside there was a blue Boy's Lucky Bag, a comic and a packet of sherbet-filled Flying Saucers, exactly the kinds of things he would have chosen for himself.

His parents had been almost as pleased as he was. 'Och, Santie's very clever! He knows what girls and boys want, doesn't he?' his dad had said. A lot of other parents agreed with him. Santie took a lot of interest in young people. He had a very special way with them, people had often said. It mattered to him that they followed the right track and that they didn't hang round with the wrong people.

After that first visit to see Santie, David had started to wonder if Santie had a 'Bad List', and what would happen to someone if they were on it. He'd decided to ask his dad.

'He certainly does, David,' he'd been told straight away. 'And mind you don't get yourself on it.'

A lot of adults made empty threats. But as he grew older, David would discover that Santie was as dedicated when it came to following through on punishments as he was in his shopkeeping.

Just after his tenth birthday, when David had heard rumours at school, his dad broke the news to him that it was really a child's parents who brought their Christmas presents.

'But what about when we go to see Santie in the shop?' David asked. '*He*'s real, isn't he?' His dad had laughed. 'Of course, David! It's the man who owns the shop dressed up. He likes everyone to call him Santie all year round, but he only wears his special suit at Christmas.'

Not long afterwards, he'd gone into the shop with his dad to buy a new sledgehammer. As they'd come to pay, his dad had said to the man at the till, 'So, how's about you, Santie?'

Santie was clean-shaven and had exchanged his red suit for dark grey trousers, a white shirt and a maroon tie with a gold tie clip. The suit jacket was neatly hung over the back of a chair behind the counter.

'Och, not so bad now, John. Always busy. But sure, that's business for you, isn't it? That's a good sledgehammer you've got yourself there. You make sure your dad passes it on to you when he gets too old to use it, won't you, David?'

Santie wrapped the tool carefully in thick brown paper and tied it up with twine.

'We've had to tell him the truth about Christmas,' David's dad had said.

'Have you now?' Santie had replied. 'Och well, it'll do him nay harm. Comes to us all, sooner or later. And he's already his own man, aren't you, David?'

The way Santie spoke to him made David feel good and instantly taller. His dad spoke to him in the same kind of way sometimes, but it felt even better coming from Santie.

'Though of course you know I'll still be looking out for you. Santie can always see about getting you the things you need. That's right, isn't it, Dad?'

His dad nodded. 'It certainly is. In fact . . . There's something I've been meaning to have a word with you about Santie. David, why don't you take yourself over there for a minute and have another look at the tools? I'll not be long.'

As David had pretended to look at the tools, he'd watched his dad and Santie out of the corner of his eye. His dad had gone round to the other side of the till. His face was serious. They'd both lowered their voices. David couldn't hear what they were saying. After a brief conversation, his dad reached into his coat and gave Santie what looked like a brown envelope, which Santie quickly tucked under the counter.

'C'mon David! Let's be having you,' his dad then called to him, waving him back over. 'Thanks a million, Santie,' he'd said earnestly, more loudly, shaking Santie's hand.

'No problem, John. Don't give it another thought. We'll make sure that gets sorted out straight away,' Santie had answered. He made a clicking noise at the side of his mouth, winked at David and put his hand into his trouser pocket. He then shook his hand too, palming him a large gobstopper and a brandy ball. 'Mind you don't get too drunk on that and disgrace yourself and your dad!' he'd joked.

Once you've been introduced to someone, you can start to notice them everywhere. It's hard to know if, by coincidence, your paths really do cross more frequently, or if the person was always around to the same extent and you've only just become more aware of them.

From then on, he'd noticed Santie much more often out behind the wheel of his big heavy Volvo. The car was also parked sometimes outside different houses on the road where David's family lived. He saw him leaving the Headmaster's office at his school. On a Saturday, he'd be talking to groups of teenagers around the town, at the park, the football pitch and, in summer, down at the travelling fun fair. Every Twelfth of July parade, Santie was close to the head of the procession through Stewartsford, marching alongside local dignitaries and their supporting young bands, immaculately groomed and solemn in his dark suit, V-shaped sash, white gloves and black bowler hat.

The week after David's dad and Santie had spoken in the shop, David and Sammy were playing out one evening after school. About half a mile or so from David's house there was a derelict cottage. Behind it in the overgrown garden there was a small greenhouse, full of weeds and shattered glass, next to a weathered old hen house. It was all supposed to be out of bounds, but David and Kev and Sammy occasionally sneaked in. They'd picked gooseberries, hard pears and sour apples and sat talking on the cool floor of the hen house under the deserted perches. It still smelt of chicken shit; there were bits of fluff hanging on inside the wood-wormed nesting boxes.

That evening, they'd been on their way along the narrow path leading down the side of the cottage and they'd heard voices that seemed to be coming from the back garden.

'Quiet, Sammy!' David had whispered. 'Let's go down the field instead.'

To one side of the path, there was a thick, tall hawthorn hedge. You could crawl through a hole at the bottom of it and get into a small field.

If you walked down the hedge on the field side, in places you could get a good view through to the garden without being seen. Immediately behind the hen house there was a square of cracked concrete with weeds poking through it, then an area of tangled brambles and old raspberry canes. That bottom edge had obviously become a dumping ground. They'd found all kinds of things there – an ancient lawnmower, broken tools, an old doll's pram with no wheels, piles of bricks, bits of wood and rusted metal.

'Let me have a look first,' David had hissed to Sammy.

Through the hole in the hedge he'd seen two men in dark anoraks wearing black balaclavas standing on the concrete behind the hen house. On the ground in front of them, on their knees, bound with rope, were two teenage boys.

It was Keith and Tom. They were both fifteen and usually spent their time hanging around the town. They'd got a reputation for being 'hard men', the ones always looking for a fight.

David had remembered his dad had been talking about them to his Mum over the previous couple of weeks. Someone had been wrecking people's back gardens at night, including theirs, and one of the neighbours had told his dad he was pretty sure it was Keith and Tom. Plants had been pulled up, sheds broken into, paints and chemicals tipped all over the place, gates and fences damaged. His dad had lost a lot of good plants. Whoever it was had just picked them for the sake of it and left the leaves torn and the stems mashed, strewn over the path. You didn't grow your own for it to get it spoiled like that by some young layabouts.

Behind that hen house, Keith and Tom had looked like terrified rabbits.

'Och *please,* mister. Please don't do anything to us. Just let us go, will you?' Tom had pleaded.

'It wasn't us. Honest to God!' Keith kept repeating.

The two hooded men were standing over them like hangmen. David couldn't see their faces but there was something familiar about their voices.

'So what do you think?' the taller man asked. 'Do you think they deserve another chance or not?'

The smaller man stood for a while in silence. 'Do you know what *I* think? I think they've used up all their chances. I think we need to learn them a wee lesson. You see these good strong pickaxe handles, boys? Now, I wonder if you can guess what we're going to use these for? I'm sure pair of bright boys like yourselves'll have some ideas?'

Keith and Tom had both started crying, their eyes and noses running.

'Och don't cry, boys. You're too old for that, now,' the taller man suggested quietly.

'I'll tell my dad on you. He'll . . . he'll . . .' Keith started off in a broken voice.

'We know your dad. He's a good hard-working fella. I don't think he'd have a problem about bad boys being learnt a lesson,' the other man carried on. 'And I don't think he'd like the sight of all that dirt coming down your nose. I think we should help these boys wipe their noses, don't you?'

The taller man nodded. Suddenly, without further warning, he lifted the pickaxe handle he was holding and smacked Keith hard across his mouth. Straight afterwards, the other man did the same to Tom. The boys could only groan and roll their heads with the pain of the blows, their mouths and noses bubbling with blood. The men then moved round behind them, pushed them down hard onto their faces and carried on mercilessly, wielding the pickaxe handles until the boys lay limp and bloody on the concrete. Afterwards, they stood back, threw down the shafts and each lit a cigarette.

'They'll not be doing any more wrecking for a wee while, if they know what's good fer them,' the taller one said, pulling down his anorak hood. He took a half bottle of something from his pocket, unscrewed the cap and offered it to his partner in crime. By now, David had recognised him. It was one of the assistants in Santie's shop, his special Christmas helper.

David had shuddered with fear. He knew he had to make sure he and Sammy weren't seen. He motioned for Sammy to copy him as he slowly got down and lay in the thick weeds at the hedge bottom. They waited there, hardly breathing, until the men were gone before they ran from the field.

Chapter Eight

Gillian

I take a cup of tea back upstairs and sit in bed with it, still thinking about what I heard earlier on and wondering what was going on with David. The most likely explanation I can think of is that he was having some kind of nightmare. My worst nightmares – worse even than those I had after Mum and Dad died – were those I had when I was at art college.

I became a vegetarian not long after I went to London. I'd been working on a project involving a collection of drawings of animals and spent hours sketching at the zoo. The more I looked them in the eyes, the more I felt uncomfortable about eating meat. Of course, I wasn't eating lions or giraffes, but when I thought about it, eating cows and lambs and hens didn't seem much different. It came to the point when every time I ate meat, I felt sick and guilty. Awake and asleep, I was haunted by animal faces, eyes as communicative as humans', searching, fearful, entreating.

It was a sudden decision – irrational and overly sentimental as far as a lot of people were concerned – but one I felt compelled to make. It wasn't something my family understood.

'Don't be going all flowery-power on us

now, will you, Gillian?' I remember Dad teasing me, with a wink. 'I mean, if you've made up your mind, it's not for us to try to change it, but people've always eaten meat, haven't they?'

'A good farmer loves Nature,' Mum added. 'He thinks the world of his beasts. Even if he has to send them to slaughter. It's his livelihood, isn't it?'

I knew what they were saying. Our lives had always been tied up with the countryside. Like a lot of people we knew, hunting, fishing and gathering was in our blood. If you respected Nature and allowed animals and birds a good habitat and quality of life, there could be give and take. If you were shooting a rabbit, you made sure it was a good, clean shot. If you hooked a fish, you killed it, as soon as you could. You were grateful for the produce of the land, your vegetables, your meat, whether they came from the wild, the butcher or the grocer. You ate every last morsel of turbot, fought over the parson's nose and the wings of the chicken, gnawed your ox tails, cleaned out your marrow bones.

In spite of my abiding confusion, shortly afterwards I joined Animal-Protect, one of the various animal rights groups who'd recruited quite a few of the students to their ranks. I knew better than to tell my family about it. Dad had no sympathy for animal rights activists. 'Those eejits do more harm than good. What they need is a decent day's work.'

We had regular meetings in each other's flats, talked into the early hours about how we felt and our ideas for change. I suppose a lot of it was about the camaraderie, the feeling that we belonged to something that could make a real difference, that wasn't just another trivial pursuit for students. We were particularly encouraged by how groups like ours had played a part in bringing about changes in legislation concerning the long-distance transportation of livestock.

To begin with, we were just handing out leaflets, manning stalls and approaching people to sign petitions. As time went on, things became much more heated. There was more pressure put on us to move towards violent types of protest, to threaten people who conducted research and take part in targeted attacks on those who were seen to be in a position to change things and had failed to do so.

My relationship with Jes, an older, mature art student who was intensely committed to the cause and increasingly convinced of the need to forcefully drive home its message, made things even more complicated for me.

We'd met in one of the bars in the student's union. I've rarely described a man as beautiful, but Jes was. He was tall and slim and had what I can only describe as a bewitching otherworldly quality, that made me think of *The Lord of the Rings*. He had jet black shoulder-length wavy hair, thick brows and eyelashes, pale green eyes. While his face quickly grew heavy, dark stubble, the background of his skin was milky white. He always wore a tiny gold hoop in one ear. Jes was a Londoner with Irish ancestry which he was proud of and referred to often. It was even included in his initial chat up line. *That's an Irish accent, isn't it? That's what I like to hear.*

It wasn't long before I believed I'd met 'the love of my life'. I was drawn to Jes's passionate nature. If he was doing something, he gave of himself one hundred per cent. He was particularly good at drawing people and practised everywhere slavishly, in sketchbooks, round the edges of newspapers, in chalk on pavements. Lead singer in the band he'd formed at college, he wrote his own songs of rebellion and put his heart and soul into his performances. When it came to sex, it was as if he guessed the exact details of my fantasies, embodied and actually improved on them. He understood how to build sexual tension, the charge in a long-anticipated kiss. Even when I was with Matt, in spite of the reasons why Jes and I split up, I still thought about kissing him. No matter how guilty I felt, I couldn't stop those irresistible images filling my mind.

Inevitably, when Jes made the decision to join Animal-Protect, it wasn't something he embarked upon lightly. He wanted others to share the intensity of his own enthusiasm. I loved to hear him talk, the beautiful seriousness of his face, the way he could hold people's attention.

'They depend on us to be their guardians. They can't speak for themselves. They need our voices,' he'd say, as he deftly rolled a thin cigarette. He was haunted, he said, by the possibility of reincarnation. 'Just imagine if you were to come back as an animal. You're packed into the back of a filthy, jolting truck. You arrive at the slaughterhouse. You don't know that's what it's called, of course, but it reeks of death. It stinks of the sweat and piss of stressed animals. You smell a history of fear. You don't quite understand what's going to happen, but you know it won't be good. That scent of fear gets into you. Your heart starts to race, your gut churns. There's nowhere to escape. All you can do is stand, suffering, and wait.'

When I voiced my reluctance to take part in any kind of threatening or violent action, Jes was keen to persuade me that sometimes a truly worthy end justified unpleasant means. 'Taking a peaceful line doesn't always work, Gill. Sometimes people have to be *made* to see the truth, even if it comes the hard way. If anyone should know that, *you* should. Coming from where you come from, I mean.'

Increasingly, it became a source of tension between us. No matter how clear I tried to make my position, Jes urged me to agree with his. I still admired his drive, but I started to realise that it could be double-edged.

I'd repeatedly told him that as far as Northern Ireland was concerned, I'd never sought to affiliate myself with either side or cause. I was a humanist if anything, without religious beliefs. While I could envisage situations where I might be provoked into defending myself or loved ones, I didn't believe in premeditated acts of violence. I knew that Jes didn't completely believe me. I think he'd already invested in the idea that I would be driven by raw feeling as much as he was, that being Northern Irish somehow guaranteed it. It was part of his romantic image of me that he couldn't easily give up.

I suspected that Jes was starting to do things that he didn't tell me about. He met frequently with other, more dominant members of the group. They'd drink late into the night together and when I asked him what they discussed, he'd just laugh, or tell me not to be so jealous. Jes didn't think he owed anyone a full account, not even me.

Things came to a head between us when a really ugly story appeared in the local papers. Following the suicide of a research scientist, it emerged that the man had had a number of letters from an anonymous animal rights group, calling into question his life's work, which had included trials of drugs on animals. He'd also been told, in punishing detail, of plans to harm his wife and family. I'll never forget the contorted face of the man's widow on the front page, racked with grief. I felt dreadful that day. It wasn't my doing, but I still felt implicated. I made up my mind to stop campaigning from then on.

That evening, I took the paper round to Jes's flat, mentally rehearsing the words of my announcement. 'Hound Dog' – our nickname for another art student, also a member of our animal rights group – was leaving as I arrived. Their mood seemed upbeat, congratulatory. Hound Dog was slapping Jes enthusiastically on the back.

'Have you seen the paper?' I asked Jes as soon as we were alone in his flat. It was a tiny, basic rented student place, with damp carpets, the bare minimum of furniture and Jes's distinctive loose black and white drawings all over the walls. 'Some poor scientist's committed suicide. Apparently, he was being tormented by an animal rights group. They're pretty sure that's what made him take an overdose. It's really horrible.'

Jes turned his back on me. 'Want a coffee?' he asked, with no reference to what I'd said. He lived on strong black coffee, without sugar. 'Kettle's already boiled.' He continued walking towards the kitchen.

'Jes? What's the matter? Didn't you hear me?' I shouted after him.

'Yeah, I heard,' he answered, still walking. 'So, what's there to say?' he carried on, nonchalantly.

I followed him into the kitchen, struggling to make sense of his response. It made me feel odd, panicky. Jes, moving away from me, turning his back, giving me nothing when I needed to see his expressive face, his eyes.

'But doesn't it make you feel *awful?* The thought that someone could be made to feel so terrible, Jes, that they believed *killing* themselves was the only way out? I've decided I can't be a part of the group anymore. It isn't right for me. I'm not a pressure group kind of person. I don't want to be ...'

Jes set the kettle down abruptly and swung round. 'Committed?'

He fired the word at me. I felt stunned. He'd never spoken to me with such unrestrained bitterness.

'No,' I said. 'No, Jes. It's not like that. It doesn't mean that I'm any less opposed to cruelty to animals. It's just that ...'

He nodded, looked down at the floor for a second, then stared back at me. 'It's just that you're happy, in fact, not to *do* anything about it. A polite petition or a stall, or even a well-behaved march, Gill can just about manage, but when it comes to *doing* anything more, you'd prefer to leave that to other people? Oh, do send my apologies, Jes. I don't mind the odd dabble in a bit of animal rights, a nice ladylike middle-class protest, but ... Is *that* it?' Jes's tone was sarcastic, aggressive. He kept passing his hand across his coarsely stubbled chin, in a way that made me think of someone trying to strike a match. It was a sign that he was really agitated and angry. It suddenly felt as if everything had changed.

'No, Jes. I'm not *happy*, in fact. I also don't think any of us should be inflicting cruelty on people in order to stop cruelty to animals. I don't think you'd want that either, would you? *You* wouldn't do it, would you?'

I'll never forget that look on Jes's face, the riveted hardness in his eyes. He raised his eyebrows and smiled. 'Stranger things have happened,' he said, blithely, although I knew that the four words were loaded with serious significance. I felt sick, because I *knew*. Oh Jes, I knew.

'Jes? *You* weren't involved in . . .? Those letters . . . That animal rights group wasn't . . .?'

Jes kept smiling and shrugged his shoulders. 'Let's just say, some things are best kept on a need-to-know basis. And *you* really don't need to know, Gill. That's bloody obvious.'

My stomach churned. I felt hot, then cold. 'But Jes! *Tell* me you didn't . . .'

Jes just shrugged again. 'What? For fuck's sake, Gill. Some bloke's dispatched himself. Life happens. He obviously planned to do it and he pulled it off, didn't he? He didn't have to lay that on his family. And so what, if he did get some strong letters to force him to think clearly about the things he did? To make him reflect on the punishment he dealt out to innocent, defenceless creatures in the name of human progress? What difference is a shitty little petition going to make to someone like that? It's just pissing in the wind.

113

The stuff doesn't sink in. It doesn't *go* anywhere.'

The longer Jes left my question hanging unanswered, the more gutted I felt. Tears were pricking my eyes, my voice shook. 'Just tell me you didn't have anything to do with this, Jes. *Please.* I need to know you weren't involved in anything wrong or illegal. The police are going to be investigating. If I knew you had . . .'

Jes turned, lifted the kettle and went to fill it at the sink. 'The police are going to be investigating. Mummy and Daddy said . . .' he moved his head from side to side, mimicking me in a sing-song, childish voice. 'Grow up, Gill. I mean, okay, I know some of this is probably to do with what happened in Northern Ireland when you were a child. But have you no sense of real autonomy? Of taking personal responsibility? Look. It's like I said before. You don't know and you really don't need to know. There's no need for *you* to have anything on your conscience. Do what you want as far as the group's concerned. It's up to you, okay? I'm making coffee now.'

It wasn't okay. I needed to have the truth. I couldn't live with constantly wondering if the man I loved had been part of actions that had led to a man's suicide. I couldn't believe, let alone accept, that the person I had so totally surrendered to could be capable of such a lack of compassion.

'I don't want coffee. We can't just leave this, Jes. It's not okay. I need you to be honest. Or I'll have to go.'

Jes put down the kettle again and came up close to me. He slid his arms round my waist, his voice quieter, softer then. 'Come on, Gill. Life's not always so simple. There are arguments on both sides. The victim is the perpetrator and the perpetrator is the victim. You know this stuff. People get caught up in their own feelings, in their historical moment. Things get messy. Nobody's immune, nobody's blameless. Maybe in the future, I'll do things differently. But why don't we just forget about this now? Don't let this spoil everything. What we have is worth more than this stuff, isn't it? Give us a kiss?'

As he leant in to kiss me, it was as much as I could do to resist. The world that I thought I knew was shifting. I felt lost and stabbed with sadness. Even so, the smell of Jes, the feel of the live wire of his body disabled my thinking, connecting me to memories of our abandoned sex, of willingly losing control.

But this time I had to force myself to stand my ground. I thought of the photograph of the scientist's widow's face in the paper, wrung out with sheer exhaustion and pain. I shoved Jes's hands off my waist and moved away from him.

'You're right. Life's not so simple. It's bloody confusing. And Gill's obviously as spineless as they come. And maybe her Northern Irish background *has* put her off violence a wee bit? It's probably made her more of a coward, more inclined to sit on the fence. One of the worst sins possible. *Jes* is defined by his *passion*! He has to fight with all his being for what *he* believes in. But, actually, do you know something? *You're* the one who spoiled it, Jes. You say you want me to have a sense of autonomy, but I have to share *your* sense of morality. You're such a hypocrite.'

Jes's face twitched, I guessed with a mixture of hurt and anger, although I knew then I couldn't even guess any more about what he was thinking. He folded his arms, leant back against the sink, crossing his legs. His tone became aggressive again. 'Okay. Well, why don't you just fuck off then, Gill? Join the W.I. and make wholesome cakes and jam for charity. Don't come back. Let's make this easy for both of us.'

There was nothing easy about it. But I lifted my coat and left.

Afterwards I agonised for a long time over whether or not I should pass on my suspicions about Jes's and the group's likely involvement in the incident to the police. I couldn't bring myself to do anything about it. As an activist myself, I suppose I could've been considered at least partially culpable. But the main reason was that, regardless of how things had ended between us, he was someone I'd loved. It was the best I could do at the time to cope with the loss and try to move on.

My morning tea's gone cold now. I put it down and get into bed. I try to get into the crime novel I'm reading, but I can't concentrate. I don't think I'll be able to sleep either. After a while I hear a car pulling up on the gravel outside, a door slamming. It must be David.

I get my map of the lough. I've been thinking about going to this place our family often visited, towards the tip of the other side of the peninsula. We'd park overlooking the sandy beach, have a swim then get dressed and carry a picnic over the rocks, round some smaller shingled bays and find a sheltered, hidden place to sit.

On the foreshore, there were cushions of grass, stonecrop, trefoil. You'd find birds' eggs, in slight hollows among the stones, so well camouflaged you had to be careful not to walk on them. There were stunted lichened blackthorn bushes at the edge of the barley fields, laid low by the winds lifting off the sea. Mum and Dad would sunbathe after lunch. Back in those days when our parents, Nature and play held us together, we girls entertained ourselves for hours, collecting crabs and making fish and chip shops. We'd shovel seaweed and stones into cones made from Dad's *Chronicle*, sprinkling them with sand and sea water 'salt and vinegar' from washed-up beer cans and Coke bottles. Or we'd lie on our fronts, raking the tide lines of broken shells for a single cowrie or a pelican's foot shell, sun scorching our legs and backs. In the summer those sheltered bays were like nests, where you felt safe, sleepy and content.

Chapter Nine

David

The past is strong, like the muscular pull of a sea current. Or the arm of a grown man wrestling yours across a table when you were a child. You knew then you'd have to give up eventually, unless the man decided to be easy on you and let you think you could beat him. When you became a man yourself, you couldn't always be as strong as you wanted to be. But your mind and your muscles were no longer a child's. You could choose to fight back. There was a bit more of a chance you might win.

He starts the engine, does a quick U-turn in the road. He'll have a shower, get on some clean clothes and head out again.

It's only just after eight when he gets back to the cottage. Gillian's curtains are still drawn. As soon as he gets in, he makes himself a coffee, pouring in the sugar straight from the bag. His Auntie June would've hated seeing him do that. And he'd have had a cuff round the ear from his mother. Sugar was spooned carefully from a sugar bowl, tea was brewed properly in a warmed pot with a cosy, butter was skimmed off a dish, not from the packet. 'We might not have much, but I'll not have anyone saying our boys were dragged up,' his mum would often say. 'You'll need to get a wash and take that brush to your nails before you'll get your tea, Davie. And there's a clean shirt ironed, on a hanger on front of the wardrobe.'

She'd probably be proud enough of him in that respect at least. He'd never been obsessive about hygiene or the way he looked, but he knew when he needed a shower. He kept his nails and hair short and clean, always shaved before work, didn't mind a nice shirt and jacket. Sophie had even got him into the habit of wearing a bit of after-shave. It'd taken until then for him to touch the stuff. Skinny Kev had once tried to cover him with some of his precious stolen body splash, but David had pushed his hand away. 'Girls like it. It gets them in the mood, you know? For *loving.* I'm telling you, Davie. You think I'm pulling your leg, but it *does.*' Perfume for men was a load of 'nancy boy nonsense', his dad had told him. A real man didn't like it, or need it.

He throws his clothes off on the bed and gets into the shower. There's plenty of water pressure and he makes it really hot. He doesn't mind growing a beard on holiday - but he lathers up plenty of soap, scrubs himself all over with the flannel. They used to have a strong lemon soap like that at home, yellow streaked with white, on a little suckered blue soap holder on the side of the bath. The smell of it starts him thinking again about putting salt and lemon on shrimps. Which gets him remembering those shrimping pools on the other side of the peninsula. There used to be good fishing a bit further round, off those rocks. He could be lucky and get a few pollock. It might make him just stay in the present, give him a bit of respite, at least for a while. He'll have to go into Stewartsford first and pick up some mackerel for bait.

Downstairs, he makes himself toast and another coffee. It doesn't take long to put together what he needs: a packet of cold sausage rolls, an orange and a packet of biscuits, a couple of cans of Coke, binoculars, sun-cream, the shrimp net, his tackle box and the rest of his gear.

It's really warming up outside. The inside of the car feels airless, so he leaves all the doors open while he loads the boot. He leaves the cottage just after half past nine, calls in for the bait and then drives to the other side of the peninsula.

The tide's on the turn. He's made his way round by the sea's edge and manages to get out along a narrow ridge just clear of the water, onto a promontory of rock. He'll have to keep his wits about him and make sure he doesn't get cut off, but there's room for him to lay his gear out there, a background of rock behind him and a good depth to throw a line into. It's a good deal fresher than it is in by the shore, but after the heat of the drive, he doesn't mind. He'll try a bit of spinning, use a baited spoon. He puts together his rod and reel, cuts some strips off the mackerel, wraps it back up, sets it in the shade behind his box. Once the line is made up, he casts out, not too far, but beyond the weed. He lifts the line, keeps the lure moving. If he gets a fish, well and good, although this time it's as much about being out there, just spinning. Fishing reminded you that small fry, or at least the likeness of one, could win the day, even if most of the time the sly big boys usually got away.

Gillian

I must've drifted off. I'm woken by my mobile ringing.

My bedroom in the cottage is really warm, the curtains edged with brightness.

'Hello?'

'Gillian? Are you al*right?*' It's Laura. 'You haven't just woken up, have you? It's quarter to twelve. I thought you said you were on a *working* break?' She sounds irritated.

'Yes, I am, Laura. But I woke very early. So I went back to bed.'

'Oh? So why was that then?' she asks sharply.

'Och, nothing really. The guy next door was up and about. He was making a bit of noise, so . . .'

Laura sighs. 'That's not very good, is it? Maybe you need to have a word with the owner? Or the fella himself? You're not paying an arm and a leg to be disturbed like that.'

'It's okay, Laura. Actually, I'm not paying that much. And it's only happened once. He's usually pretty quiet. I've met him, actually. He's fine.' I can already guess what's coming next.

'You've met him? Oh? So, is he on his own too? Where's he from? Is he *married?*'

It's like a reflex for Laura - she can't help herself giving me the third degree. It's just how she's wired, even if it's annoying to be on the receiving end.

'He's from Manchester. He pretty much keeps himself to himself. We've only met briefly. Anyway. Everything okay with you? I didn't expect to hear from you again so soon.'

Laura clears her throat efficiently. 'I've had Claire on the phone. She's too caught up to phone you, so I said I'd speak to you instead. She's invited everybody over to her house tonight. She wants us all to have a meal while you're over. She's putting a lot of pressure on herself, Gillian. I'll be going a bit earlier to help her get ready. She says you're to be there at half past five.' It's an announcement and instruction, rather than a request.

I take a deep breath. 'Right. Okay, well, bit short notice, but...' The words are out before I can stop them. It's as if I've triggered a land mine. Laura explodes.

'So what do you think it is for *Claire* and the rest of us? All *you've* got to do is flipping turn up! I don't *believe* you sometimes, Gillian! What planet are you on?' Her voice is at its most animated when she's giving me a dressing down.

'Okay. Sorry. I'll be there. Will I phone Claire back myself?' For the sake of an evening there's no point in me arguing about it.

'No. Sure, I told you she's too busy. We left it that I'd contact her only if you weren't coming.'

'That's fine. I'll get her some flowers and a bottle of wine.'

'She's got a notion for rosé at the minute.' I can tell my prompt compliance has taken some of the wind out of Laura's sails. 'See you later then, Gillian.'

Through the curtains I can see Derek McEvoy, climbing onto his tractor in the front yard, driving off down the lane. He doesn't have to make excuses for spending a day by himself in a field. There's not a cloud in the sky. I should be out there, making the best of what I own of the already shortened day. I'm going to drive over to that beach, walk round to one of the sheltered bays and sit on the shingle.

Being self-reliant and confident about being out and about on my own has always been important to me. I don't walk down unlit alleys in Liverpool on my own late at night— I'm certainly not naïve enough to believe that rape only happens to other people – but in some people's minds, perhaps I take more risks than I should. It's just that I wouldn't have the same quality of life if I couldn't walk alone along a beach or a path through the countryside.

It's after one when I get there. I park in the usual place, overlooking the beach. Like a lot of parking places, it used to be just a rough bumpy bit of grass where you could pull off the road, but it's more managed for visitors now, with mown grass and wooden rails. I take a bottle of water and an apple with me, get down onto the beach and walk towards the rocks.

There are moments in your childhood you have a feeling you'll always remember. When you wanted to guarantee that the same experience would be repeated exactly, later in your life. Even at that age you knew that such a moment was as good as moments could ever get. Sitting on the hot stones in one of those shingle bays, it seems as if I'm travelling back in time, to one such moment in this place. From the field behind, the fully charged soprano vocals of the skylark. The hushed accompaniment of breaking waves. The heat, soaking in. Slowing and relaxing. Making you give up to a euphoric feeling of heaviness, as if your veins are filling with warmed oil or honey. As if you have nowhere else to be.

I spend a while idly raking through the banks of shells. A lot of them are broken, although there are also concentrated drifts of whole mussels, limpets and tiny flat winkles in shades of brown and yellow. Dry, the winkles look quite dull, but when you wet them, they instantly light up.

They make me think of the 70s. When Mum made a lamp base out of a heavy jar, thickly covered with Polyfilla, embedded with flat winkles, painted with clear varnish to bring out the colours.

Then I just sit still and close my eyes, losing track of time, thinking again in glass. I conjure up a background of intense greens and blues, with horizontal waving bands, filled with tones of brown and yellow.

'Gillian?' The voice is quiet, coming from behind me.

When I open my eyes and look round, I see David. A bit uncanny the way our paths often coincide. He's carrying a fishing rod and a shrimp net in one hand and a tackle box in the other, a rucksack slung over his shoulder.

'Didn't want to make you jump,' he apologises. 'Great day, isn't it?' He stays standing where he is, higher up the shore, close to the sloe bushes.

'Gorgeous. Been fishing? Stopping for lunch?'

He nods and sets down his gear either side of him. Clenches and unclenches his hands a few times, then rubs them on the sides of his khaki shorts.

'Get any fish?' I'm squinting up at him. I put my sunglasses back on.

'No takers so far, I'm afraid. But that's fishing for you. Can be all or nothing, can't it? Don't know if you fish yourself?' He runs his hand over his hair and shakes out his arms – to loosen up, I guess, after holding the rod.

'Not for a long time. My dad taught me a bit when I was child. But I haven't really fished since. And I don't eat them now anyway. I'm a vegetarian.'

'Oh, right.' I'm relieved he doesn't ask for more details. I'm not in the mood for another 'I'm-a-vegetarian-because' explanation. 'You've got yourself a good place to sit. I'll leave you in peace. No matter how hard you try to avoid me, I keep turning up on you, don't I? I'll get off and let you get your head showered, as they say.'

'I'm sure the same applies the other way round. Have to say, you're not wasting any time picking up the local lingo!' I'm even more convinced I can detect a trace of an Irish accent. I'm reluctant to give up my solitude, but it seems mean not to offer to share the beach. 'Please, feel free to join me, David. I think I've got the best spot. While I like the idea it only belongs to me, I haven't really got the right to exclude anyone.'

'You were here first. You're entitled to your space,' he offers.

'And you'd probably prefer a bay of your own.'

He laughs and bows his head for a second. 'It's too hot for debate. No person is an island, is he? Or she? I'm going to barge in, impose myself again – but only for ten minutes.' He makes his way down onto the shingle and settles on a spot, a few feet away from me.

'Have you eaten already?' He unzips his backpack, rummages around and brings out a can of Coke, then cracks it open and takes a long drink.

'I'm not hungry when it's so hot. I've got a bottle of water and some fruit. And I'm having tea at my sister's tonight, so I need to make room. She doesn't like it when I leave things on my plate. That's a sure sign of anorexia, as far as Claire's concerned.'

'So, *that's* how it is?' He nods and smiles, takes a bite out of a sausage roll.

'Yep.'

'I thought you weren't going to see your family this time?'

'I didn't plan to. But as you know, it's a very small world. I ran into my sister, Laura. The predictable chain of dominoes – she had to let Claire know. They're both not very impressed. Understatement. I've had to be fitted into schedules. Though to be fair, they didn't have to invite me and they did. It's just, things are always a bit tense. Anyway, that's later on. In the meantime, I'm going to do my best to switch off.'

'You do right.' He nods, throws back his head and takes a gulp of Coke.

I uncap my water and take a drink too.

He looks thoughtful and carries on eating unselfconsciously, clearing the pastry flakes off his mouth with the back of his hand. When his sausage rolls are finished, he bites into an orange before starting to peel it.

'A blood orange?' I notice out loud.

'No. Just the remains of last night's dinner on my fangs! We don't usually come out during the day. Though occasionally we'll make an exception. Would you . . .?'

'Fancy a bite?' I finish for him, laughing.

'You spotted me a mile off. My guess is you're had a right few bloody oranges yourself.'

'I only started eating them recently. They actually really scared me when I was a child. This boy told me the blood came from the fairy corpses buried at the centre.'

'Never trust a boy. Whatever age he tells you he is. Did your parents not tell you that? Anyway, fairy blood is invisible. So we good pagans believe. . . Although – sorry, sometimes I get a bit carried away. I wasn't assuming that you were a pagan, of course. I hope I've not said the wrong thing there? I mean, I'm all for respect where respect's due.' He grimaces slightly.

'Don't worry as far as I'm concerned. I'm not religious. Coming from this place, I decided fairly early on it was much better to be a heathen. Nothing's happened since to change my mind.'

'Know what you mean.' He nods solemnly. Then begins to smile again. 'But if you don't mind me asking you now? Would you be a *Protestant* or a *Catholic* heathen?' in a strong and convincing Northern Irish accent.

'Agnostic. Definitely a devout agnostic

heathen. Yourself?' Variations on the old joke never fail to amuse me.

'Oh, I'm just bad. Rotten to the core. Beyond redemption. My place in Hell's already booked. Mind you, they say the company's going to be pretty good.' He gets up and offers me a share of the orange, presented in a 'dish' he's made of the coiled peel.

We look towards the sea without talking for a while. In spite of his remark about imposing himself and the fact I still know very little about him, David has an air of confidence and an unpretentious quality that puts me at ease.

After a while he goes to his backpack for another Coke. 'Serious rehydration required. Only myself to blame, I'm afraid.'

'Late night on the town?' I suggest, although I'm pretty sure he stayed at home.

'No. Lads' night in. Just one lad turned up. Luckily, unluckily, whichever way you look at it. On the upside, there was no competition for the beer. How about you? How's your work going?'

'Fine. I've been a bit lazy this morning. I haven't brought my drawing stuff with me. Although I've got plenty of ideas. Our family used to come here a lot.' In other circumstances, I'd probably leave it there. But the effect of the heat and the atmosphere feels hypnotic, loosens my inhibitions. 'I love this place. It always had, *has* the power to make me feel at peace. Probably sounds naïve, given everything that's happened here. But whatever we try and lay on them, land, sea and sky really are neutral. Unopinionated. Aren't they?'

'I don't think it's naïve. I do know what you mean. Although I think it's an unusual person who manages to hang onto that feeling of peace. If the enemy storms a beach, it's hard for you to think of it as anything other than a war zone.'

'Though it doesn't always have to be like that, does it? If your thinking changes – if *you* change your thinking – you and the place could be freed up again. The future doesn't have to be the past. Unless it's a past worth holding onto.'

'That's true,' he allows. 'Though maybe not so easy in practice.' He takes off his sunglasses and polishes them on the edge of his shirt. He has a thick smear of sunblock across his nose, like a cricketer or a skier.

'I know. Sorry, I'm sure you just want to relax.'

'Not at all, you're fine. Certainly beats the routine daily banter, down at the fire station.'

We're back to the same joke. Part of me is tempted now to ask him outright what he really does, but I'm not sure if he'll want to get into that at the moment. For now, I'm also enjoying the game, suspending the usual framework for conversation between strangers, the expected questions and automatic exchange of mundane information. What's intended to lead to better understanding often doesn't. And so maybe there is an element of flirtation in it too. He's an attractive, intelligent man. And what's flirtation if not non-threatening play and a gesture towards new territory – even if you decide not to go there?

'Oh, I'm sure the station's pretty lively sometimes with all that adrenaline,' I continue.

'You'd be surprised - it can be really dull.' He pauses, then resumes more seriously, 'No, take it from me. This is much better. What could honestly be better than a place like this?'

We sit again in silence, this time for longer, looking out to sea.

Then he gets up, gathering his empty cans, crushing them in his hand. 'Right. I'll not outstay my welcome. I'm going to leave you in peace and head on round the shore.'

'Hope you catch something for your tea,' I tell him as he packs up.

'You never know. Could be lucky. And I'll be thinking of you, clearing your plate nicely, for your sister.'

'Cheers.'

David

The mackerel gave him a good bit of sport, but David finally brought him in. He grabs the fish firmly, unhooks him as quickly as he can, knocks him on the head against the rock to make sure he's properly dead. Must be a couple of pounds' weight, at least. He's beautiful: silvery underbelly, inky bluish-black markings, perfect streamlining. He was also a merciless predator, with a greedy appetite for the flesh of young fry. Including his own.

'Hard to beat a fresh mackerel. He's not your sea bass or your salmon, of course, but he's as proud and handsome as a tomcat and he'll give you a run for your money. Fry him up and put him on a plate, with a couple of your dad's freshly dug potatoes and a few scallions and you'll need nothing else for your tea,' Trevor, his dad's old friend from the farm, would say.

It was Trevor who'd really taught David to fish. His Dad often preferred to work in his garden when he was at home. And when it came to fishing, everyone knew there was no one craftier than Trevor. He knew exactly where to go. He could read the water, work with the rocks and the weed and the currents. He had the patience of a saint and the cunning of a devil, his dad said. Trevor could get right inside the head of a fish.

David slits open the mackerel with Trevor's knife, pulls out its guts and tosses them out for the gulls. Then he stoops down at the edge of the rock and washes the gutted body in the sea. The folding knife has a smooth sort of marbled pearly handle and a single blade, catching the light like fish scales. Trevor's wife had passed it to him when he and his dad had been at the house after Trevor's funeral. It wasn't a set of modern multitasking blades. But it was all that Trevor had needed, for everything. It was a good knife, his dad said. More than good enough for a boy like David.

David decides to call it a day. The sun's still hot, but it's almost 4.00 p.m. And there's something he needs to do before he returns to the cottage for the evening.

He drives back again across the peninsula. Instead of going in the direction of the cottage, he goes into Stewartsford and takes the road uphill, out to the main public cemetery. There's a car park there, inside the cemetery gates, but David parks on the street, about fifty yards away, and walks back along the thick privet hedge, past the pink-flowered cherry trees he remembers when they were just thin, staked saplings.

The entrance looks smarter now and the tarmac paths are better maintained, but the railings and the main gates are still dark green, the memorial benches still the same sober matt brown, bearing brass plaques. He has never minded graveyards. Even as a boy, he wasn't spooked by death the way some children were. Once you were dead, you were dead. Your troubles were over, you were out of harm's way. There was nothing, no one could hurt you anymore, nowhere you could fall.

David's parents' grave is headed by a rectangular polished black marble stone, etched simply with their names and dates of birth and death, the ground in front of it a rectangle of chippings. He should've thought to bring some flowers. After his dad died, his Auntie June and his Uncle Keith helped to make the arrangements. There were several smaller graveyards closer to the town and the hamlet where his parents had lived, but most of their ancestors and friends had been laid to rest, as his dad put it, 'on The Hill' at Stewartsford. As well as the other details on the grave stone, his Auntie and Uncle had arranged for the words, *Thy Will be done on Earth as it is in Heaven,* to be engraved on it.

On the day of his dad's funeral, after the burial, when she'd had a few whiskies, his mum had told David and Mark that when their time came, if ever they needed it, there would be room for both of them to be laid to rest in the same plot.

'Thanks, Mum,' David had said, just managing to hold himself together, not knowing how else to react. She'd forced a wavery smile and said that he was very welcome. Mark had frowned and told her abruptly not to be so bloody depressing. It wasn't long before they were burying David's mum. He wished they hadn't had to die so young. Everyone had faults, but they were good people. Straightforward, just wanting to enjoy life as best they could. His dad had once been so physically strong and energetic. Without her John to lean on, his mum had quickly fallen down, like a beautiful and delicate sweet pea, suddenly deprived of its support.

David stands for a while in silence, staring

at the headstone. A good place to come to your final rest, The Hill. Once you were dead, you were dead. He'd never been able to make himself believe there was anything else afterwards. Other than the idea of living on as a gradually fading reflection, carried on ripples of memory in the minds of those who for whatever reason kept on thinking about you.

"Bye for now,' he then says under his breath, rubbing his eyes as he leaves their grave. Although he hasn't quite finished at the graveyard yet.

Skinny Kev and Sammy were buried in separate plots, not far from David's parents. There's still no one else around as far as David can see. He has to keep his wits about him, like a twitchy vulnerable bird forever on the alert, constantly turning his head, looking behind him, scanning for new cars arriving on the road alongside the graveyard.

As David reaches Skinny Kev's plot, he sees that Kev's parents' names have been added more recently to the small, basic headstone. Hardly surprising. They weren't young when they'd had him.

About a year or so after David had moved to live in Manchester, his Auntie June had to break the news that Skinny Kev and Sammy had died together, when a car they were driving through the town late one night had exploded. It was tragic, his aunt and uncle had acknowledged, but they told him he had to try not to think too much about it. They didn't like him listening to the radio or watching the news too often about what was happening across the water. So many lives had been lost and destroyed. No one would likely ever know exactly what had happened to those wee boys. They would be in the Lord's hands, they'd kept reassuring David. It was very, very sad, but there was no point in David tormenting himself by dwelling on it.

David hadn't really been able to take the news on board properly. He'd felt sad and empty, leaving the boys behind when he'd had to move to Manchester. They'd been good friends and he'd missed the way the three of them had hung round together. But since those days he'd had so much to deal with. Adjusting to living with his aunt and uncle. His new school. The loss of his parents. He'd constantly felt like a fish out of water. It was hard work, having to give an account of himself, deliberately losing some of his accent so people would understand and not poke fun at him. He'd had to choose either to assume that life was all about loss and sadness, or start to grow a bit of a tough shell and do his best to carry on. Sammy and Skinny Kev, once so much a part of his world. Sammy and Skinny Kev, long gone.

It was only later when David went into the police that he'd felt compelled to search for more information about what had happened. From what he could glean, no group had declared responsibility for the incident. There'd been a bomb in the boot of the stolen vehicle the boys had been driving. It was believed that the boys had been tasked with transporting it to its destination. Their deaths had been accidental. A fault in the device had caused it to explode prematurely. It seemed that, like many other young people there at the time, Sammy and Skinny Kev had ended up as prey, being recruited by paramilitaries. Undoubtedly, they would have had no choice in the matter, knowing that refusing to comply would have been tantamount to signing their own death warrants. Had David not moved to Manchester when he did, it was completely possible that he too might have been drawn in and exploited in a similar way.

Trevor's grave is only a short walk up the hill from Sammy's. The stone is a very modest one, just for Trevor and his wife. They'd had plenty of friends, but no children of their own. On the ground in front of it there's one of those sunken flower bowls, covered with a metal grille, with the straggly remains of a few plastic flowers still stuck in it. All that time, working on the land, to end up buried under some bloody plastic flowers? Though that wouldn't have bothered Trevor and Anne. They'd been easy-going people with plenty of humour about them. Trevor was a good man. He didn't feel he had anything to prove and had gone about his own business quietly. He'd not pretended to be any kind of heroic champion, politician or pillar of the community. If they'd all been like him, the whole community would have held together a lot better for it. Like the crafty, mature fish he'd admired, Trevor had known when and where to keep his mouth shut. He'd believed in a kind, truly wise God and in helping other people. He'd never acted holier-than-thou or tried to force his own beliefs or opinions down your throat. He'd allowed David to be the child he was, but he'd acknowledged the man in the making and didn't ever seek to be condescending or to humiliate him.

'What do you think, Trevor? What would *you* do? Lie low? Cause a stir?' David finds himself saying out loud, then checks over his shoulder at once, feeling relieved there seems to be no one else around. He needs to be careful, stay aware of where he is and to think before he speaks. He has Trevor's folded knife in his pocket and closes his hand tightly around it. There were a lot of things they'd never discussed. That perhaps they could have. He was sure there'd been a lot that Trevor had noticed and understood. But it was the way it had been between them and he wouldn't have wanted it otherwise. Being with Trevor had been about sharing the pure beauty and joys of the peninsula, the sea's wild edges. Often spending time in long, comfortable silence, without feeling you had to give an account of yourself or anything else. Whatever else was going on, out there you were cut loose from the knotting tensions and conflicts of other parts of life. You were just concentrating on the gathering or the fishing, feeling that you and parts of your land, at least, were equally free and unspoilt.

'Never forget you, Trevor,' David says, almost in a whisper, as he moves away from the grave and heads back to the car.

After what happened to Keith and Tom that day behind the hen house in the garden of that derelict cottage, during those years before he'd had to leave to live with his aunt and uncle, David and Sammy and Skinny Kev had witnessed a lot more things that were never meant to be seen. Situations, they'd started to realise, that had a common denominator. Santie and his helpers.

For a while they'd avoided the cottage. David and especially Sammy had been wary about returning, but Skinny Kev was itching to get back. He had less fear – or at least his curiosity and desperate need for a bit of excitement, however dangerous, would more often override his worry about taking risks. It was like the way he'd started taking cars with some of his other older friends, going joyriding. He believed they were invincible somehow and would never get caught. He'd talked Sammy into going with them a few times, although David had refused.

'Och, *c'mon!'* Kev would keep saying, pushing them both to agree about going to the cottage. 'We'll be alright, as long as we're careful and don't let them see us.' Quick-witted in some ways, Skinny Kev could also be so stupidly naïve and lacking in imagination. What was it David's dad had often said? *Not everyone is like yourself, son. You don't always know what's in there,* he'd warn, pointing to his own head. There were some dark depths in life you really couldn't fathom, like the unseen inaccessible reaches of those crevices of the sea pools. Your hand or your net could only get so far in. You could only guess at the uncharted territory and the nature of the beauty or ugliness of whatever lay beyond.

It was a strange thing, David had always thought – that compelling need to know and see dark things, realising at the same time there was often nothing you could do to change them and that the witnessing was bound to haunt you. Was it perhaps that, in opening yourself to suffering, you felt at least that you shared some of the suffering of others? Or was the heaviness of the burden you carried the inevitable penalty for your curiosity and lack of self-denial?

Eventually, David and Sammy gave in and the three of them started to visit the abandoned place again. Instead of taking the risk of walking into something going on at the back of the cottage, they would go straight into the field alongside it and slowly and stealthily make their way down the hedge, stopping to listen and peer through. The first couple of times, they saw nothing. They'd begun to wonder if what had happened had been a one-off incident and if they were getting too worked up. But they soon discovered nothing could've been further from the truth.

Keith and Tom were just the first of many they would go on to observe taking punishment there. Boys beaten mercilessly with tool handles. Kneed and kicked in the guts and chest and heads and groins, until they were retching and screaming and grovelling for mercy. Almost strangled in the bare, vice-like hands of those brutal men. Tied up. Left alone and together. Held at knife point. Scored and slashed, maimed for life. Usually they were boys, but occasionally there was a girl, slapped and knocked about because she'd been caught with the boys, stealing or joyriding or behaving in a way that a *good wee girl* shouldn't have behaved. Like Linda. Wee Linda. A girl who'd needed to learn her lesson. *Bastards. That heartless bastard.*

David's sitting in the car now, still on the road outside the graveyard. He screws up his eyes, clenches his fists. He'd put Trevor's knife back in his rucksack, tossed onto the back seat, but takes it out again and opens the blade, polishes it hard with the car window cloth, until it gleams. The metal and the handle are smooth and warm. It's full of glintings of Trevor, of those unspoilt, clean moments of his childhood. Sealed, untouchable memories of peace and the sane untainted integrity of the Nature of his homeland. He lightly strokes the mirroring surface of that blade. The smooth, pearly handle, so beautiful.

All things bright and beautiful. Linda's pale translucent skin. Her sandy, naturally white-blonde fine hair. Her clean, lovely teeth and expressive mouth. The way she'd smiled and teased people. Just the sight of her had made him feel so good, sometimes he'd not known what to do with himself. Linda. Poor wee Linda.

'*Forgive us our trespasses, as we forgive those who trespass against us,*' they'd had to close their eyes and pray at school. '*Forgive us . . . as we forgive.*' A constant request to be forgiven. Based on the unspoken assumption that you would constantly forgive others, trusting that whatever happened, justice would be done in eternity. *For Thine is the kingdom, the power and the glory.* It was the Almighty's role to judge and be responsible for restitution. *Romans 12. Vengeance is mine, I will repay, saith the Lord.*

David snaps the knife closed, holds it tightly for a second, then puts it down in the foot well of the passenger seat beside him. He starts up the car and creeps past the graveyard, glancing in. Then faces forward and moves on.

Chapter Ten

Gillian

A bottle of rosé and a mixed bouquet dutifully in hand, I arrive at Claire's house just before six. My face and shoulders have really caught the sun. I've no doubt at some stage I'll have Laura's malignant melanoma lecture, but my afternoon at the shore has cleared my head and left me much less tense.

Claire's home – a spacious four-bedroom bungalow on a fairly modern development on the outskirts of Saintwood. New PVC everywhere, an oversized conservatory at the back. Pale, stain-free carpets, spotless tiles and laminates. Silk flower arrangements and plastic pot plants. It's devoid of character. Not that I'd tell her that out-right, of course. Even if I don't share her aspirations and I often don't like her, she's still my sister. She's invested so much physical and emotional energy in the place. She's hardly unusual in that respect. It's a shift I've noticed in many people – a concern with reflecting their up-and-coming status through forever upgrading their home and possessions. It may be a nostalgic view, but people seemed less preoccupied with having picture perfect homes and gardens when we were growing up in the 1960s and 70s. It seems a bit sad to me, but Claire's heart is in this bungalow, inseparable from the fittings and furniture. I'd never deliberately try to undermine her pride and joy. 'Claire's wee palace', my dad used to say with a tolerant, ironic wink, as well as, 'Always the last word, you know.'

'Hiya, Gillie! How's you?' It's Tony at the door. Smart, in a crease-free lilac shirt with gold cufflinks, a purple tie, and charcoal-grey suit trousers. Saturated in cloying aftershave, as always.

The central heating's on, no matter what the weather. The hall smells of cooking meat. Laura will be in the kitchen – Claire's Control Room. The two of them will be finishing preparing the meal, inevitably exchanging canned criticism on the subject of husbands. Robbie, on the other hand, will be in the sitting room in his comfy chair, eyes fixed on the TV, right hand squarely enclosing the remote control, a pint of Carling on the small table by the armrest. He'll be having the first of two cans allocated by Claire, on nights when she's doing a 'special tea'. On other nights if he's lucky, she might just spoil him and allow him one.

'Hi, Tony. I'm fine, thanks. You?'

'Great, thanks, Gillie. Can I take your cardigan for you now?'

'No. It's okay. I didn't bother to bring a bag – I've got a few things I might need in the pockets.' I slip my sandals off automatically. Claire's house rules.

'Now, that's what I call a sensible girl. You'd

not catch Laura without her handbag. Carts it about with her everywhere! Honest to God, it's about the size of a suitcase. But then you can't expect us men to understand your girlie things. We prefer to travel light.' *Like hell you do, Tony.*

'Or so you boys like to tell us *girlies*, anyway,' I come back. I've no problem with 'girlies' a lot of the time, but I hate it when it comes from Tony. His over-familiarity makes my skin crawl. I cringe every time he calls me Gillie. It doesn't matter how often I tell him I'd prefer Gillian, or at least Gill.

'Make yourself at home, Gillie. It's a kids and teenager free zone tonight! My Mum's got our two at her place and Nicola and Roger are out with their friends. Laura's in the kitchen with Claire. I'm front of house! Robbie's in the sitting room. Why don't you go through? Can I get you a wee glass of wine, or something?' I give Tony the wine and the flowers. 'Och, that's very good of you! Claire'll be chuffed with the flowers. And she's definitely on the rosé at the minute. Aren't you the clever girl now?'

'Laura told me,' I state baldly. I've no time for even mild flirtation with Tony.

'Och, you shouldn't have said anything. You could have got that one past me, Gillie. You're far too honest, for your own good.' *And do you know what, Tony? You're a dishonest little shit,* I feel like answering, but I just smile slightly. 'So, what's it to be, Gillie? A glass of rosé, or a wee white wine instead?'

'Actually, I'll have a glass of white. But only a very small one. I'm driving back.'

'Okey-dokey, Gillie. I know what you mean. I prefer the drier stuff myself – a nice crisp wee glass of Sauv blanc? You go on in. I'll be there in a minute.'

It's another of Claire's house rules. The kitchen door at the end of the hall is closed. Apart from Laura, no one else goes for a chat in Claire's kitchen until after tea.

'Hi, Robbie!' Robbie is installed in the sitting room, as I anticipated. He looks heavier than he was, literally pushing his shirt's capacity to its limit. He has a habit of lowering his chin when he speaks, which makes his already deep voice even deeper.

'Och, how's about you, Gillian? Sorry, don't mind me. Just catching up on the footie. Glad you could make it. Sit yourself down there. Bit of a surprise, you being over and us not knowing, like, but och well, these things happen. We're all entitled to do our own thing.' His eyes home back to the TV.

Although I find Robbie's lack of gumption irritating, he's a good-natured, unpretentious man. He has to absorb a lot from Claire. He reminds me of those reddish-brown soft sea anemones you find stuck on the sides of rock pools. When we were girls, we used to joke that they looked like floppy bosoms. They have soft tentacles that close gently round your finger. They retract into their own centres when they're uncovered at low tide. I used to feel sorry for them. Simple and vulnerable watery creatures. Not feisty like crabs or shrimps.

'I know Claire and Laura are probably still annoyed with me, but I wasn't meaning to offend anybody.' I sit down on Claire's immaculate beige leather settee. Robbie's always less at ease when he's sitting face to face. He feels more comfortable with a parallel arrangement, ideally both of you watching TV at the same time.

'Not to worry now, Gill. Sure, the two of them'll be over it soon enough. Is Tony getting you a drink?' Actually, Robbie knows as well as I do that Claire and Laura don't quickly forget. But in order to manage living with them, Robbie has to pretend they do. He has to let life wash over him as he feeds to maintain the shock-absorbing cushion of his rounded frame and withdraws into himself when threatened with too much of a challenge.

'Yes, he is, thanks. So, how's work? Tough times for the banks. Can't be easy for you and your staff. I imagine you have to deal with a fair bit of flack?'

'Och, sure it's like everything else, Gillian. You've just got to keep your head down and get on with it. Go with the flow, as they say. Today we even had a taste of bubbly – one of the girls was leaving, so we all had a wee glass at the end of the afternoon. Don't tell your sister, mind. I'll not be allowed my other can. So, how's about yourself? Managing to break even at the studio?'

'Actually, I'm doing much better than I expected. There seems to be a demand for well-finished decorative glass at the moment.' We both continue talking to the screen, as if it's some kind of benign, reassuring intermediary.

'Glad to hear it, Gillian. Long may it last. Now, here comes your drink. And about time too. You've not been growing the grapes out there now, have you, Tony?'

Tony comes in, holding two glasses of white wine by their stems, passes one over and sits down beside me on the settee.

'Did you not find those bigger glasses, Tony? Gillian'll be wanting a *decent* glass of wine,' Robbie tells him, after a sip from his own pint. He has a line of beer froth above his upper lip. It makes me think of sea foam.

'I was instructed to use these ones by your more glamorous half, Rob,' Tony returns smoothly.

'Right you be then. It'd be more than my life's worth not to agree with you.'

'It's fine, Robbie,' I say, 'I told Tony just to get a small one. I have to drive myself back. I can't have more than one.'

'Whatever you say, Gillian. You're in charge. As long as you're happy . . . Oh, here comes trouble!'

It's Claire and Laura, each with a glass of

rosé in hand, in their posh dresses and high heels. 'Hi Gillian!' they say almost in unison, standing in front of the TV, blocking Robbie's view, although he continues to stare at the same spot.

'You've really caught the sun there on your shoulders, Gillian,' Laura immediately observes. 'What've I told you about using a proper sunblock? There's no excuse for not knowing about the risks these days now, is there?'

'I thought I'd put plenty on, but obviously not enough.' *Don't you ever get bored with saying the same thing, Laura?* I keep thinking.

'Thanks for the wine, by the way. You didn't need to do that, Gillian,' Claire says. Even she seems keen to move the conversation on. I sense she has an agenda of her own. In contrast to Robbie and Laura, she's lost weight. I guess she's conscious of the fact, by the way she stands straight-backed, a hand placed on her noticeably flatter stomach. 'I've been doing the Weight Watchers. I'm being very strict with myself. I'm only allowed a small glass of wine on a special occasion. What do you think, Gillian? I've lost a fair bit now, haven't I?'

'You certainly have. Good for you, Claire.' I leave it at that. Any encouragement and Claire and Laura will happily launch one of their favourite diet conversations. Even a night of family bickering is better than an evening of brain death.

'She keeps trying to get me to go along with her,' Laura adds in, doing her best to keep the theme going. 'Suppose I should, really. I can't believe what I've put on recently. I'm disgusting. It's doing nights. I eat like a pig, don't I, Claire? And Tony's not much help. He never gives me any support if I do put myself on a diet!' Cue another moment for Tony and Laura to showcase their time-served happy couple act.

'But you know what I mean, don't you, Robbie?' Tony engages Robbie. 'A fella can't get it right whatever he says. Whatever you say, say nothing. That's a man's best policy, isn't it?'

'Och yes. Spot on, Tony,' Robbie confirms. I suspect he's more interested in getting back to his viewing of the sports' results.

'Am I not always telling you I love you, Laura? Just as you are?' Tony carries on, getting up from the settee and slipping an arm round Laura's waist. She pretends to be bashful and puts her head against his chest. It's what she and Tony do, in company.

'You'll need to be a bit more careful about where you steal your lines from, Tony.' Robbie decides to send up an intelligent tentacle. 'Isn't that . . .?' Good old Robbie.

'He's right, Tony. *Bridget Jones*,' I agree.

Claire frowns at Robbie. 'Right, enough said,' she decides. 'Tea-time everybody. We've already put the starters on the table in the dining room. Tony, bring some wine through for us. Robbie, your second can's in the door of the fridge. Help yourself when you're ready.'

'Och will you look at that now, Gillian?' Robbie says to me behind his pint as we sit down at the table. 'The starter's *melon balls!* Nothing fills you up as much as a melon ball, does it now? Especially when you get a whole quarter glacé cherry with it.' The extra glasses of champagne combined with the Carling must be going to his head. Robbie doesn't often try for more than one act of rebellion in an evening. He should know better than to think Claire will miss the trick.

'I've done some nice skinless chicken breasts, with plenty of steamed vegetables, and vegetarian stuffed tomatoes for Gillian. I want everybody to be able to eat their mains. You'll be finding yourself on your way to the chip shop, Robbie,' Claire reprimands. He puts a whole melon ball into his mouth. 'Och, for goodness' sake! That's just ignorant, Robbie! You're supposed to cut them up with your knife and fork. You'll choke on that!'

Robbie chews and swallows the mouthful quickly. 'Keep your hair on, will you, Claire? Sure, there's nothing to eating a wee bit of melon.' He finishes his starter straight away and sits silently after that, eking out his pint. Poor Robbie. He just wants a really good feed and permission to get quietly pissed.

'That's it, Tony. Top up everybody's glass. Apart from mine,' Claire orders, covering her own glass with her hand. 'And Robbie's, of course. He's just on beer. Although I'm still deciding whether he deserves that other can, or not.' She looks in Robbie's direction, but he doesn't react. 'Gillian. You'll take another drink, won't you?'

'I'm driving back. So I'll have to stop at one,' I state, bracing myself. It won't be the end of it.

'Och, just go ahead and top up her glass, will you, Tony?' Claire tells him. 'I've done a special tea, for crying out loud. You can stay overnight, Gillian. We've got one of those blow-up double beds. Or if you want to get back tonight, sure we'll get you a taxi. Leave the car here. One of us can pop over and ferry you back to collect it, sometime later on tomorrow.'

'No, I've had enough, Tony, thanks. Claire, it's really good of you to offer, but I want to go back to the cottage tonight. I'd like to get started at a good time in the morning. And anyway, I don't need another drink. You're not having any more wine yourself, are you?' I'm determined not to let Claire bully me into staying.

'But that's different, Gillian. I *can't*. I'm on a diet, aren't I? Go on. Keep Laura company on the rosé. Tony's not so keen on it and we don't want to waste that bottle, now, do we? C'mon Gillian. This is *your* party.'

'No, Claire. I'm fine with driving myself back tonight. Let's forget about it now. This melon's really lovely and sweet.' I know already she won't buy it. *Like hell this is my party, Claire.*

'Do you know your problem, Gillian?' she asks. *Here we go.* She picks up her rosé, drinks half

152

the glass and keeps holding it up. She touches the corners of her lipstick. She hasn't even started her melon.

'No. What, Claire?' I return, wearily. I wish I was back on that sane bloody beach.

'I'll tell you. It's all this 'I-must-have-my-personal-space' stuff! I mean, don't you think that was at the root of all your problems with Matt? Maybe even *more* so than his infertility issue? And who knows how much the former led to the latter?'

'Claire. C'm'on now. She doesn't have to have another drink if she doesn't want one. You've spent a lot of time on the meal. Why don't we just *eat?*' Robbie suggests.

Discussion of Matt's 'infertility issue' has always been too much information for Robbie.

'Too right. Live and let live,' Tony puts in, almost in a whisper. Ideally, he likes to keep Claire on his side.

'*No.* You two just stay out of this!' Claire cuts him off. 'I'm talking to Gillian. And I'm trying to make an important point, so I am. I am, aren't I, Laura? You can see what I'm getting at.'

'Of course I can,' Laura sympathises. 'I do think you could make a compromise this once, Gillian. Okay, you need to do your own thing. You're over for your wee working break and everything, but this is about *family,* Gillian. A wee extra night with family wouldn't do you a button of harm.'

I'm trying my best to stay calm. While Laura was speaking, Claire has finished her wine. She doesn't tolerate alcohol well and her diet won't help.

'I'm sorry,' I say, alternating eye contact between Claire and Laura. 'I'm not going to change my mind. I'm not having any more wine, okay?'

Laura tuts and rolls her eyes.

'Suit yourself, Gillian! It's your loss,' Claire tells me, springing up from the table. 'Right. Pass me your plates. I'm not having that chicken spoilt. Are you not eating that bit of cherry, Gillian?'

'Sorry. I never liked glacé cherries – you know that.'

Claire looks at Laura and sighs dramatically.

'Can I give you a hand with the plates, Claire?' I offer, already knowing the answer.

'No. You're alright. Laura and I'll manage, thanks. We know what we're doing. You just sit there and talk.'

'Don't be giving *me* that! Tastes like bloody polystyrene,' Dad used to say, about cottage cheese. I've been presented with four hollowed out raw tomato halves filled with it, sparingly sprinkled with white pepper. Robbie gives me a sympathetic look. His own disappointment at the sight of his pale skinless chicken breast is unmistakeable. Claire smacks back his hand as he reaches for another boiled potato to compensate.

'You've had your share, Robbie. Tony hasn't had his second one yet.'

'Och, not to worry, Claire. I've got more than enough here. Let the man have another spud, if he wants,' Tony offers, as a peace-keeping gesture.

'That's not the point, Tony! This is exactly why I've got to keep his drinking reigned in. It affects his appetite and God knows, he's carrying way over what he should be already.'

'Though you won't be depriving your fella of his second can?' Robbie asks, tentatively, fearing the worst.

'I should but, och, go and get the blessed can and get it over with, will you?' Claire gives in churlishly. 'And you may as well pour me another glass of rosé, Tony. Dieting or not, I'm not having that good bottle wasted.'

'So, what have you been up to, Gillie?' Tony begins, as he fills Claire's glass. I appreciate his effort to change the subject, although I resent the fact that he's chosen to focus in on me. 'Laura says you've met the fella renting the place next door? Any chance of a holiday romance there? It's about time you allowed yourself a wee fling. It'd do you the power of good.'

I should never try to second-guess Tony. His stupidity never ceases to amaze me.

'Not my style.' I could leave it there, but I'm running out of patience, let alone kindness. I just want to make obnoxious Tony squirm. 'No, I

155

prefer to leave *flings* to other people, Tony.'

He frowns at me slightly although he's still smiling, pleased and caught up in a feeling of his own cleverness. Claire and Laura exchange glances. Robbie returns with his can, keeps quiet, concentrates on pouring his beer carefully.

'Okay, point taken, Gillie. In your case it wouldn't be a *fling*, would it? I mean, you're not married or in a relationship, so the world's your oyster, isn't it?'

'Now, Tony,' Laura comes in, gently chiding. 'Don't be winding Gillian up. Maybe you're getting a wee bit personal there.' *That hasn't bothered you before, Laura.*

'Not a problem, Laura,' I say. 'Personal's okay by me. I think Tony's right, actually. I'm young, free, single. I'm entitled to a little bit of what I fancy, aren't I, Tony?' I look him straight in the eye. He shifts his gaze. I wonder if something's beginning to get through. He reaches for his wine and raises it in front of his face.

'Course you are, Gillie,' he says, in a more subdued tone. He takes a drink and suddenly becomes preoccupied apparently with preparing a forkful of food.

'Tony's an auld married man,' Laura goes on. 'He's just jealous.'

'Though I don't think you need to be jealous, do you, Tony?' I persist. 'You've got everything you want, haven't you now?'

He makes a point of continuing to chew his

food, gesturing that he needs to empty his mouth before replying. Laura takes over.

'It's such a shame you haven't had the support of a lasting marriage, Gillian. You both have to work hard at it, of course. It takes two to tango, as they say.'

It's cruel but I can't resist. 'Bit of a challenge otherwise. Would be a bit tricky if they'd said it had to be three.'

'You're right there, Gillian,' Robbie throws in, unexpectedly. He's beginning to sound slurred. Occasionally Robbie can say something very apt, even if he doesn't know how apt it is. 'Three's a crowd. Mind you, it's never stopped some fellas playing away from home.'

Following Claire's third insubstantial course – a scoop of bitter lemon sorbet, garnished with a tinned mandarin segment – I suggest I help her and Laura clear up. She still obviously hasn't forgiven me for not staying overnight.

'No, Laura and I'll be fine. Have a look down the garden if you want. See what you think of the new decking we've had done.'

Robbie returns to watch TV. I assume Tony's gone to the bathroom.

I seize the chance to get outside. The lawn's perfectly cut and strimmed, the metal planters are filled with grey slate and white and jade-coloured ornamental grasses. Like the house, Claire's garden is modern and minimalist. I make my way down the flagged path and sit on one of the chrome-framed chairs around a glass-topped table on the decking, under a tilted white canvas parasol. It's a relief to be outdoors, on my own again. Until I see Tony on his way down the path. He's put on a long navy cardigan and is holding what looks like a glass of whiskey.

'Getting a wee bit chilly, isn't it? The decking looks fab, doesn't it, Gillie?' he starts off, trying to recover his usually resilient patter, although I can tell he's still preoccupied. He sits down opposite me at the table, sets his tumbler on one of Claire's coasters and pulls the edges of his cardigan together.

'It does. Nice to have the extra space outside. Though you know me, Tony. I'm not very domesticated. I'd always prefer to go to the beach instead. You don't completely appreciate a place until you come away from it. I have to drive quite a distance to get to a good stretch of the coast these days. There are still so many beautiful secluded places along the shore here.'

'Certainly are. There's no place like it in the whole world. Here's to yourself, Gillie.' He toasts me and takes a mouthful of whiskey, nods wisely in agreement with himself as he swallows. 'Look, Gillie. I wasn't trying to wind you up earlier on, you know. I certainly wasn't prying or anything.' As I suspected, Tony wants to find a way to worm back in, to return to our conversation over tea.

'Oh, no. I didn't say you were prying, Tony, did I?' I haven't made any decisions yet, but I don't feel inclined to make things easy for him.

'Well, no, but you seemed sort of *annoyed* with me, for some reason.' He lifts a coaster and turns it over in one hand against the table. 'I mean, if I've done something to offend, just tell me?' He looks at me directly, as if butter wouldn't melt. I stare back, say nothing, just raise my eyebrows.

'For crying out loud, Gillie! Whaaat?'

'Okay then. I *saw* you,' I state. *Let's just cut the crap, will we?*

'What do you mean, you *saw* me?' What did I expect? *Lie* is Tony's default setting.

'On the shore, Tony,' I answer.

'On the *shore?*' He lifts his glass and sips his whiskey again, exaggerates a puzzled expression. He's going to run with it. See what he can get away with.

'Yes, Tony. I saw you and *Kelly*, on the shore together, earlier in the week. You didn't see me, but I saw you.'

Tony's eyes dart about. I've seen him doing it before. He's in the process of a calculation. He gives a forced laugh. 'Och, *that?* Around lunchtime, was it?'

'Yes.'

'That must have been the day we were having that wee working lunch. That's right. Come to think of it, the two of us took ourselves off for a stroll round by the shore afterwards.'

'I think we both know it was more than that, don't we, Tony?'

'Och Gillie! You're winding me up, aren't you? You're not seriously suggesting I would . . .? I mean yes, Kelly and I do get on pretty well. She's keen to learn as quickly as she can about the job. She's only young and . . .'

'She's young alright!' I interrupt him. 'She must be half your age, if that.'

'She's nineteen. A mature nineteen, going on twenty. With the right mentorship and encouragement, Kelly'll really come on. Nothing wrong with two colleagues having a bit of banter and a wee flirt for a laugh, is there?'

'The kind of wee flirt she gets her dress and her knickers off for, you mean?' *Game over, Tony.*

Tony lifts his glass and gulps down the rest of his whiskey. He puts his elbow on the table, covers his mouth with his hand and keeps nodding. He knows he's caught, but his eyes start darting again. He hasn't given up hope. Time for the humble card, a confiding tone.

'Och, sure . . . Nobody's perfect, are they? And we're both adults here, aren't we? It was nothing. You've got to believe me, Gillie.'

'*Believe* you, Tony? After you've spent most of the conversation lying?' *Catch yourself on.*

'Honestly. It was nothing, I swear. It didn't mean anything much to either of us. You're not going to tell Laura, are you? Och, please don't say anything.'

'So, you'd rather the two of us just kept this a wee secret, Tony?'

160

'Well, what do you . . .? *Could* we, Gillie?' He takes his hand away from his face and looks at me, hopefully. *You sick bastard, Tony.* 'Now I wouldn't want you to do something you didn't want to on my account, but och, you know what I'm saying, Gillie. Jesus! The *thought* of what this'd do to Laura if she found out . . .'

'Exactly. Shame that didn't occur to you a bit earlier though, isn't it, Tony? I would've thought, what with you being the original Mr and Mrs, you'd be able to predict each other's reactions to just about any scenario under the sun. And this is a fairly basic one, isn't it?'

'So, have you decided what you're going to do, Gillie?' Tony asks with an edge of impatience. His remorseful reflection is short-lived. His main question is about whether or not he'll be let off the hook.

'I'm not sure yet, Tony,' I tell him, shrugging. 'At the moment, to be honest, I can't really be arsed thinking about it. This the last thing Laura needs to hear from me. However badly we get on, I don't enjoy seeing her upset. On the other hand, I don't like the fact that my sister's being lied to. Know what I mean? Or maybe you don't. But do you know something?' I lean towards him, lower my voice. 'This is *your* mess, Tony. You'll have to clean up your own shit,' I hiss. I've had enough. I get up from the table.

'Och don't go, Gillie. We've got to talk this through.' He puts out his hand, to touch my arm. I move away.

'There's nothing more to talk about, Tony. You work it out. I'm going home.'

I leave Tony standing by the table, his head thrown back theatrically. I'll tell Claire and Laura I'm not feeling well, that it's probably down to a bit too much sun.

As I reach the house, Laura's putting on a cardigan, on the point of coming outside. She's not happy when I explain I need to leave. 'Sure, we've only just eaten, Gillian. You can't be going already. It's only just past nine. Claire and I were just coming out to join you and Tony for a chat.'

'Sorry, Laura. I need to go. I'm really not feeling good.'

She gives me a critical eye and sniffs. I feel sad for her, but I can't stand the thought of staying any longer. I need to get back to the cottage.

Chapter Eleven

David

The mackerel will do him for his tea with a few of McEvoy's potatoes. He needs something stronger than beer tonight, so he'll call into the offie for a carry-out. The sweet taste of Irish whiskey always suited him better than any smoky Scottish malt.

Stewartsford centre is busy with rush-hour traffic and he has to queue for ages at the lights on his way back out again. Linda's family used to live in one of the two-up, two-down town terraces coming up now on his right. The house looks very much as it did – the old buff-grey render, black front door with the knocker and dusty gloss. And what look like exactly the same off-white nets in the street-facing windows. The terraces were tiny inside and they wouldn't have had much room, especially given the size of Linda's mother Wilma, who you rarely saw without a fish supper or a pastry in her fat hands. Wilma had been gorgeous when she was younger, people'd said, but she'd let herself go over the years and her shape had eventually gone under forever, in Skinny Kev's words, 'like the sinking of the Titanic'.

Linda had been a couple of years ahead of David at school. She and her friend Anne had been the girls most of the boys had fancied and he'd been no exception. Among other girls jealous of their pulling power, Linda and Anne had had a reputation for being 'too full of themselves', teases and flirts who dressed, out of school, like 'cheap pros'. As far as David was concerned, the girls, and especially Linda, were just beautiful, clever, lively and full of fun. He'd never seen anything wrong with them wearing short skirts and other clothes that showed off their long slim legs and curvy figures. What was wrong with them enjoying dressing the way they wanted and being as sexy as they were? He'd resigned himself early on to admiring Linda from afar, accepting she was older, in many ways more streetwise and mature than he was. When she and Anne had started going with older boys, then flirting with men around the town bars, including some of the young English soldiers, he'd known that she was well out of his league. But he'd not criticised or resented her for it. Some of the older people were bound to tut and judge because it wasn't their idea of how nice, self-respecting girls should behave, but it was probably always going to be like that between generations, with people forgetting how it was when they'd been young themselves.

'Makes you glad all the same you've just had boys sometimes,' he'd once overheard his mum saying to his dad one evening when they were washing up. 'Those wee girls need to be careful, the way they're all over the boys, hanging round with the men and carrying on with those army lads. They need to be careful they don't give someone the wrong idea. If I was Wilma, I'd not be letting my girl out dressed in skirts as short as that, wearing all that make-up. Asking for trouble, isn't it? But Wilma's not herself anymore, poor woman. She's hardly able to look after herself, let alone her daughter.' His dad had agreed, 'You're right, Jean. They're only wee girls, but some people don't think it's decent – they think it lowers the tone, like. They need to catch themselves on, before it's too late. We're not the only ones noticing. Know what I mean?' he'd added at the end, lowering his voice slightly. David hadn't quite understood what his dad had been getting at, although it wasn't too long before he would find out.

One late summer afternoon, when David and Sammy and Skinny Kev were lying on look-out on their stomachs in the field next to the garden of the derelict cottage, they'd heard voices approaching on the other side, getting closer.

'*Pleeease!* Leave us alone, will you?' they'd heard first, in Linda's pleading, frightened voice. 'You're hurting my arm!'

'What are you going to do to us?' had come afterwards, from Anne, panic-stricken.

The boys then saw two men each dragging one of the girls by the arm behind them. In spite of their black balaclavas, David had realised at once that they were the same men who had

165

beaten up Tom and Keith. The girls were dressed lightly in short cotton summer dresses and heeled sandals, arms and legs bare.

'Och, pleeease just let us go. Tell us what we've done wrong and we'll not do it again. Honest to God!' Linda was begging again, but it wasn't making any difference to the men.

'Bit late for saying sorry now though, isn't it, Linda?' Santie's chief Helper told her. 'Away on!'

The men pulled the girls towards the ruined greenhouse and hurled them roughly inside so that they fell forward onto their knees, onto the shattered glass and splintered wood on the floor. Then, while his accomplice stood outside and lit up two cigarettes in his mouth at once, the chief dealt further with the girls, grabbing them both by the backs of their necks, pushing, grinding their faces down hard against the ground, muffling their screams of agony.

'Boys a dear, my arms aren't as strong as they used to be, girls. That'll have to do for now. Gissa a fag, will you?' Santie's special Helper let go of the girls, backed out of the greenhouse and took one of his mate's ready prepared cigarettes.

'Nice one! Is that us now? Fancy a fish supper on the way home, once you get your breath back? I'm starving!' Leaving the girls lying crying on the floor of the greenhouse, the men had headed off.

Anne and Linda had gradually picked themselves up and turned round in the direction of the boys. The fronts of their pastel dresses were stained brown and dirty green with soil and grass, covered with bits of rotten wood and flaking paint. Their arms, legs and faces were cut and scratched. Linda's especially – she had a deep gash near her eye, blood and make-up running together down her cheek.

'C'mon!' had been Skinny Kev's immediate reaction. 'We can't just leave them down there like that,' he'd hissed, starting to move to get up. 'We'll have to go and help them!' Sammy had turned pale, obviously sick with fear.

'Sssh! Shut your mouth, will you?' David had hissed back at Kev. He'd been shit-scared too, but he'd had to stop Kev and pulled him down hard, so he couldn't get up.

'Don't be so fucking stupid, Kev! They've only just left, haven't they? And if they find out we've been watching, they'll beat the living daylights out of us! And that's if we're lucky!'

Kev had understood. He'd made a noise of repressed frustration in his throat and buried his face in the grass, but he'd stayed where he was. The girls had come out of the greenhouse and were clinging together sobbing, so shocked and upset they couldn't speak. The boys had stayed on, waiting, listening for the sound of the men's footsteps going into the safer distance, then the sound of their car starting up round on the road. David was just on the point of suggesting that it was probably safe at that stage to go and comfort the girls, when there was the noise of what sounded like another vehicle arriving. Soon after that, they heard the sound of heavy, brisk clicking footsteps, coming down the side path. It was Santie.

The girls sprang apart and backed away from him.

'C'mon now, girls,' Santie had started off in a quiet way, as he approached them, hands in trouser pockets. 'Sure, you know we're only looking after you! We don't like people calling our nice girls hoors, do we? And you'll not be forgetting your lessons in a hurry now, will you?'

'Pleeeease don't do anything else to us,' Anne begged him, trembling, wiping her nose on the back of her hand. 'We'll not do anything you don't like any more, promise. But please just leave us be now!'

Santie nodded calmly and waved his head towards the cottage. 'Get yourself home now, Anne. And mind you won't need to mention anything about the wee lesson to anyone. I think we can keep this between ourselves alright, can't we? And we don't want to have to remind the pair of you about this again, do we?' He was wearing his smart suit and tie – the same kind of suit he would wear on Sundays – standing with his back to the boys, linking his big square hands behind his back.

'No, course we'll not tell, Santie,' Anne told him nervously.

'Right you be then, Anne. Off you go now,' Santie dismissed her, in a more abrupt tone.

'Promise we'll be good, I swear. C'mon, Linda.' Anne had linked arms with Linda, obviously keen to get away before anything else happened.

'Actually, I need a quick wee word with Linda. On her own. I'll not be keeping her long but there's no need to wait,' Santie then told Anne, putting a hand on Linda's arm. 'Off you go now and be a good girl for us, mind.'

The girls had exchanged bewildered looks. 'I don't mind if Anne stays,' Linda had suggested. 'Whatever you need to say to me, it's alright.'

'That's very good of you to say that Linda, but we've a wee thing of our own to discuss. So off you go now, Anne. Don't be getting into trouble for being late for your tea.' There'd been no point in Anne trying to change Santie's mind.

When Anne had gone, Linda stood with her head down, waiting for Santie to speak, her grazed, bleeding arms crossed over the front of her stained dress.

'Shame about your nice wee dress, Linda,' Santie began. Keeping one arm behind his back, he moved closer to her and reached out his other hand. He laid it against her, the gap between his thumb and other fingers forming a V shape high up under her neck.

'Pleeeease. Pleeease don't do that,' Linda started to whimper, reaching up to take his hand

169

away.

'You don't think Santie would hurt you, Linda, do you?' he answered, in an apparently gentle voice, the same sort of tone he'd used to talk to children when they'd come to sit on his knee in his shop. 'Santie understands. He knows the sort of things you wee hoors like.' His hand slipped away from her neck, down her chest, coming to rest over her breast, cupping it, then grasping it tighter, squeezing it in his broad, thick-fingered hand.

'No! Stop it! Please, I don't want you to. Please let me go home now,' Linda's voice was quaking, the expression on her face a mixture of disgust and dawning terror.

Santie's hand kept on moving down, over the skirt front of her dress, reaching at her hem, gathering it up. He was bending his knees, then roughly pushing his hand up under Linda's dress, pulling her towards him with his other arm. 'Santie knows what you wee hoors like,' he repeated, with a hacking laugh.

Linda struggled against him, trying to get away, trying to pull his groping hand from between her legs. 'Leave me alone! You can't do this. I'll tell my family. They'll tell the police. I'll, I'll tell your *wife* and your family on you!'

Santie just laughed even harder. 'And do you think she'd believe a shameless wee hoor like you? I've got some very good friends in the police, Linda. And I know your family. And who do you think they're going to believe? Wise up! You're a very lucky wee girl. You don't have to pretend to Santie you're not enjoying yourself. There's nobody here but us.'

David had almost been on the point of vomiting. His heart was pounding. He could feel Sammy, like a fear-rigid animal holding his breath, beside him on one side, Skinny Kev's body shivering with the tension of controlling his pent-up anger, containing the urge to burst through the hedge and hurl himself like a raging, tight-muscled dog at Santie. David hadn't wanted to let Santie have his way any more than Kev. He'd felt like a cowering, big girl's blouse of a coward, lying doing nothing, watching the whole sickening scene panning out, from behind that hedge. But he'd also known there was a good chance they'd do more harm than good by showing themselves and intervening. There was no telling how many other people as well as Linda and themselves they'd end up hurting by doing the right thing. Santie had the influence and the weight of so many behind him. He knew all kinds of dangerous characters who'd have been more than ready to help him out and repay his favours. There was no denying how much damage he could do if he'd put his mind to it.

'So, how's about we find ourselves some-where a wee bit more private, Linda?'

They had to just listen to Santie carry on talking to Linda, as he forced her backwards, towards the old hen house. He grabbed her by her lovely hair while he threw the cracked, rattling wooden door open and shoved her in ahead of him, fumbling with his trouser belt, pulling the door shut after them.

'No! No! Don't do that! You're hurting me,' was all they could hear next.

Then Santie's forced, cruel, gun-fire laughter. The noises of the struggle inside, that the boys had only been able to imagine. Thuds against the shed walls and floor. The heavy crash. Followed by repeated creaking of wood. Santie's bestial puffing and grunting. Linda's strangled calls and clawing and flapping about, like the hopeless, ineffectual protests of a cornered, overwhelmed bird, refusing to spare itself pain by deciding to surrender. *That filthy, brutal, sick bastard.*

Linda and Anne were very different from then on. They'd stopped going out, stopped flirting and giggling. They didn't seem bothered any more about how they dressed or looked. It was as if their souls had been snuffed out.

As with all the other clandestine punishments, the effects of which were always put down to accidental or fighting injuries that those involved only had themselves to blame for, there'd certainly never been any repercussions for Santie. If people had ideas, they'd kept them to themselves. Some big boats weren't worth rocking. He'd carried on, driving round in his big red Volvo, serving his people. The untouchable community champion, polishing his badges, a law unto himself.

The potatoes and fresh mackerel are good, but David has lost his appetite and doesn't enjoy them as much as they deserve. Once the nightmarish memories begin to kick off, they gather their own force, colours and details sharpening, building and darkening. The mind can be a distilled, bespoke Hell, with no respite, no sure means of forgetting. Unless, like his poor tormented mother, you come to the conclusion that there is nothing else for it, but to escape, once and for all. He'd been so sad, for her and for all of them. Mark had despised her for doing what she did, but David had never judged or blamed her. Who could really presume to know the pain of another person's mind, and oblige them to bear a life of indefinite suffering? Anyone can find themselves at the mercy of uncontrollable circumstances. And the givens of their genes and chemistry. Some may just have more luck than others. Hand on heart, given his mother's grief, mightn't he equally have considered taking the same way out? What was it Trevor often said? *There, but for the Grace of God, go I.*

There'd never been any question in his mind about the value of a good over-the-counter anaesthetic from the offie. And sure, it might knock a few years off your life, but who could tell how many more you'd be subtracting by not allowing yourself to take the edge off your distress?

He leaves the fish bones and skin on the plate by the sink, searches the cupboards for a glass for his whiskey and finds a short, thick-bottomed tumbler. He thinks he might put his jacket on and find somewhere to sit outside. It's getting a bit cooler, but it's still a decent June evening and it'd be a pity to sit indoors. There's no sign of McEvoy around the yard and it doesn't bother David if he has to say hello to the man. He's always been pretty good at giving people the message when he's not in the mood for conversation anyway. And if he sits out of sight, over the gate, in the corner of that high-walled empty field close to the yard, he's unlikely to be disturbed.

As he crosses the yard with the glass and bottle of Jameson in hand, McEvoy's dog spots him and gets up. 'Fancy a wee whiskey, do you?' he whispers to her. He eases back the bolt on the field gate as quietly as he can and the dog follows on his heels.

He was right. It's private and sheltered, sitting in the early evening sun in the corner with his back against the high stone wall. The dog stretches out alongside him on the warmed, close-cropped grass and closes her eyes. She's obviously just looking for a bit of undemanding company. He sets the tumbler on the ground, pours himself more than a good measure of whiskey and knocks it back, then pours another one to enjoy more slowly. He should have thought to bring his sunglasses, but can't be bothered to go back in and just closes his eyes against the sun, trying to blur his thoughts, telling himself it won't be long before the whiskey starts to offer its dependable, unconditional sympathy.

He'd not seen Linda or Anne since he'd left to live with his auntie and uncle, and had often wondered what'd become of them; where they'd ended up living; who they'd married. He'd tried to hope that they'd managed to cope with what had happened, that Linda especially had found a way of detaching herself from such an abhorrent experience and had not come to blame or hate herself for it. Imagining that she had coped was the only way he could stop beating himself up for his failure to defend her. He'd felt there was no choice at the time, but the thought that Santie would walk unchallenged, head held high to his grave, was like a stabbing blade in the gut. No matter how much David had wanted to distract himself over the years, the blade stayed and turned, goring more deeply each time he thought about the prospect of such an eternal injustice. *For Thine is the Kingdom, the power and the glory.* Whatever you believed and whatever you could or shouldn't take into your own hands, it was unbearable to think you would never ever know how, or if, some wrongs had been righted. Peace could only come from knowing that the punishment fitted and equalled the severity and perversity of the crime, that the abuser would suffer just as much as the abused. How could such crimes ever, ever be *forgiven?* Where was the virtue in opening your heart to those whose acts were completely heartless, or trying to dissuade yourself from harbouring a healthy barrier of hatred?

David downs the rest of his whiskey and immediately pours another one. He leans back against the wall, lays his hand on top of the dog's back, tries to breathe slowly. The whiskey's starting to take effect, softening things slightly in his mind, padding his mental furniture. What's in there is still the same, underneath, but it makes it temporarily a touch more possible to let it be there.

'You're not such a bad wee dog, are you?' he says out loud, stroking the animal's thick black and white coat. His eyes start to feel heavier and he begins to drowse off.

He wakes with a start, to the sound of a car arriving in the yard. He feels quite knocked out with the whiskey, which has him checking his watch to find it's gone twenty past nine. He forces himself to get up. Okay to have a few drinks, but he can't afford to completely lose it. The dog slips through a hole at the bottom of the gate and runs back into the yard, with a couple of sharp, greeting barks. It's Gillian's car. He thought she'd said she was going for a meal at her sister's and didn't expect she'd be back so early. She's already out, slamming her door, looking seriously fed-up, in as far as he can read her expression. She's wearing a simple white T-shirt and black jeans, and slings a light cardigan or jumper over her shoulder as she locks up.

'Hello!' he finds himself shouting over at her from the gate, holding the now empty whiskey glass on the top bar. 'Cheer up, will you? May never happen,' he tells her.

'Oh, Hi. Too late. It *has* already happened. But never mind,' she replies, forcing a quirky smile, although she sounds irritable. 'Drinks on the *pacio?*' she jokes, mispronouncing the word, poking fun half-heartedly at the middle-class social ritual, pointing at his empty glass.

He smiles, aware that he's already half-cut and it probably shows. 'Nothing as grand as that for the likes of me! A dram or three in the corner of a field. They don't call *me* proud.'

She stays by her car but looks a bit less preoccupied. Stares back at him, narrows her eyes, seems half-amused, half-quizzical.

'Me neither!' she says. 'But then I don't mind people knowing I was born in the corner of a Northern Irish field. And no matter how long you've lived away from the auld sod, it's always in you, isn't it? No matter how hard you try to cover or lose it, it'll come out, one way or another, I suppose.'

She's twigged. Relaxed by the whiskey, he's let go of trying to control the remnants of his

Northern Irish accent. There's nothing he can do now to backtrack.

'So, whereabouts do you come from over here? If you don't mind me asking?' she continues.

He may as well come clean with her. 'You're alright. I came from just the other side of Stewartsford originally, but it's all a very long time ago and I didn't think it was worth saying, like. I've lived across the water most of my life anyway,' he explains, conscious his mouth's dry and he's slightly slurring his words.

'Though once you get talking, you've still held on to quite a bit of your accent, haven't you? I've tried to hold onto mine, I suppose. But anyway, wasn't meaning to pry – none of my business. Take it from me, I know what it's like, wanting to cut off and do your own thing!' She sounds more irritable again, sighs, looks down.

'So, you had a jolly time at your sister's then?' he asks, guessing by the look of her that she didn't.

'Bloody marvellous!' she answers, obviously not meaning it. 'One of the best. Reminded me of how much I'm missing out on.'

'Good as that, was it?' he nods, grinning, acknowledging her irony. 'Sorry I couldn't have been there.'

'I'm pretty sure it wouldn't 've been your thing. Whiskey in a field being a much saner option.' She's smiling, seems to appreciate the banter.

'Yes, Okay. So I've had a few. Though drinking outside always makes the stuff go to your head a bit quicker, don't you think?' he adds at the end, smirking, looking at her directly. A bit on the flirtatious side, but what the hell?

'Or that's your excuse anyway? But don't worry, I'll not breathalyse you this time or ask to see the level on the bottle,' she plays along.

'Much appreciated. Now, you wouldn't take a wee drink yourself, would you? The bar's not so grand, but I've got a nice quiet table here in the corner. You'd be very welcome, if you want to fetch yourself a glass? I'll not be telling on you either. Gets a bit lonely like, drinking on your own. Go on! It'll do you the power of good!'

He's not holding back now. No harm in a bit of fun, as long as you know when to stop.

'Och, I don't know. I'm going to get off early in the morning. And I'm not always so good with whiskey. A small hot one before bed now and then for a cold is okay, but . . . Look, what I mean is, nothing personal, but I probably should be getting in.'

'You could always get yourself the hot water and I'll supply the whiskey? Only saying. Not trying to make you give up your good intentions. Your call.' He's pushing it a bit, but he's pretty sure she's not the type to be persuaded into things she doesn't want.

'Well . . . Why not? Don't expect me to be up to much by way of conversation after this evening's fiasco, though. Talk about *punishment.* I'll be back in a minute,' she says, as she turns towards her cottage.

'No worries,' he calls after her. 'We can both just sit and look at the dog and stare into our glasses.' He needs to make sure he keeps a grip.

Chapter Twelve

Gillian

I get a glass with some sugar and boiled water and put on my cardigan. It's much cooler now, in contrast to the earlier baking heat.

'Sure, a wee hot whiskey'll do you nay harm!' Dad would say, late of an evening, when I went over to stay with them, especially if he thought I was looking pale or tired.

He'd set out three short glasses in a neat line on the kitchen worktop. His was a generous double with a splash of tap water. Mum's was a small one over ice. Then he'd set a teaspoon in my glass to take the heat and prevent it cracking. He'd stir in Demerara sugar with boiled water, before pouring in the Jameson or the Bushmills, clinking the spoon against the rim at the end so as not to waste a drop of the precious nectar, the colour of peat infused rain water. 'Get that into you!' he'd tell me. 'Then get yourself up those stairs to your bed and get your head down. You'll not go wrong with that.'

I've never managed to make a hot whiskey the way Dad did. Although I know it wasn't just down to technique or the actual ingredients. It was the whole ritual, the fact that he was making it for me. It was about his voice alongside it, the comfort of its particular familiar phrasing and lilt, the kind of natural poetry that had been around me ever since before I was born, like my mother's quieter physical way, her hands and her heartbeat. Part of Dad's style was about repeating certain words and details of stories. They were like lyrical refrains that you expected and depended upon. Especially since I'd moved away, I realised more how it was something other Northern Irish people would often do too. To someone outside the culture, it perhaps seemed repetitive or unnecessary at times, but it was an important part of an atmosphere and a way of living with whatever came along, of weaving yourself, your family and others around you together.

For a moment I wonder what I'm doing, heading outside to sit and drink whiskey in the corner of a field with a man I scarcely know at all, but I'm still feeling the drive of my anger at Tony, which frees me up in other ways and makes me more decisive. It makes me care less and tell myself to just get out there.

As I leave the cottage and walk across the yard, I see Derek McEvoy standing, with his back to me, leaning against the gate, the dog by his side. He's obviously talking to David, who must be sitting down now in the corner of the field, behind the wall. The dog notices me straight away and barks, alerting her owner at once.

'Och, Hello, Gillian!' Derek calls out to me

cheerfully. 'How's about you? Having a wee drink to yourselves? Nice night for it!'

'It is, isn't it?' I answer. 'As long as I'm in time for last orders!'

'No need to worry about that! The landlord's quite easy going. So I've heard, anyway,' he jokes, moving to make space for me as I reach the gate. 'A nice wee hot whiskey?' he comments, with a knowing look.

'Yes,' I say, talking to David now as well. He's sitting on the grass behind the wall, with another glass of whiskey poured. 'Assuming there'll be some left,' I add, nodding in David's direction.

'Right enough! You'd better get your share before he finishes the bottle. Not that I'm against anybody taking a drink. I'll get out of your way now. Don't let that water be getting cold. Even a Northern Irish man knows you can't make a hot whiskey without hot water. See you later then. I'll take the dog out of your road as well.'

'See you soon, Derek. And we'll keep the music down,' I finish, grateful to him for not prolonging the conversation.

'Let me get that gate for you,' he offers, sliding back the bolt, letting me into the field, then shutting it behind me. 'Going to be another good day tomorrow, by the looks of it. You've been lucky with the weather. Bye for now.'

'Was it the Last Supper, then, at your sister's? Or do you think there's still hope?' David asks, as he adds whiskey to my sugared hot water. We're sitting about a foot apart, side by side on the grass, backs against the dry-stone wall. 'How's that?'

'That's plenty, thanks,' I tell him, putting a hand over the top of my glass. His joke about the Last Supper makes me smile. Whatever their belief or lack of belief, Biblical references can be an engrained part of a Northern Irish person's vocabulary in both serious and humorous conversation. I take a sip of my whiskey, enjoy the warmth of it in my throat. 'There's always everlasting hope, I'm afraid. It doesn't matter how totally unenjoyable a meal or a conversation is. There'll always be another one.'

'Sure, that's families . . . that's people for you,' he says quietly. He breaks eye contact, swallows another mouthful. For a moment, it's almost like a bit of a shadow passes over his face.

I can't think how what I said would've offended, but then, perhaps for some reason I did. 'Sorry. You must think I'm a right bitch, talking about my sisters like that, especially when they invited me for a meal at such short notice?'

He blinks, seems to come to again. 'Oh, no, not at all, Gillian. Sorry. Something just crossed my mind there for a minute. Nothing to do with you. I mean, no problem, feel free to go right ahead there. Sounds like your sisters take some handling?'

'They certainly do! Mind you, they'd

probably say the same about me. As you say, every family has its problems. At least we're still in touch. It's just so bloody annoying, the way they have to see me only on their terms. Doesn't feel like anything ever changes. We just go round and round in the same boring, bickering circles. Sorry, whinging on. Cheers, thanks for the drink. So, how did you get on with your fishing? Catch anything?'

'A nice mackerel. Already on board,' he says, patting his stomach. 'Just washing him down.'

'Lovely part of the coast that, isn't it? We used to go there a lot as a family when I was younger. How about you?' I enjoy the cut-and-thrust of humour and word play, but I can't help wanting to know more about him and it's difficult to completely put aside personal subjects, including the past, especially when it's potentially common ground.

'Yes, it's a beautiful place. Sometimes I went there with family. But more often than not I'd go with Dad's old friend, Trevor. He taught me nearly everything I know about fishing. And I went with my mates too. We used to go shrimping and crabbing and just mess around the pools and on the rocks.' His voice is low and almost wistful now. He sighs, sets down his glass and doesn't refill it. Lays his tanned hands either side of his stretched-out legs on the grass, looks ahead.

'Still in touch with anyone?' I ask.

'No. Like I said, my brother moved off ages

ago to the States. We still send each other the occasional letter or card, but nothing else. Most of the people I knew here have moved on. Most of them to that so-called 'better place'. There'll still be the odd relative of a relative and friend of a friend around, but I never made the effort, so . . . As I said, I've spent most of my time over in England. I was only fourteen when I moved. And as far as the two lads I mentioned are concerned, well . . .' he pauses again, puts his chin on his chest, closes his eyes for a second, then turns towards me, raises his eyebrows as he speaks in a wry tone. 'Let's just say . . . unless you know any good mediums . . .?'

'Oh no. I'm sorry.' I feel awkward. I know how it can be when people churn things up for you, even if they don't intend to.

'No problem. You weren't to know. As I said, it all happened a very long time ago,' he explains, rubbing his eye.

I'm sensing that no matter how long ago it was, whatever happened in his past still matters to him. 'Yes, although things can still affect you, can't they? I mean, it's awful when people die young.' As I'm saying it, I'm wishing I could just shut my mouth. I hate it sometimes when other people get you to talk for the sake of acquiring information, leaving you afterwards to deal with all the hurt or fury they've stirred up. Feelings you think are safely dormant can erupt sometimes with unexpected force. And I can be as guilty of activating painful memories as anyone else. At the same time, there's something about him I like and my questions aren't stemming from idle curiosity. I'm becoming interested in him and what he thinks.

'You're right there,' he comes straight back, without resistance. 'Of course, you know anybody can go at any age, but when someone's so young, it feels wrong. Especially when it's a violent thing. It was back during the worst days of The Troubles. The car the two of them were in blew up. The bomb wasn't intended for them – their deaths were accidental, in as far as any death's accidental when you're made to transport a bomb. They were blown to kingdom come. The only thing you console yourself with is that they wouldn't have known anything about it. Which is more than be said for some people's suffering on their exit. Oh Christ, I'm getting fucking dark. Like I said before, I'm a master conversation-stopper.' He puts his hands either side of his head and runs them back hard through his hair, screwing up his face.

'No, you're not. I was asking, wasn't I? Anyway, life can be dark, can't it? There were certainly plenty of dark moments back then. You're allowed to feel dark and talk about it when terrible things happen. It'd be more of a problem if you didn't.' I'm feeling less awkward now. Maybe partly because of the whiskey, but also because I'm drawn more into what he's saying. Talking about serious things can come easier to me than small talk. There's a peace somehow, a self-forgetting that comes when you connect with a person in discussing what really matters.

'Yes. I think so too. Thanks. Not everyone wants to go there though, do they? An ever-smiling face may be more desirable. Or at least, easier for other people to live with.' He looks a bit less tense now.

'In some ways, maybe. Though we can't always live to please other people, can we? And people worth bothering about don't want or expect to live with an ever-cheerful person. I'm not saying relationships are just about constantly offloading problems, but . . . surely there has to be some room for being yourself in your own life, your dark sides as well as your light?'

'Yes, you're right,' he says, looking me directly in the eye, then shifting his gaze towards the field. 'There certainly should be.'

I guess that he just wants me to leave his words unanswered. We both fall silent again for a while.

'So, apart from . . . How does it feel to be back?' I ask.

'Alright. Yes, there are darker memories. Though as far as the countryside goes, it's a hard place to beat. And I needed to come over and . . . But anyhow, how about you? Feeling any better about that family situation? You know, on the beach, you were saying you didn't know what to do? About some *knowledge* you had, that you didn't want? Feel free not to reply, of course.'

Fair play. It's my turn to be churned up. Although I'm churned up anyway, when not absorbed in conversation. I still don't know what I'm going to do, or how much I should confide in him. Doesn't sound as if he's still in touch with anyone here and he doesn't seem the gossiping kind. I'm tempted just to pour the whole thing out and have done. But why should Tony's stuff be allowed to spill over into my time?

'Oh that? Still an ongoing dilemma. There have been developments since we spoke. But I still don't know what the hell I'm going to do.'

'You didn't mention you were MI5.'

'I thought you'd probably guessed anyway. Seriously, the whole story would probably bore you to tears. I wouldn't want to waste your time.'

'No worries on that score. I'm used to that. A fireman has to take all kinds of things in his stride. Having his time wasted being quite run-of-the-mill,' he says, smiling, giving me a knowing look. He's police. I'm ninety-eight per cent certain.

'Right. So, you're one of those firemen who keeps the peace as well?'

He says nothing, just lifts his head slightly, widens his eyes and raises his brows.

'Okay, got you.' I'm tired and let myself relax back more heavily against the wall. I keep getting flashbacks of the moment I discovered Tony and Kelly on the shore. I know sooner or later I'm going to have to make up my mind about what to do, especially if I'm going to tell Laura. *But not now. You can piss off, Tony. No, not now.*

'Can I pour you another drop?' David asks, his words sounding slightly slurred and drowsy. No need to judge a man for having a few drinks on holiday on the edge of a field. A man trying to confront some darker memories. And if he's police, there's probably a lot more where that came from.

'Just a drop,' I tell him. I probably won't drink it, but it's more about making the gesture than the drinking itself. He starts to pour and stops immediately I raise a finger.

'I'll put the bottle here, so you can help yourself if you want. No standing on ceremony.' He sets the half-full bottle on the grass between us.

We sit quietly, in parallel, looking ahead across the dimming field bounded by stone walls, with hawthorn hedge in places, the smell of damp summer night in the air. We still know very little about each other. I'm sure there'll be all kinds of things in his mind, as there are in mine, held back. But there's a quality in the atmosphere between us I've a gut feeling is genuine. Even if we're not saying everything, it seems like on both sides there's a willingness to let go of deliberate pretence. In the mix of light and dark, play, wit, and emotional disclosure in our dialogues, there's a growing mutual agreement that we can be ourselves and cut the small talk.

No standing on ceremony. It seems that, like

me, for his own particular reasons, he's at a point when he's weary of empty conventional gestures for the sake of others' approval. Without completely giving up on the desire to make a positive impression. I'm still not forgetting he's a man and I'm a woman. I'm aware of having a persistent buzz when I'm with him – while at the same time feeling more grounded, somehow. How I tend to feel when I'm in the company of a man I find physically attractive, with whom there's the potential for a deeper connection too.

Of course, I have no way of knowing exactly what he's thinking, but I'm as sure as I can be that the intention, to simply relax with no other fixed expectations of each other, is mutual. We sit on in comfortable silence. Hearing the sounds of birds coming in to roost, the condensing, mingling smells of leaves, grass, earth and stone.

As it grows darker, the field, hedges, walls and sky merge together into a more even, deepening tone. In the way that the blanketing whiteness of snowfall unclutters a landscape by covering details, a darkening night can bring a sense of unbounded space which can connect with the place inside yourself that feels free.

'I need my bed,' I say after a while, getting to my feet.

He nods. Lifts the bottle and gets up too. Lets me out in front of him through the gate and carefully, deliberately, bolts it after us.

'Thanks for joining me, Gillian,' he says, as

we cross the yard. We pause when we reach the cottages and stand on the gravel between our front doors. 'Sleep well. Get your head down now. And I'm sure your work'll go well tomorrow. I'd shake your hand now, only . . .' he lifts his whiskey bottle in one hand and his glass in the other by way of explanation.

'I'll not hold it against you! Enjoy whatever you're doing too. And thanks. For the whiskey and the craic. It was good,' I reply, briefly touching his shoulder with the edge of my glass before turning to go inside.

Chapter Thirteen

Gillian

I'm dressed and downstairs by 9.a.m., still in two minds about where to go this morning. I'm wondering whether to drive further along the road towards the less sheltered end of the lough side where the car ferry crosses to the west. Or to a much closer National Trust country estate our family used to walk round in the summer, to do some sketching in the gardens or by the lake.

The gravelled yard outside is already dry and flooded with sunlight. I catch the back of Derek on his way down the lane in his tall-wheeled red Massey Ferguson tractor, his posture upright, dog tucked in the cab up beside him. I've no doubt Derek has his moments like everyone else, but this morning, he has an upbeat air about him. He's his own man. On the go, in charge. Busy, ready to face his world.

Last night I dreamt about swimming in the lough as a girl. Mum was much further out, waving at me. She wanted me to join her. I kept swimming and swimming towards her. I was in my old plastic beach shoes – you had to wear them because of all the rocks and sharp broken shells you had to cross before you got to the impressionable base of muddy sand with fine waving threads of Eel grass.

It seemed to take forever to get to any kind of swimming depth in the lough. You'd paddle, wade, then get down, under the water. Once wet, you'd be cooler with the wind chill if you stood up. You'd walk forward on your hands, kicking your legs, then make an effort to begin swimming, your stomach barely clearing the ground in the shallow water. Telling yourself that when you stood up, you'd be at waist depth, at least. Really knowing that the water would probably still only be up to your knees.

Mum had this thing about swimming into the path of the sun on the water. She was right – it felt close to my idea of a heaven too – the sun's rays holding you in a sure, generous, warm stream. And if you kept swimming, with your body horizontal, you didn't touch the colder depths below. You didn't have to worry about any of the slithering eels or fish, or the big crabs' pincers under the rocks and weeds down there, because you would stay above them, out of harm's reach. We'd have such fun out there. Drops of sea water would sparkle on Mum's chest, above the line of her halter-neck turquoise swimming costume, reminding me of the 1950s, rainbowy glass crystal necklace she'd kept in her underwear drawer in an ink-blue box with a white satin lining.

I decide for the sake of a shorter drive to go to the estate. I think I might sketch the mute swans against the background of the lake.

There are only a few cars in the car park when I arrive. The facilities for visitors are much more developed than they used to be.

'Are you a member?' the smartly dressed thirty-something woman at the ticket desk asks in a quick, professional manner.

'No. Though I should be really,' I say. 'This place has always been a favourite, ever since I was a child.'

'Och, has it now? So, would you like a ticket for the gardens and the house, or just for the gardens?'

'Just for the gardens today, thanks.'

'And can I give you a wee map?'

It always feels strange and almost on the verge of impertinent being offered a map or a leaflet about somewhere you feel you know like the back of your hand, where you've been so often over the years you can't help feeling some sense of ownership.

'No, thanks. I'm sure I'll find my own way around. As they say, the map isn't quite the territory,' I reply, taking my ticket and heading outside.

The front of the grand nineteenth-century house looks onto spacious lawns. Beyond, there's a lake, an arboretum and less formal areas of woodland.

Today the lawns hold the heat of summer. There's a subtle scent of warmed conifer and freshly cut grass.

There are a few walkers about, but it's the kind of place that absorbs us well and it's usually easy enough to find yourself a secluded spot. It's still and quiet, apart from the echoing calls of wildfowl and other birds against the distant intermittent hum of a lawnmower.

I stop about halfway round the lake and sit close to the water's edge, just taking it all in.

After a while I begin to sketch, putting in colours and pencilling a few notes for myself. There are endless possibilities for designs in glass. Lines of the weeping willows bowing towards the water. Profiles of the trees and reeds, their colours reflected in the lake. At the end of the curving wooden jetty, I see the figures of a man and woman leaning close together over the handrail, throwing food to a squawking crowd of ducks.

As a pair of adult swans move closer, I work quickly to capture the shifting S-shapes of their bodies, how their forms move together and separately, their changing bright configurations against the darker background of their territory.

Knowing that swans stay with their mates for life has always added to their aura of romance. Returning to the idea unfortunately jogs another opposing, intrusive train of thought about catching Tony and Kelly on the shore, and how it would affect Laura if she found out. I try my best to blank it out, determined for now at least not to allow Tony to sabotage my peace.

Not far from the lake, where formal gardens meet wilder, less managed woodland, there's a striking statue of a white stag. When we were little, we'd picnic on the grass beside him, and Claire, Laura and I would take turns to sit on his back, with Dad's help. I instantly felt more important up there, bolder, as if I was drawing on the deer's strength. 'Watch he doesn't throw you off or run away with you now!' Dad would joke. Claire would tell him not to be silly, that it was only a statue. Laura, being frightened of heights and most animals – apart from small dogs and hamsters – would plead to be helped down again immediately. I, on the other hand, had to be persuaded to leave the stag. I would close my eyes, imagining that we were running away together through the woods, that there was nothing to fear, because he was my protector and no animal or person would dare question his authority. He might have fought and raged at others, but to me he was a pure trustworthy hero, loving, gentle and understanding.

I decide to visit him and leave the lakeside. He's still exactly where he was, still dependably impressive. I decide to sketch him, from different angles. I can already picture a big feature window or a framed glass hanging, shot through with the curved, scything shapes of his antlers. I draw from a distance, then end up lying on the ground, under his head, looking up, just focusing on his antlers against the cloud-curded blue clearing of the sky. It's just he and I again, sharing an exhilarating, magical world apart. Glass is the perfect medium to convey something of its spirit.

David

He'd hoped the drink and the distraction of company would help him escape his thoughts for a while. Knowing that, realistically, it'd take more than whiskey and conversation to settle his conscience. He enjoyed being with Gillian. They were clearly different, but they had common ground, coming from Northern Ireland, both having moved across the water. And they definitely shared a similar, ironic sense of humour. She didn't interrogate, but she wanted to go beyond the superficial and didn't retreat from darker subject matter. She had a way of reading between the lines that meant he didn't have to explain everything. He was certain they'd never met before the holiday, but she was one of those people you felt you'd known somewhere previously and they'd known you. Maybe just because the more idiosyncratic elements of their characters reflected each other? A surprising, disarming sense of déjà vu.

He's been awake on and off since seven, making himself lie on in the hope of resting. Headachy, drifting in and out of dreams, mostly disturbing, the same preying images always on his case. Hard to believe it's Friday already. Tomorrow he'll have been at the cottage for a week. A week of thinking and feeling, confirming a burden of unfinished business to be sure, but a week too long without a plan, let alone decisive action.

He opens the drawer of the bedside cabinet and takes out his wallet. Behind the scratched plastic window of a pocket inside, he carries a faded, browning photo of his parents. It was taken not long after she and his dad were married, his mum had told David.

His brother's note is folded, stuck into one of the pockets opposite the photo, with his credit card. Mark had always been the same. He'd never written more than a few lines of a card or a letter, certainly never more than one side of a small piece of plain notepaper. Lines widely spaced, that rarely told you anything more than you already knew. Token gestures towards communication, although his parents had read and reread every word, keeping the letters carefully gathered in the wooden letter-rack with the brass horse's head on their mantelpiece. 'He's not telling us about what he's actually *doing*,' their dad would say occasionally, not always as contented with *Dear* and *Thinking of you*. Although their mum had quickly talked him round. 'Och, sure he's just so busy,' she'd say, with 'And as long as he's safe, that's the main thing, isn't it?'

David pulls out Mark's letter and sets it down on the bed, snaps his wallet closed and throws it into the drawer. He could do with some water, then plenty of coffee. He's seriously dehydrated. He pulls on some shorts and a T-shirt, lifts the letter and takes it downstairs with him. It's on Mark's usual thin paper, but it feels heavy in his hand. The knowledge it carries has been weighing even more heavily on his mind since it arrived through his letterbox in Manchester. *Ecclesiastes 3: To everything there is a season, and a time to every purpose under the heaven.* To everything?

There's an unwashed Guinness glass by the kitchen sink. David swills it out, fills it to the brim with cold water and drinks the pint quickly, leaving the tap running, before refilling it.

The letter lies folded, waiting for him. Waiting for his attention, for his decision. He hadn't noticed the table surface was wet. 'Shit!' A splash of water soaks through the paper, showing the familiar lines of Mark's careless handwriting in blue pen. He sweeps it up, blots it against his T-shirt. Still knowing it'll take more than a bit of water to wash away those words indelibly recorded in his mind. That casual question, followed by the clipped unforgettable sentences. *By the way, not sure if you knew or not? A couple of the lads from home have been back in touch for a while through Facebook. Apparently Santie's got terminal cancer.*

He hasn't got long, so they say. He's at home with the family.

He'd had to keep rereading those sentences when he'd first opened the letter. *Santie's got terminal cancer. He hasn't got long, so they say.* The words were just senseless sounds in his head at the beginning. But once the initial numbness and disbelief passed, ideas and feelings had arrived that had nothing to do with pity, let alone grief. How could you feel sorry for someone who'd been the cause of so much pain? For a man who'd deliberately engineered the suffering and humiliation of others? The impending death and prospect of the permanent banishment of such an abuser should surely be a source of pure relief. If only his mind had been content to simply leave it at that.

Santie's got terminal cancer. If only that could be sentence enough for the man. But how could it be? *He's at home with the family.* How could that bastard be allowed to quietly slip away like that, unchallenged? His family and community mourning, commemorating his life. His pride and reputation intact. His medals polished. And even if he was called to account in Heaven, why shouldn't he be judged on Earth? Why shouldn't he die suffering?

So, what are you going to do about it, Davie? You didn't do anything then, did you? So, what are you going to do about it now? The same nagging questions in David's own younger voice, echoing, demanding that he answer. The answer requiring a decision. *Romans 12. Vengeance is mine, I will repay, saith the Lord.* Without a decision, the same questions gathering force. Threatening to torment him, indefinitely. *Forgive us . . . as we forgive . . .*

He makes himself a strong black coffee with three sugars and sits stirring it at the table, his hand on top of the letter. Feeling his anger surging again, intensifying for being contained, adrenaline priming him to fight. If only he knew how and with what. His hands tighten into fists, at the same time knowing fists can't do the job. Why should it cost him to punish the raping, twisted monster? How can he settle the score, without destroying his own life in the process?

He has a shower and decides to drive into the town to get some more fuel, beer and food. Nothing fussy. A sliced loaf, a dozen eggs, a packet of bacon and bag of potatoes to keep him going. Something undoubtedly stereotypical about an Irish man not being able to go for long without his boiled potatoes, but he'd always been attached to having them. And there wasn't much that could beat the local freshly dug new spuds with a bit of salt and a slice of hard butter. He'd often helped his dad dig them in their garden, their hands shaking excitedly as they'd unearthed each plant's crop like a hidden clutch of soily eggs. He'd clawed through the ground, making sure they'd got them all, some as small as marbles. There was something pure and innocent about those pale-skinned tubers, never seen or touched before you took them out. Later when they'd had them for tea, they'd fallen into contented silence, appreciating the floury texture and comforting, subtle flavour. Agreeing there was nothing like a locally grown new potato. Feeling a sense of superiority and pride in the accomplishment of the soil, the ground of their own origins.

On his way into town, David passes the church hall again. It was Santie's church. Even in the sunlight the place looks grim and uninviting. Windows like dull eyes behind their metal grills. Always a poster with a Bible verse on the board. The lower edge has started to come unstuck and torn.

When he was younger, it's seemed as if Biblical texts were like seeds scattered everywhere. They weren't just outside churches. You'd find them on smaller plaques on telegraph poles, round towns and at roadsides, painted on brick walls and on the sides of houses. You didn't need to go to church or Sunday School to get your readings or lessons from the scriptures. Whether you were a Christian or a downright atheist, the texts became part of your own thinking without you having to make a particular effort to learn them.

David's parents had gone to the smaller, older church below The Hill, not far from the graveyard. He'd been made to go with them every week and to the Sunday School, while he'd been at primary school. After that, the two of them still went by themselves most Sundays.

Sammy and Skinny Kev weren't forced to keep going either. Having this freedom gave them all a different, more cheerful feeling about the weekends. It'd seemed immediately better, having the extra free day to be outdoors, especially before you had to go back to school on the Monday. He'd felt sorry for the other children who'd still had to spend half their day cooped up inside, not being allowed to hang around with their friends.

When they weren't on the fields or by the shore, the boys would sometimes observe the coming and goings outside Santie's church, hiding, at a distance. On Sunday mornings, the roads outside that plain grey church on the edge of the town had been lined with cars, bumper to bumper, like straight rows of dominos. Each car and its passengers claiming their own place in the long-established order. Santie and his family had always been among those parked closest to the entrance. They usually arrived early, at least half an hour or more before the service.

Santie's wife, Ruth, in her Sunday best coat and hat, would go straight into the church with their children, Stuart and Mary, who were older than David. Ruth would organise Sunday School. Stuart and Mary would hand out hymn books by the door, the way they'd done every Sunday since they were little. They always wore dark browns –

close to the colour of plain church pews – with sensible, low-heeled lace-up shoes. They were both thin and pale-skinned, Stuart's short-back-and-sides never seemed to grow. Mary's straight mousy hair was parted in the centre and tied in neat bunches. She'd had the same plain style at five and at sixteen.

People had always said that Ruth was a good and thoughtful kind of person, the sort who looked after other people's children and took cooked meals to older people if they were sick or just out of hospital. She was the kind of respectable woman you'd hardly ever see out after six o'clock in the evening, unless she was at the church or visiting someone. She was all about the home and the family.

One Sunday, the boys had noticed that she'd left her gloves behind by accident on the wall close to the family's car. It'd been David's idea to pick them up when she'd gone and take them back to her. They were plain, but nice gloves, and he'd imagined at the time if it'd been his own mother, she would've been upset to lose them. He'd never forgotten the feel of them in his hand, the smooth, cream-coloured fine leather. They'd had long slim fingers and lines of white stitching on the fronts. Skinny Kev'd told him not to bother, that he should just keep them, but he'd gathered the courage to knock on the door of the family's home on the estate and explain where he'd found them.

Ruth had opened the door to him herself. She'd been touched that he'd thought to be so honest and responsible, she'd said. It made her own and the Lord's heart glad, knowing that there were special boys like him about, who knew what was right and what was wrong. She told David to wait while she went to get something for him as a thank you. She'd returned with a home-baked fairy cake smelling of sweet, freshly cooked eggs, with a centre of rich vanilla butter cream.

Whatever happened inside the church was left to the boys to try to piece together on the basis of hearsay and imagination. During the service, Santie would turn very quiet, people had said. He'd stand or sit respectfully with his head bowed, even when they weren't saying prayers. Apart from when it came to the time for the Sunday collection, which was his particular responsibility. If you knew what was good for you, apparently, you made sure you never forgot to bring your collection money. Santie liked a nice full plate. He had to have a quiet word if you forgot, or didn't give as much as he knew you could afford.

Whatever happened inside, outside, before and after the service, Santie would be working his way up and down the pavement. Talking earnestly. Meeting and greeting. Patting backs, shaking men's hands. Pressing the flesh. Listening to the widowed old ladies, with a sympathetic expression. In his smooth grey suit and ironed shirt. His tie with a gold pin and his clicking, long-toed leather shoes. Before and after, it was always the same. Handshakes, nods and winks. Santie organising, making arrangements. Rallying, comforting, On the move. Getting things done. Solving problems, seeing to the needs of his community. The way he'd seen to Linda, that day in the hen shed? A wee private matter to be kept between him and his Lord?

So, what are you going to do about it, David? You didn't do anything then, did you? So, what are you going to do about it now?

Chapter Fourteen

Gillian

It's getting busy in the estate café, the tables filling up quickly with animated chattering couples and groups. Families with toddlers spreading themselves out, parking their tank-like prams and all the other paraphernalia apparently essential for modern parenting. It's jarring after the peace and space of the gardens. Not because I generally dislike children. Today I'm just not in the mood for crowded rooms and fractiousness, so I decide to buy a sandwich and coffee to take outside instead.

I'm back at my spot on the lakeside when my mobile rings. It crosses my mind I should just ignore it, but I'll be annoyed with myself for having to return the call later.

'Gillian?' It's Laura. Her voice sounds different. Quieter, more nasal.

'Oh, Hi Laura. Are you alright? Have you got a cold?'

'Did you and Tony have an argument or something?' she asks sharply straight away, not acknowledging my question.

'Sorry? What do you mean?' I try to keep my tone even.

'I mean, you were being quite snide with him at the table. He was only having a laugh with you. You know, about having a fling with that fella renting the cottage beside you? And then after you went home, he wasn't his usual self.'

'In what way?'

'When Claire and I said we were going back into the lounge, he said he wanted to stay outside on his own. And he was *freezing* when we went home,' she adds at the end, with a level of concern more appropriate to announcing he'd had a heart attack.

'Was he? That's a shame.' *I don't need to do this now, Laura.*

She carries on, not seeming to notice my lack of genuine sympathy, intent on delivering her own spiel. 'I kept asking if there was something bothering him. He said there was no problem, he was just shattered from work. But he still wasn't right this morning when he left. There's definitely something on his mind.'

'Well, maybe you need to ask him again, Laura, if you're still worried,' I suggest, only just a word ahead of myself in knowing what I should say.

'Of course I am!' she bursts out now. 'He's my husband, isn't he?'

'Yes. He's no one else's. I mean, I . . .' *Here we go.*

'When *we* said, 'til death do us part' we *meant* it. We took solemn *vows*, Gillian! Though I don't suppose you were married for long enough to know about that yourself!'

She has to turn things round, doesn't she? Push into what she thinks is my weak spot, to defend her own vulnerability. 'Why don't we just forget about *my* failed marriage for the moment and concentrate on yours?' My words are running ahead of me now, but I'm past worrying about it. 'If you care so deeply about each other, why don't you just go ahead and talk?'

'What do you mean *if?*' she reacts immediately. 'And there's nothing failed about *our* marriage!' The old circles again. Going nowhere. *Make it all about me, Laura. It has to be my fault whatever it is, not yours.* Always the ball in my court, up to me to drive things forward. To get over and beyond the net. To be the hard-hitting, guilty one.

'Look, Laura. As you said yourself, Tony's *your* husband. It's for the two of you to sort it out. It's not my problem!' I'm losing it now.

'*What?* So, are you saying there *is* a problem, Gillian?' We're both losing it. Her voice is becoming more and more high-pitched.

'Talk to *Tony,* Laura!' I strike back. 'For God's sake, just have the bloody conversation!'

'What do you mean, Gillian? Is there something going on here I don't know about? What is it?'

I can picture her face, the way she's holding her frown. She's starting to sound more desperate. I'm so pissed off with her, but I can't deny her the truth any longer.

'Right. Okay, Laura. You're asking me, so I'll tell you. I wasn't going to, but if you want the truth, yes there's a problem. You and Tony have a problem.'

I pause, hear her inhale sharply. *'What, Gillian? Tell me. Now.* You've got to tell me what's going on.'

'I caught Tony with someone, Laura. I bumped into them, down by the lough, by accident. I think Tony might be having an affair with her.'

'What?' she says spikily, obviously trying to hold herself together. 'You must've made a mistake. I mean, it must've been somebody else you saw. I know you've always resented what Tony and I have. But this is just going too far.'

The idea that I could be envious of Laura and Tony's relationship makes me want to laugh back at her. I try to stay calm but I'm running out of patience. 'I don't resent what you have with Tony, Laura. Take it from me, I'm not jealous, in the least. Do you really think I'd be stupid enough to lie to you about something like this?'

'I don't know, Gillian. Sometimes I think I really don't know what you'd do any more. But I think it'd make you happy if Tony and I were struggling. Some people thrive on seeing other people suffer. And I think you'd like nothing more than to see us break up, the way you and Matt did. What's it they call it? Sodden Freud or something?'

'Schadenfreude?' I offer.

'Whatever, Gillian!' she retorts, sulkily. 'You're always the clever one when it comes to words, aren't you? But anyway, that's not the point.'

'Too right, it isn't. But then why stick to the point if you prefer to avoid it?' I snap. I'm looking across the lake. If I'm jealous of anyone at the moment, it'd be one of those swans gliding with such dignity over the water, set apart from the knots of human lives.

'I'm not avoiding anything, Gillian. I just want the God's honest truth.'

'Which is what I was trying to tell you, Laura. No. It wasn't someone else I saw. I definitely saw Tony and *Kelly*. I confronted Tony about it last night. He denied it at first, but eventually he admitted it. He didn't want me to tell you.'

'So, let me get this right. You're saying, you *knew* and you decided to keep me in the dark about it?' she asks, more aggressive again now.'

'I didn't know what to do for the best, Laura. I was still trying to decide. You might've even done the same thing yourself if it'd been the other way round.' I don't blame her for being angry but I still feel like hanging up. I've had enough. This is about Tony, not me.

'And let my sister go on making a fool of herself? I don't think so, Gillian!'

'Look. I know it's crap, Laura. I didn't feel

comfortable, knowing and not telling you. I'm sorry, but it wasn't that easy. Whatever you do, sometimes you're never going to get it right. And I didn't want you to be upset.'

'Doesn't seem to have bothered you before.' Always the old sniping instinct.

'Do you know what, Laura? Actually, I've had enough now. I came here to do some work, have a bit of space, get some peace. This is Tony's fault, not mine. Speak to Tony.'

'Oh, don't worry, Gillian. I won't keep you from your work any longer. Only your sister's life. Nothing really important. We mustn't get in the way of your precious art.'

I know she's really hurt. Her pride won't allow her to be direct with me about how fragile she feels behind her pointed defence. And I'm her old familiar scapegoat.

'I'm sorry, Laura,' I tell her, trying to keep my heart open. 'This is a nightmare for you. And of course, your life's important to me. I wish I'd told you straight away. I certainly didn't intend telling you over the phone like this. Want me to come over and . . .?'

'No. It's okay,' she answers abruptly, close to crying. 'I'll be alright. And the kids'll be back soon. And anyway, I'm not totally convinced. Even if you did see them, you probably read things into it that weren't there. *We'll* deal with this, Gillian. You carry on there and enjoy yourself. You've hardly ever here anyway. So, no need to get

involved. Why break the habit of a lifetime?'
Laura, queen of the wee-and-crap cliché.

'You know where I am,' I state, trying to
stay in neutral, knowing there's no point in me
saying anything else. Laura is going to say what
she needs to say and hear what she wants to hear.

'Claire or I will be in touch next week.'

'Don't feel obliged.'

'We'll do another tea for you before you go
home.' Whatever the circumstances, the feast
must go on. 'Bye in the meantime, Gillian,' she
finishes, brusquely ending the call.

David

He's waiting in the queue of traffic at the lights
close to the town centre when he notices the
plump figure of an older woman stop outside the
door of what used to be Linda's family's house.
From a distance, she looks remarkably like Wilma.
She sets her two bulky plastic carrier bags down
either side of her, fishes in her handbag for her key
and is inside by the time he drives past.

He'd assumed Wilma probably died years
ago. She'd hardly had a healthy lifestyle. Even
before he'd left to live in Manchester, she'd
obviously been out of breath even walking along
the street. People had felt sorry for her. Her bare
legs and ankles – she never wore tights – were
heavy, tight and swollen. As Skinny Kev'd said,

'Wilma's legs are as red and shiny as a couple of Gillespie's beef sausages.'

Linda herself was bound to have moved out ages ago. But he can't help wondering if it is Wilma and if she would be able to tell him where her daughter is and what happened to her. He'll go to the car park close to the town square, get the shopping and leave it in the car. Then walk back to the house and knock on the door. It might well be someone else, but it's worth a try at least.

As he noticed when he passed the pavement-side terraced house before, it's hardly changed since he was a boy. It has the same bubbled black paint on the front door and wooden window frames, smoke-yellowed nylon nets behind the murky panes. There's even the same off-white silk roses in a cream vase, a china bell and a chipped Scottie dog ornament on the windowsill inside. He wonders for a moment if he's really doing the right thing, but he won't press the woman to talk unless she's happy to.

He bangs on the blackened metal knocker, lightly at first, then harder when there's no answer. She's definitely at home, but given her size and reduced mobility, he'll have to give her plenty of time. He has banged on a right few doors, especially in his earlier days in the police, often in pretty stressful circumstances, mentally rehearsing what he needed to say, bracing himself for the effect his words would have on those behind the door.

'Hello?' the woman says, in a quaky voice when she appears. She looks at him directly with a puzzled expression, obviously wondering what he wants. She's taken her coat off, is wearing a thick, older style of woollen yellow cardigan, over a mottled black and blue tent of a nylon dress. Her hair is cut in a short, functional kind of style, dry and frizzy, a mix of blonde and white. Closer up, she does bear some resemblance to Wilma, but her face actually looks surprisingly younger than he'd expected. Her make-up free skin is smooth. Wilma would be somewhere in her mid-seventies or so by now. The woman in front of him looks more around her mid-fifties or a bit younger even perhaps – though it may just be because she's carrying more weight. Thinner women can often look older and more gaunt about the face.

'Hello.' He suddenly feels more anxious. He might be making a mistake. Wilma didn't really know him. She'd be well within her rights to tell him to clear off. Why should he expect her to disclose information about her daughter to a virtual stranger? 'Sorry to bother you, but . . . ' She's just staring at him, her lips parted slightly, one hand on the door handle, the other in the pocket of her custard-coloured cardigan. 'It's just, I was passing and I was wondering . . . I don't know if you'll remember me or not . . . *Wilma?*'

'Oh no,' the woman replies immediately, quickly shaking her head. 'I'm afraid Wilma passed away quite a while ago. Sorry to have to tell you if you didn't know. Did you know her from the shop or something?'

'No. I knew her daughter Linda a bit. She was a couple of years ahead of me at school. I've not been here for a while, so I was just wondering if her mother was still here. Sorry to have bothered you.'

As he speaks, her expression begins to shift, as if something's occurring to her.

'You're not . . . ? It's not *Davie*, is it?' she asks, looking him up and down. 'Used to hang around with Kev and what's his name?'

'Sammy. Yes. That's right. Yes, it's David, Davie. So you're . . . ?'

'*Linda,* Davie! It's *me*, Linda. Long time ago and I've obviously changed a lot, but I'm still here.'

He tries to disguise his shock, but she's bound to have noticed his reaction. 'Sorry, Linda. You'll have to excuse me being slow on the uptake these days. I mean, I was thinking you'd have probably moved somewhere else. And you and your Mum were always a bit alike.' Digging himself an even bigger hole.

'Probably even more like her these days. It's okay, Davie. I've changed a lot since school. And not for the better. Anyway, you're welcome to come in for a cup of tea if you're not rushing?'

'Well, only if you're sure. You're probably in the middle of doing something?' Probably not such a good idea to go in if she's got the husband and family at home.

'Och no, you're alright. I'm on my own since Mum died, so you'll not be imposing on anyone. Come in and I'll make us a drink.'

'Thanks. And don't worry. I'll not stop long,' he tells her, as he steps into the house. The place smells old, damp, of chip fat and cigarette smoke, like somewhere forgotten and frozen in a 1970s' time warp that never sees the sun. David follows Linda down the narrow hall, with grubby magnolia wood-chip and a swirly patterned, plucked nylon brown carpet, through to the dim back room. She tells him to take a seat while she goes to make tea in the kitchen. He sits on one of the armchairs either side of the hearth. There's a worn three-piece tan suite facing towards a beige tiled fireplace, the cold remains of a fire in the grate behind a misshapen mesh fire guard. A scratched wooden sideboard is covered with ornaments, mainly ceramic horses and dogs and photographs in basic metal frames. An unframed oval mirror hangs by a heavy chain above the fireplace. A mirror can often make a room seem bigger and brighter, but this one is dull and speckled with black spots.

Linda. In her early teens, everything about her had seemed fresh and hopeful. *All things bright and beautiful.* She was everything a girl of her age should've been. Becoming her own person, having a good time, getting on with other people. Enjoying her sexuality, the way boys and men noticed her. *The Lord God made them all.*

Wasn't Linda only being who she was and doing what she was *made* for? What was 'hoorish' about having a bit of confidence in yourself, getting charged up on other people's appreciation of you? Who would've thought back then that he'd ever mistake Linda for her mother?

Chapter Fifteen

David

'Here you go, Davie. Help yourself now. Sorry I've not got any fancy biscuits.' Linda sets down the tray on the upholstered brown buttoned pouffe next to his chair. On it there's a plain blue mug each of strongly brewed tea, a chrome milk jug with matching sugar bowl and a plate with a stack of digestives. She puts four heaped spoonfuls of sugar into her tea, takes a biscuit and lowers herself awkwardly into the other armchair.

'Thanks. Nothing wrong with digestives,' he acknowledges, taking one.

'I knew I recognised something about you when you came to the door. You were only, what? Thirteen, maybe fourteen or so when I last saw you? You're looking well. Lucky you.' She sips her tea then dunks the biscuit.

'Thanks. Kind of you to say so, but I wouldn't go that far. I've seen better days.' He smiles at her, takes a drink of tea - hot, dark, well-stewed. The same way his Mum made tea. 'Sorry to hear about your mother. You said it'd been quite a while?'

'Coming up for five years. She'd had heart trouble on and off. The doctor kept warning her about smoking and piling on the weight. But she couldn't bring herself to change. They were the only things that gave her pleasure any more, she said.'

Linda's eyes suddenly fill with tears. She sets her tea on the edge of the mantelpiece. There's the end of a squashed white toilet roll tucked in beside her between the seat cushion and the arm of her chair. She winds a piece of paper off round her fingers, pats her eyes and wipes her nose. 'I'll have to be careful I don't go the same way myself, the doctor says. I could do with losing a few stone like, but never mind. What will be, will be. Sorry, didn't mean to get upset on you like that. We never knew each other that well, but it's thoughtful of you to look me up.'

'You're alright, Linda. No need to apologise. Probably not fair of me to turn up like this out of the blue, after all this time. And get you thinking about your mum again.'

'It's okay, Davie. It just doesn't take much to set me off. A lot of people didn't have much respect for Mum. They thought she was just a lazy auld stupid woman who'd let herself go over the years. And left her daughter to her own devices. But I loved her, you know? I knew what she'd had to deal with. There was a lot more to Mum than met the eye – reasons why she found it hard to cope. How about you, anyway? Whereabouts do you live now? What do you do? Got your own family now, I'm sure?' She sounds more together now, spreads her fleshy fingers across the high mound of her stomach. In spite of her size and the way her features have lost their sharpness, he can still see something of Linda as she was, in her eyes, in the way she looks at him directly.

'I'm across the water. Dull job, as jobs go. My parents are both dead long ago, buried up on The Hill. I was married for while, but we got divorced. We didn't have any children. Not much to tell.'

'So, are you just back for a bit of a holiday or something?' Linda shifts forward in her chair, reaches for her mug on the mantelpiece.

'Yep. I needed to come back for a bit, for one reason and another.' *So, what are you going to say now, Davie? Where are you going to take it from here?*

'Staying with relatives?' A Northern Irish instinct in conversation, checking up, making sure you're alright, that you're with family.

'No. I've rented a cottage actually. Nice place. Just been doing a bit of walking and fishing.'

'Good for you. Wish I was that fit. Though I've nobody to blame but myself for getting into such a state.'

No one to blame but that raping bastard who took the soul out of you when you were sixteen? 'Don't be hard on yourself now, Linda. C'mon. You're alright.' It feels like he's saying it for himself as much as her. He tries to block it out, but images of that forsaken hen house are coming back to him again with the sounds of Linda fighting Santie inside, like the sounds of a panicky bird flapping and fluttering about, trying to escape being caught. She makes him think of a hen now. Not a well-fed spirited one with glossy feathers, but a bedraggled older hen, scratching in dry gravel. In spite of her size, there's something faded and frail about her. 'So, got kids yourself? If you don't mind me asking?' He already suspects what her answer will be.

"No, I never got married. What with looking after Mum and everything. Just how things turned out, I suppose. You start off with grand ideas when you're younger, but your life doesn't always work out the way you expect, does it?' She puts her mug down, pats her eyes again with the wad of toilet paper.

'Sorry, Linda. Shouldn't 've asked such a personal question. None of my business.' *So why are you here, Davie? Why are you here?*

'No problem. Makes a change, somebody asking, being interested, like. I never met the right fella. Help yourself to the biscuits – don't wait to be asked. So, didn't you have an older brother?'

'He moved away to live in the States a long time ago. He still keeps in touch with a couple of his old friends here, on and off, but his life's out there now. Wife and kids, his own booming business.'

'Lucky for some, isn't it? Cutting loose from it all,' Linda comes back, resignedly, with half a smile.

'Oh yes. He was always a born survivor, my brother. He's done pretty well for himself. Once he's made up his mind, no stopping him.' He catches his dad's words in his own mouth. 'We send each other the odd letter. And I mean that, literally! He's a man of few words.'

'Better than nothing.' She shifts from hip to hip, as if her back's uncomfortable, which it's bound to be.

'Actually, talking about letters . . .' He may come to regret it, but he's going to have to say something. 'I heard that apparently Santie's on his way out with cancer? Don't know if you knew?'

'Don't think there's anybody who doesn't,' Linda confirms quietly, breaking eye contact, looking down at the crumpled piece of toilet roll in her hand. 'They're saying it won't be long, though he's not one for giving up easily. There's people gathering all the time at the house, apparently. He was such a big man in the community. Word is he's had a bad stroke as well. He's not able to talk or do anything for himself. Though they say he's still with it in his mind.'

Her apparent equanimity in talking about her abuser is like a smooth layer of ice over a seething pond. He wants to break through it, to say something real. Even if it feels cruel. Though, hasn't she been broken enough already?

'Right. Still in the same house?'

'Och yes. He always stayed in the same place,' she says wearily.

He can't keep holding back. 'So . . . good riddance, eh?'

She looks up, startled. '*What* did you say, Davie?'

'I said, good riddance. As in good riddance to bloody bad rubbish.'

She stares back, her mouth open. 'What do you mean, Davie?'

He lowers his voice, but not the strength of his contempt. 'I mean, it's about time the man was gone. *You* know what I mean, Linda,' he tells her, looking her in the eyes. 'When it came down to it, the big *community man* was a merciless bastard, wasn't he?'

She looks down, fidgets with the disintegrating toilet paper.

'Och, shush now, Davie. You shouldn't. You have to watch yourself. Walls have ears. However much things seem to have changed on the surface since we were children, some things aren't that different round here.'

'No one's going to hear us, Linda. The walls of these houses are thick as they come. You've got to be able to tell it as it is somewhere, don't you? If it's only in your own home. Or even if it's only in your own head.' He's almost whispering. In spite of what he's telling Linda, he doesn't discount her feelings, however irrational. He understands her fear. 'You see, I know what he did to lots of people. And I know what he did to you, Linda.' It's out there now, no taking the words back.

'*What?*' She looks bewildered.

'I hated myself. Even though I knew I would've done more harm than good,' he carries on. 'I've never stopped wishing I'd been able to do something about it.'

'About what, Davie?' Linda frowns slightly.

'About what Santie did to you in that old hen house, Linda. You know, after he'd told Anne to go home?' How can she not know what he's talking about? He knew what he'd seen, what he'd heard. 'You didn't know we were there, but Sammy and Kev and I were in the field, on the other side of the hedge. We saw him take you in there. We heard . . .'

'Och that? Sure, that was nothing.' She shrugs slightly, looks down. 'I was a silly wee girl. I didn't get anything I didn't deserve. You've nothing to feel bad about.'

He can't quite take in what she's saying. He saw and heard what'd happened. And so did Sammy and Skinny Kev. Not that their knowledge was any use now. There'd been no doubt in their minds that Santie had forced himself on Linda. They couldn't 've made a mistake. Could they?

'Linda, you did nothing wrong. Nobody deserves to be treated like that. We saw and we heard what he did to you,' he repeats. 'We saw him undoing his belt.'

'Sure, Dad used to take his belt to me almost every week. Probably just sounded worse than it was. I think I tripped. Must've made a right noise. Don't worry, Davie. Forget about it. These things happen. Want me to make you another cup of tea? Or would you rather have a coffee this time?' she asks, seeming ready to put the subject behind them.

He can't keep on and on. This isn't all about him. He wants her to confirm his understanding of what happened, but he can't get forceful or any more graphic. From work he knows well that victims of rape have their own ways of living with the past. Some rage and scream for justice. Some suffer amnesia or dissociate. Others outwardly deny the truth, knowing it all, but locking the past away, for fear of what disclosure will do to them or their families. And for fear of further antagonising their abusers. He's almost a hundred per cent certain he's right, but he won't pressurise her. She has to choose to talk and the depths she's prepared to go to. As it is, when he leaves her house, she'll be left alone with her feelings and memories, holding herself together. Continuing to confront and push information at her would feel like another form of abuse in itself.

'No, you're alright, Linda. I should be making tracks really,' he explains. Although it feels awkward moving off so soon after raising the subject with her. 'Sorry. Hope I didn't upset you by raking over things from the past. Still keep in touch with anyone else from school these days?' He wants to try and get things on a more even keel before he goes.

'A couple of people, yes. Though a lot have moved away, like yourself. I see a few of the girls. Anne and I still meet up at least once in the week. She's got her husband and the girls to look after, but we'll still have a cup of tea in the town, do a bit of shopping.'

'That's good.'

They sit on for a while, talking about this and that, mostly how the town has changed over the years, about how all the new housing is taking over the farmland. Linda sees him to the door when it's time for him to leave.

'Nobody's getting into your place in a hurry!' he tells her, gesturing at the door, trying to stay light with it. The door has a security 'spy hole', three bolts as well as a snib and a chain.

'Well you can't be too careful these days, can you? There's some right weirdos about. I just put the chain and the snib on during the day, but I like to do the bolts before I go to bed.'

'You do right,' he says, nodding. 'Good to see you now, Linda. Look after yourself, won't you?'

She has undone the chain and is on the point of undoing the snib. But then she turns back towards him, lifts her head. Looks at him for a moment, without saying anything, her eyes slightly narrowing, obviously preoccupied. She brushes down the front of her dress, as if to dust off crumbs; takes a breath.

'You know something?' she asks him. Her

voice is more energetic and decisive than it's been since he arrived.

'What?' he answers, putting his hands into his shorts' pockets, with no idea what she's going to say next.

'You're not . . . You *weren't* wrong, Davie. Santie was behind a lot of horrific things that happened to people. He ruined so many young people's lives. What happened that day with Santie and me in the henhouse . . . it *wasn't* nothing.'

She's looking straight at him. Her eyes begin to water, but she sniffs and blinks fast to stay in control.

'Linda. You don't have to. Don't feel you need to . . .' he says, although he still wants her to keep talking.

'It's okay. I didn't think I could, but you were right. What you thought happened that day did happen. He raped me, Davie. And I know I'm not the only person he hurt either.'

'No, you're not.'

'There were so many boys. He was behind so many beatings. And there were other girls too. He was even . . . He was interfering with Mum and her sister as well when they were younger, before they put on all the weight.' There's something sharper about the way she's speaking now. The way she's holding herself is different too. Her head and shoulders are up and back, her spine straight. In many ways she's altered, of course, almost beyond recognition, but in her upright posture there's more of the upbeat Linda he'd once so admired.

'I'm sorry, Linda,' he says simply, wanting her to say what she needs to, in her own time.

'I've never told anybody else about it to this day,' she carries on. 'Probably for a lot of the same reasons as yourself. I knew I probably would've done a lot more harm than good. You shouldn't have blamed yourself. Everybody knew how it was. But they were too frightened for themselves and their loved ones to do anything about it. He was so clever with it. He was well in with the paramilitaries. He saw to it that they had the money, the young recruits who'd do as they were told. He had plenty of contacts high up in the police. They helped him, he helped them. They made their own version of the law to suit themselves, didn't they? He was the community man who went to church every Sunday and marched proudly on the Twelfth. But, as you said, he was a bastard. An evil, bloody-minded monster with a massive crack in his brain. Yes, good riddance. And you know, I hope . . .' She's in a flow, but suddenly checks herself.

'You hope what, Linda?' He wants to hear it. She needs to say it.

'God forgive us, Davie. But I hope that man burns in Hell. Slowly.'

'So do I, Linda,' he acknowledges at once. 'And sooner rather than later, eh?'

It feels such a relief to hear her speak like that, with such fierce hatred. Listening to that single sentence alone justifies him being where he is now. It doesn't compensate for what happened to her and the others all those years ago, and his nagging regret for not being able to protect her. Santie would've assumed he'd taken Linda over completely, left her forever defining herself as one of his powerless victims. But there's a health and strength in her anger. A sign to them both, especially to herself, of her wish to hold on to her own identity. To separate herself, mind and body, from her abuser.

'Yes. Sooner the better,' she affirms.

'You know, if you ever needed . . .There are people you could talk to, in confidence, for support, like. And if you felt you wanted to, legally you'd be within your rights to . . .'

As he's saying it, he knows, for the same reasons they've both stayed silent for so long, that any attempt to prosecute now would likely carry more potential costs than benefits. Now and after his death, Santie won't be without his loyal supporters. Taking any formal legal action would make her life an ongoing nightmare. He's also guessing she's not the sort to go in for any kind of psychotherapy. It's not part of her language, what she feels at home with. At work, it's the kind of thing they're taught to broach with people who've been involved in traumatic incidents. He does know some people, including colleagues, who've been helped by having counselling with the right kind of person. He wouldn't knock it. Although he's never been convinced it would help him personally. He's always been more of a one for getting a skinful and drowning his sorrows, then trying to just get on with his life, baggage and all.

'Och, no. There'd be no point now. Thanks, but as we were saying, he'll be gone soon.'

'Do something for me, will you?'

'What's that, Davie?' She gives him a quizzical look.

'Just hold onto that thought of yours?'

'What thought?'

'Santie, being punished, in Hell fire.'

Back at the cottage, David makes himself fry some bacon and a couple of eggs for his lunch. He'll put them between slices of bread, drive down to the car park just along the road and find a place to sit and eat on the shore. Being in Linda's dreary airless house and seeing that dull grey closed church again makes him feel even more like being outdoors by the water, with the sun on his face. The thoughts will still be with him, but out there he feels cleaner, less penned in with them. Out there the land has his back, offers the present moment to distract him and balance painful memories.

Once on the sea front, he makes his way round past the spot where he killed the gull. He finds a place to sit, above the shoreline. There's a slight breeze, but it's warm and sheltered down in the long grass. The tide is on its way out again. There's a couple, maybe mid-twenties, sitting a bit further along. He can hear the babble of their talk and the occasional rise of laughter, but they're too far away to be overheard. There's a little fair-haired boy in blue shorts and a green T-shirt, probably around three or four, obviously theirs. He's hunkered down, not far in front of them, poking about in the stones with a stick. Quiet, totally absorbed. He often wonders what it'd be like to have his own children. He'd grown up expecting he would one day. He'd probably have been a lot better off if he'd met someone in his twenties like that, had a family of his own and not given so much of himself to his police career. Although he'd have to have found the right kind of person of course. Sophie had never shown much interest when he'd brought up the subject of children. Even if their marriage had lasted longer, he couldn't imagine she'd have become any more enthusiastic. She was more naturally house-proud than maternal.

His colleagues were forever telling him he should've had kids. He was so good with theirs, they said, on the rare times they got together outside work. You could tell he preferred the company of kids and dogs, they liked to joke. He knows there's something in that. You obviously get the less likeable manipulative ones, but he appreciates the way kids can be direct and simply themselves. He hasn't much time for the games often involved in adult society.

He's glad he saw Linda. At least he was able to offer her a listening ear. She'd trusted him enough to finally share some of the burden of her dreadful secret. And to admit that her mother and her aunt had been abused too. She'd clearly understood why he hadn't felt able to intervene, recognising that they and so many others had lived in silence, threatened by the violence and tyranny of Santie, his helpers and friends.

He'd seen Linda dignified by her anger. Her life had been damaged and shaped by her suffering, but not completely irreparably. However tenuous the thread, she was still connected to the idea that she deserved to be heard and to defend herself. Having finally confided in David and knowing that the man who had hurt her would soon be gone, Linda seemed to have no expectation that anything else needed to be done. Why isn't that enough for him?

Chapter Sixteen

Gillian

I find it impossible to settle down to work again after talking to Laura. I feel restless and irritable. Part of me is sorry for her. Her critical remark about my 'precious art' is part of her usual armoury. I should have grown a tougher skin by now but she still has the power to make me feel guilty and just plain selfish, forsaking her for something as self-indulgent as sitting by a lake sketching swans. How I make my living has never been 'real' work as far as Laura or Claire are concerned.

I don't feel like eating any more. I pack my sandwich and sketchbook into my bag and wander around the gardens, distracted, only half-seeing things, trying to work out what to do next. In the end, I head back to the cottage.

It's just past three. David's car isn't there when I arrive. He's probably out doing something sane and interesting. I wish I could just stop thinking for a while. Between last night's fiasco of a dinner party and my tense conversation with Laura, I feel pretty wrung out. I'm not usually one for sleeping during the day, but I decide to lie down for a while and try to drift off. At first I can't help telling myself it's a bit sad and a waste of time, but as I lie curled up in a pool of sunshine on top of the duvet, I think about the lithe cat that sometimes relaxes on top of one of the broad stone gate posts at the entrance to the lane leading up to Derek's farm house. When you watch her, you can't doubt she understands how to feel at ease in her body. She lives by her wits. And feels fully entitled to sleep when she's tired.

It's nearly six when I wake. My mobile's ringing. I meant to switch it off but forgot.

'*Gillian?*' It's Claire.

'Yes?' I'm not in the mood. Although we'll have to talk sooner or later. And maybe it's best to just to get on with it. Whatever her angle, I'm determined to keep things brief and to the point.

'I've had Laura on the phone, Gillian. In *floods.* She told me the two of you spoke earlier on and what you'd said about Tony. I don't think you've got this right, Gillian. But even if it's true, you've really upset her. Couldn't you have just kept things to yourself?'

No show without bloody Punch. I take a breath. The best thing is to try to stay emotionally detached from what I say. It won't be right for her, whatever it is. Easier thought than done.

'For what it's worth, I'm sure I *have* got things right. Tony has been messing around, Claire. I confronted him and he admitted it. I know what I saw. So, actually, it's not *me* who's upset Laura. It's *Tony.* Though, let's be honest. Whatever I say or don't say, I'm bound to get it wrong. If I don't tell her, as Laura said herself, I'm keeping her in the dark. If I do, I'm the cruel sister, jealous of her perfect marriage, aren't I?'

Claire is quiet for a moment, then gives one of her self-important coughs. 'I don't expect you to totally understand this, Gillian.' She pauses, obviously expecting me to object, but I keep my mouth shut. 'Sometimes things happen in a marriage. Sometimes a couple has a wee blip. But when people love each other, they can work things out. One wee mistake doesn't have to mean the end of the world.'

'Or even the end of a *marriage?*' I suggest ironically, though she probably won't get it, especially as my part of the dialogue is almost irrelevant anyway.

'Laura and Tony have always been a deeply committed couple, Gillian. Even if there has been a wee problem – and I'm not saying there has now – there's not a doubt in my mind they'll weather the storm and be even stronger for it. Especially if they have our support. Every marriage needs the support of family and community. That's why we take our vows in public, isn't it?' She's in full flow now. Although Laura and Tony's particular situation has given her the starting point, she's in stock phrase territory, channelling collective wisdom, feeling good and righteous for it. She's in Claire's Family Homily mode.

Right,' I confirm, without feeling. I should just leave it there, but I can't. 'Yep. Then we can all help each other paper over the cracks, can't we? Tell you what? Next time we have tea, remind me to bring a big economy packet of wallpaper paste and a bucket, instead of a bottle of rosé?'

'Och, don't be so flipping childish, Gillian! This is your *sister* we're talking about. And all you can do is make a stupid, immature joke about it?'

'Just as logical, if not more so, as the alternative.' *Why not just tell it as it is?*

'You always think you're so bloody smart, don't you, Gillian?'

My careless tone is guaranteed to wind her up. 'Well, as telling the truth's not an option, being as it's not *supportive* to the status quo . . .'

'You're twisting my words now, Gillian! I never said you couldn't tell the truth, did I?' she retaliates.

'That's true. But you'd prefer me to keep it to myself, wouldn't you? Even if Tony's having sex on the shore with a girl barely half his age. Better if you just forget about that, Gillian, and believe in Laura and Tony's everlasting romance and public commitment?'

'Och there's no point in talking to you, Gillian. There are some things you can't understand. You've always been the same. It's like part of you is missing. Switched off.'

'Thanks for the feedback,' I reply flatly. 'Mustn't keep you any longer on the phone. Tony'll be home by now. They're probably trying to get through to you as we speak. And say hi to Robbie for me, won't you? He'll already be looking forward to his cans tonight. Bit of give and take? Always helps a marriage, doesn't it?' I can't resist it, even if she'll ignore the comment.

'We'll put Monday tea in the diary, Gillian. I told Laura you could come to ours again if it made it easier on her, but she insisted it was her turn. It's how she is. She keeps going, keeps her head down, no matter what's happening.' The good old solid sisterhood. Three's an awkward number.

'You could always come here instead,' I offer. 'I could make a few salads, get bread and cheese and stuff. Nothing grand, but something different maybe?' The offer's already dead in the water. And actually, I'm relying on it. Having them at the cottage would be a real ordeal.

'No. That wouldn't work for us, Gillian. It's too much of a trek at that time of the day. The men need a proper tea after work. I know Laura would say the same.'

'Right. Okay. See you on Monday, Claire.'

You've always been the same. Like part of you is missing. Switched off.
Claire's words play on in my head for a while, no matter how determined I am to move on. I wonder myself if I lack sympathy at times. How much of that is really true, I don't know. Claire and Laura have both fixed on the idea for so many years, pointing to my ability to detach myself as a fault. I've always found it hard to function without

my own space. I've never been one for game-playing and as time goes on, I find people who can't be upfront more and more annoying and just plain tedious. But I don't think I'm uncaring if people genuinely need my attention. I think I'm still capable of love.

I go downstairs, pour myself a glass of red wine, open the front door and stand looking out across the yard. There's no sign of Derek or his dog. I imagine they're both back up at the farmhouse having tea. It's slightly cooler now, but still bright. I love the peace you often get later on a summer's day, the subtle, more subdued feeling when people and creatures start to turn in and become quieter.

I've been standing there for about ten minutes when David drives into the yard and parks in his usual spot.

'Anything interesting happening on the street?' he asks me, smiling as he gets out of the car. He's caught the sun across his nose and forehead. He's wearing longish shorts and a T-shirt, slings his rucksack over his shoulder as he slams the car door.

I was just thinking myself of how I'm following the time-honoured tradition, often of older women and men, of standing in doorways watching the world go by, hopeful of gathering the makings of a story or a morsel or two of the local gossip. I'm thinking that a series of figures framed in doorways could work well in glass.

'Nothing much so far. Feel free to do something worthy of gossip yourself. Though no pressure, of course. How was your day?'

'A fairly quiet one. How about you? Get some work done?' He takes off his sun-glasses and puts them on top of his head.

'A bit. Though not as much as I was hoping. Usual ongoing family stuff.'

'Starring the ugly sisters?'

'Yes.'

'So, how's Cinderella?'

'She's had enough of cleaning the hearth and doing her sisters' dirty washing. She's in desperate need of a kind godmother – or even a godfather. She's not fussy.'

'Stick to the godmother. A godfather can be dodgy. Never fear, you will get to the ball!' he adds, in a funny high-pitched voice.

'Not sure about a ball. That would involve other people. It might just be more of the same. A remote castle or an island would be better. Somewhere with a bridge you could pull up once you'd got in your supplies. Otherwise inaccessible.'

'Pretty drastic!' he says, laughing. 'Though some situations require extreme measures?'

'Certainly do. I'm not asking for much. Know what I mean?'

'We could always run away together, if you like? Sorry. No answer required there,' he quickly adds, lifting his palm towards me, indicating that he knows outside the context of our banter where the boundary is.

'That's a shame,' I reply. I've only known him for a week, but I feel comfortable. We're both unattached. I don't see why we shouldn't have a bit of fun. 'Actually, sounds like the best offer I've had in a while. So . . . Like a glass of wine? I was just going to do an omelette or something basic for tea. You're welcome to join me if you want.' At the back of my mind I have an image of Claire and Laura. They're looking at me, nodding, exchanging winks and knowing glances, nudging each other the way they did in their teens when there was a romantic scene on TV.

'Yes. Thanks, Gillian. That'd be great,' he answers straightforwardly. 'Won't outstay my welcome.'

As we go inside, I do my best to blank out Claire and Laura's faces. Pull up a mental draw-bridge.

David

He's glad she's asked him in. When he'd planned to come over and first arrived, being alone and keeping himself to himself had seemed like the best thing to do. But as time's going on, he's finding it tough being in solitary with his memories and thoughts. It helps to be outdoors, but sometimes no matter how self-sufficient you are, you actually do need the company of another human being. He'd tried to relax down by the shore, but he'd kept replaying his time with Linda – what she'd said, how different she'd looked. Although it had helped to finally be able to talk to her and to think that she no longer felt alone with what had happened, the thought of Santie slipping away peacefully, unpunished, still torments him. While the idea of Santie in Hell brought Linda comfort, it doesn't feel enough for David. Hardly surprising, since he doesn't believe in Hell anyway. As far as he knows, life happens on Earth. Rightly or wrongly, he wants to actually see evidence of Santie suffering, with his own eyes.

Gillian's obviously an intelligent woman, self-possessed, up for a bit of banter and fun but not the type to bow down to a man or throw herself at him. Their conversations absorb him. Help him set aside other things. She shares responsibility, doesn't expect him to do all the work. And there's no point in pretending she's not attractive. He's likes the fact she's confident enough in herself not to wear make-up all the time. Some women can't be seen without it. Sophie was like that. She usually already had it all on by the time he opened his eyes first thing in the morning. She'd seriously sulked and pouted when he offered, as a joke, to chisel it off for her at night.

'Get yourself a glass from the end cupboard, there? Help yourself to the red wine. Or I've got a bottle of white in the fridge if you'd prefer? Okay if we sit down for a bit before I do the tea?' she asks him, taking her own glass with her and crossing the lounge area to sit on the settee.

'Of course! No rush as far as I'm concerned,' he tells her, helping himself to a small glass of wine.

'Go on. Pour yourself a proper glass. And you can top mine up while you're at it,' she suggests, draining her glass and holding it up towards him.

Chapter Seventeen

David

He sits down on the settee with her, leaving a seat cushion between them. She looks good in tight jeans and an olive-green top, her arms and her face lightly tanned, cheeks a bit flushed from the wine. Her shoulder-length, brown-black hair looks like it's just been brushed through, but sexily under-groomed. She's neat rather than thin, has slim arms, smallish breasts, no excess weight on her hips.

'This is good, isn't it?' he says, holding up his glass, looking at the colour of the wine against the light from the window. The dark red of ripe pomegranate seeds. 'Closest the vampire in me can get to blood – legally, I mean.'

'Probably should be the lighter white with the omelette. Though have to say, I don't worry too much about the done thing.'

'You leave that to your sisters?' Always a risk, joking about people's families when you're still only getting to know them. Even if they struggle with their relatives themselves, they'll often defend them from stranger attack. Though he's fairly sure she'll be okay with the comment.

'Exactly. Serviettes have to match tablecloth. Slippers must be worn at all times, except in bed. Height of wife's heels must take account of husband's height. Chocolates and flowers must be given without fail, at anniversaries and Valentine's. Wine glass must be held by stem.'

'Of course! Rituals that ward off evil. Matters of life and death.'

'Oh yes. We have standards, David. We have our standards, when it suits us.' It feels like these last words, shot through with bitterness, are spoken really just for herself. She's making short work of her glass of wine. He gestures towards the bottle on the coffee table and she nods for him to give her a refill and to top his own up too while he's at it.

'Sounds a bit like me, to be honest. Sometimes you need to let yourself off the hook?' He's meaning it quite lightly, at the same time wondering if it sounds a bit pedantic or if it could reinforce something serious she's feeling unhappy about. But she doesn't seem to mind.

'I know, only . . . I mean, I'm all for being flexible too, but when it comes to some things, if you know something's wrong, you can't suddenly say it's right, to suit whatever's happening at the time.' He's obviously missing a piece of the context she's speaking from. But there's no denying she's pretty fired up about it. And less inhibited in expressing herself now.

'I think you're right. Though I'm guessing you're not just talking about standards in serviettes and wearing slippers here?' He smiles slightly. But he doesn't want her to think he's laughing at her, or standing back, detaching himself.

'No, I'm bloody not. Although some people have the same strength of feeling – or lack of it – no matter what kind of standards they're talking about. Sorry. Didn't mean to go off on one there. Probably should just come out and tell you what I'm talking about.' She seems distracted now and annoyed with herself.

'No need to go there if you'd rather not. Something to do with that situation you mentioned during the week, maybe? About having knowledge you didn't want, and being unsure about how to resolve a dilemma?' He only wants her to explain if she wants to.

'Yep. Aforementioned dilemma and my point about standards definitely connected. May as well tell you. You don't strike me as the type to blab. Even after the best of a bottle of whiskey.' She pauses, takes another drink.

'It'd take at least three bottles to properly loosen my tongue,' he jokes, then adds more seriously, 'No. I don't blab.'

'Cutting a long story short, I caught my brother-in-law with this young woman last week on the shore. Obviously post-coital.'

'Oh God.' He likes the way she tells it unflinchingly.

'I didn't know what to do for the best and

whether to tell my sister or not. I confronted my brother-in-law last night and he finally admitted I was right. Laura phoned me this morning saying he seemed different, and I ended up telling her. She was obviously upset and not wanting to believe me, blaming me for telling her and also for not telling her. I just came off the phone with my other sister, Claire, before you got back. Marriages have these "wee blips" she told me. Looks like we'll all be forgiving and forgetting. Even if we don't.' Her words are spilling out. She's clearly been needing to talk.

'So, your brother-in-law will get a bit of stick from your sisters, but the show must go on?'

'Yep, in a nutshell. Sounds really insignificant, but . . .'

'No. Not insignificant. It must've been a right shock, running into him like that. Not a good position to be in. Last thing you want when you've come away to do a bit of work and get some peace. That would really wind me up. I'd be raging with the guy, even if he hadn't meant to involve me.' He's guessing they're probably similar in this re-spect – independent, but with strong consciences, prone to brooding over things.

'You're right. I'm bloody furious with him. It's like I'm having to pick up most of his tab too at the moment. It's nothing to do with me, but that doesn't stop Laura and Claire making me feel bad about telling the truth. I've never particularly liked him anyway. He's always been such a smug, patronising stupid little shit. Sorry. Told you I'd bore you to death.'

He gets why she feels the need to apologise, because he probably would too, but he's happy to listen. It feels good she trusts him enough to tell him about it. 'It's fine. You're not boring me. Carry on.'

'Thanks – but no, I think I've said more than enough on that theme already. My stupid brother-in-law has had more of my energy than he deserves. So, how about you? Do anything interesting today?'

She opens the wine again and he accepts another glass. She pours the rest for herself. He notices the outer edges of her top lip are slightly stained. There's something disarming about it for him. She's the type who'd probably want to be told, but he's not quite sure if he should point it out or not.

'In town for a while in the morning. Then came back, made a butty and went down to the shore. Just round from the little car park – you know, where the gull was, where we first saw each other? Had a short stroll. Lazy day, to be honest.' Though not a lazy morning at all, if he's really honest.

'Good word, *butty,* isn't it?' She's smiling, bright-eyed, getting drunker. The smudges at her mouth edges have grown slightly. She sets her glass down over-cautiously, but still not right on the coaster.

'It is that,' he comes back, in his version of a Lancashire accent.

'What sort of butty?' She's obviously wanting to cut loose from the family stuff, just wants to have a bit of a laugh.

'Bacon and double egg,' he says. 'Heels of the loaf. Plenty of butter. Four rashers of streaky. Lashings of red sauce. Has to be the leading brand for me, I'm afraid.'

'You can't beat lashings, can you?' she carries on cheekily, tipsy, laughing at herself.

'Nothing like them.' He's quite happy to go along with her. The wine's hitting him a bit now too, though not as much as it's affecting her.

'You're bad,' she teases him. 'And you've made me really hungry now,' she continues mischievously. She drains her glass, sets it down sharply on the table and edges forward in her seat. 'It's about time I made us the omelette. Happy to share? Or will I do us one each?' She's funny, cute. Turning him on.

'Sharing's fine by me. As long you definitely have your share. Can't stand it when women pick and poke at their food. They should just get stuck in and enjoy it.' He's set himself up for a comment there, but he doesn't mind.

'Oh, don't worry, David. I'm not that picky.' She laughs, runs a hand through her hair, a finger across her lips. Using his name, coming on a bit stronger. No problem.

'Tell you what? Why don't you let me do the

cooking? I'm not bad at omelettes, even if I say so myself. And if you're not too fussy, well . . .' He doesn't mind and he's more comfortable letting her know he doesn't assume she has to be the one cooking.

'Yes, why not?'

'As long as you know I mainly cook for myself these days. The result may not meet your expectations.'

She gives him seriously full-on eye contact but doesn't say anything straight away, which gives the moment an even stronger charge. She just smiles, nodding slowly.

'Oh, I'm sure it will. Need me to help?'

'No, it's okay, I think I can manage. Can I get you a drop more wine from the fridge while I'm at it?' He doesn't want her to think he's pushing her to drink any more, but the decision's hers.

'Go on then. Probably shouldn't, but sometimes you just need to get out of your head for a while, don't you?'

'Never a truer word. Cheese okay in the omelette? Want me to do a few fried potatoes with it, or a bit of salad?'

'Cheese is good. A bit of lettuce and tomato's fine for me. But feel free to help yourself to potatoes if you want them.'

He gets her a glass of white wine from the fridge. She toasts him with it then relaxes back, putting her legs up on the settee. He feels her watching him as he turns back to the kitchen. If it had been her heading towards the fridge then no doubt he'd have taken the opportunity to take in a view of her from behind, so even if he does feel a bit self-conscious it'd be hypocritical of him to blame her if she was doing the same.

'Quite an advantage, isn't it? Having more or less the same kitchen yourself as the person you're cooking for? McEvoy must be obsessive enough. Cutlery, plates, pans, all in exactly the same places in my cottage.' He cracks six eggs into a bowl and whisks them briskly with a fork. You need at least three large eggs each in an omelette, or you're left feeling a bit hungry and cheated.

'No. That'll be *Mrs* McEvoy. The vases of flowers, the nice bed linen, the properly clean bathroom. All a woman's touch.'

He takes her bait for the sport. 'So, don't you think a man's capable of cleaning a bathroom properly? Or choosing a decent duvet cover?'

'No. Well, certainly not of cleaning a bath and toilet to *my* standard,' she states, pretending to be serious.

'Back to standards again, are we?' He grinds some pepper into the beaten eggs, then sets out plates and cutlery. Washes some lettuce, quarters a couple of tomatoes, grates a pile of cheese.

'Definitely not. Let's not go there again. Any plans for tomorrow?'

'Depends on the weather. Might go fishing again. Or drive along and take the ferry over to the other side of the lough. Seeing your family before you go back?' He's making the omelette now, tipping the pan. His Mum taught him. He was good at omelettes, she'd kept saying. She'd sometimes chop a handful of fresh chives and parsley from the garden for him to sprinkle on top.

'Laura's doing a tea on Monday. Not really looking forward to it. Sitting across the table from Tony puts me off my food at the best of times.'

He serves up the omelette, passes over her plate and cutlery, then goes back for his own.

'Don't wait for me. You've got to eat an omelette straight away,' he tells her.

She sets her plate on her knees and starts eating hungrily. He does the same. It's good to sit and eat with a woman, enjoy your food and not feel that you've got to make small talk.

'You're definitely more of a chef than I am. This is lovely.'

'Thanks. Fairly limited repertoire, I'm afraid. I'm not a baker, though I can make pancakes. Not bad with eggs, chicken, fish, steak. And I can do a roast dinner.'

They clear their plates quickly and he stacks them over beside the sink. They both relax back on the settee. He's sitting closer to her now than before. Not a deliberate move, just the way it happened. Without thinking he lets his arm fall onto the back of the settee, behind her shoulders.

'Oh, sorry,' he apologises as soon as he realises. 'Bit clumsy there. I didn't mean to . . .'

'It's okay,' she says, sounding relaxed, looking straight at him. 'I mean, it's okay with me, if it's okay with you. And before I forget to say, you've got a bit of a smudge of red wine. Here and here.' She touches her own mouth exactly where she has the wine marks herself, which makes him smile. 'I wasn't sure if I should've said earlier or not. I mean, I'd like to know myself. But I didn't want to embarrass you.'

'No problem,' he says, wiping his mouth with his hand. 'Lets me off a hook, actually. You know you've got . . .?' He nods at her, then points to the sides of his own mouth again.

'Oh no, have I? Sorry. Not a good look. You should have told me.' She sets down her glass, puts her finger on her tongue, then rubs the sides of her mouth.

'I think we'll somehow survive the wine moustache crisis. I don't go off people that easily, if I like them.' He's feeling more and more like just letting go. He's at ease, safe, comfortable. She's got something about her. They have a real connection. Given the least bit of encouragement, he'd go for it with her, right now.

'You've not quite managed to . . . Here, let me.' She wets her finger, reaches towards him.

He doesn't move. Lets her touch and rub either side of his top lip. *I Surrender . . .* The old Rainbow song, crazy and tender in his head.

'As long as you let me . . .' He touches her top lip gently, tracing it with his index finger.

'Why wouldn't I?' she replies, almost in a whisper.

Fucking hell. What more of a come-on does he need?

Chapter Eighteen

David

He shifts his arm down off the back of the sofa, draws her over towards him. Brushes his lips lightly against the space between her nose and mouth, before kissing her top lip. She runs her hand up the side of his face, angling her open mouth to meet his. They start to kiss, gradually more and more deeply. Her mouth tastes good. She smells of a sweet natural flowery scent, not the sickly kind of chemical-smelling perfume some women wear.

'You smell gorgeous,' he tells her.

He strokes her breast with the back of his hand, then slips his hand up under her T-shirt. He's pretty sure she wants it as much as he does.

She holds her hand over his, stopping it. 'Let's go upstairs, David? Don't want to shock Derek - if he happens to be sweeping the yard . . .'

He gets to his feet, gives her his hand, pulls her up. They go up to the bedroom.

He can't think when he last felt so good, in his head and his body. He knows it's because it's not just about the physical sex. It's about the intimacy, the way it's followed on from the banter and conversations, both funny and serious. About how she's keeping talking to him. Not in any scripted way, but in her own voice, without the impersonal romantic clichés, using his name. It wasn't as if he'd not enjoyed sex before, but with other women, even with Sophie, he'd felt somehow divided, as if part of him wasn't really there. It'd sometimes felt as if he could have been with any woman. Which was undoubtedly as much his own fault as anyone else's. He'd not taken time. He'd not held out for the kind of woman he'd really needed. With whom he stood a chance of meeting in mind and body.

She's moving backwards, bringing him down onto the bed with her. They kiss harder.

'Bloody hell! Did you lie in the bath and deliberately shrink these?' he jokes, as he helps take off her jeans.

'Old habits die hard,' she says. 'It's a kind of modern chastity belt challenge. He who perseveres wins. If he doesn't die of frustration in the process.'

They lie facing one another. He touches her cheek, reaches into her hair.

'I don't mind at all,' he says, smiling.

'You don't mind . . .?' She lightly rakes through the hair on his chest.

'Persevering,' he whispers. 'I'm okay to persevere, if you are.'

'Yes, I am, but only if . . .' she pauses, looks up at him directly. 'Only if you tell me what you *really* do? I'd just sort of like to know whose hands I'm in. If you're happy to trust me with the information, of course?' she adds.

'Don't think I'd be *here* if I didn't,' he replies.

'In spite of my irresistible allure?'

'Well yes ... Although I think we both know you've already guessed I'm just a dull bloody copper? Wouldn't have blamed you for wanting to keep going with your fireman fantasy.' She smiles, blinks hard – it's a habit he's noticed she has.

'Oh, I think I can manage a policeman as well. I mean, *instead*.'

Gillian

I love the solid feel of him lying at my back, his breath at my neck. His particular presence, the cocktail of warm skin, fresh sweat, low-key aftershave that reminds me of green pinecones.

The taste, sound, smells of him, of the two of us, everything mixes together. I close my eyes and surrender to the moment. An orange-red disc of light flashes into my head before the irresistible peaking, the warm waves and relief. Peace spreads through me. He half yells, half cries, grips me tightly, buries his head in the curve of my neck as his breathing and heartbeat gradually settle.

Afterwards, he brings his arm around me and I put my head on his chest. 'Good thing the guy next door's gone out tonight - with these thin walls,' he says, his relaxed voice deeper.

'Certainly is.' I'm feeling so euphoric, unwound.

'A bit more than I expected when you asked me in for an omelette,' he jokes, stroking my upper arm. 'Do you always give your guests such good hospitality?'

'It depends.'

'On what?' he's laughing, my head feeling it through his ribcage, my hand in the muscles of his stomach.

'On whether or not they do a good enough omelette. If it's not to my taste, well . . . '

He kisses the top of my head. 'So, what are the chances of your standards being met? I suppose you get a few satisfactory ones as well as the mediocre?'

I'm close to falling asleep. 'It's not often . . . That I get a really good one. As good a one as yours, I mean. I'd say what you do is pretty rare.'

He pauses, then, 'Thanks, Gillian. My pleasure, of course.' Playful, but genuinely touched. 'Sorry. Need a quick pee, be back in a minute.' He shifts his arm from under me and gets out of bed. 'Let's get you a bit cosier there. C'mon, get yourself under the duvet,' he says, before he goes to the bathroom, helping me under, pulling the cover right up under my chin, pushing it all in around me, as I lie curled up on my side, drowsing off.

When I wake in the morning, David's lying curled round my back, still asleep, his arm over my stomach. It's only just past 9 a.m. I don't remember dreaming. I must've slept through so solidly. I've got a headache, inevitably – I've never been good at mixing red and white wine. I need to get up and drink some water. I move his arm slowly, manage to slip out of bed without disturbing him. He's snoring lightly, his mouth just open. His closed eyes flicker slightly, though otherwise he's quite still. I creep quietly into the bathroom, get on my dressing gown and swallow some paracetamol before going downstairs.

I have a long drink of water, standing at the kitchen window. We didn't close the curtains last night. Derek's coming across the yard, the dog on his heels. He catches sight of me, nods and lifts his arm slightly and carries on. It's a more overcast day than yesterday, but still promising to be warm. With any luck, later on the sun will break through again.

I'm not quite sure how to get my head round what happened between David and me last night, and especially where we're going to take things from here. At the moment, I just want to stay unwound and avoid thinking. I need to hold on to how good it was and allow myself a feeling of uncomplicated happiness. Some details of the earlier part of the evening are quite hazy now. There's no doubt the wine went to my head and loosened my inhibitions, but I also know that what I felt went far beyond the effects of alcohol. It's about this particular man, about David, how he is with me. The quality of our emotional and physical chemistry.

My mind is brimming with sensual images and memories of him and what we said and did together in my bed. His hands gentle and firm on my body. The seductive and protective feeling of having him holding my back. His unguarded expressions. His firm musculature. The vigorous, lush feeling of freed-up, breath-of-fresh-air sex, making us simply be in the moment. Swept along. Swept clean like the wind-brushed bays, on the outer coast of the peninsula.

'Gillian?' David calls down to me. 'Where are you?'

'Downstairs,' I shout back. 'In the kitchen. Want a tea or a coffee?'

'Tea would be good. Want me to come down for it?'

'No, it's okay. I'll bring it up. Milk and sugar?'

'Both, please. Three sugars.' I hear him get up, pad over the landing in bare feet. 'Don't be long,' he adds, as he goes into the bathroom.

'Want me to make us some toast or something?' I ask.

'No. Just come up? I want to see you.'

I hear him lifting the seat, the trickling when he uses the toilet, the flushing. The slight singing of the taps and what sounds like him splashing his face with water in the sink. It seems such a strange thing when you think about it. How quickly some boundaries can shift and social graces relax after two people have sex. What, the previous day, would've felt 'too much information' or almost impossible somehow, the next morning feels naturally easy to accept. So saying, I can't help feeling a bit nervous as well as excited when I take up our tea.

He pulls back the corner of the duvet, lifting a pillow up against the headboard for me. I put my mug on the bedside table, pass his tea over.

'Cheers. Could get used to this alright,' he says, grinning. His hair's wet and more spiked at the front from him splashing his face.

I climb in beside him, still in my dressing gown, and lift my tea. 'You okay?' I ask, taking a drink.

'Yes. You?'

'Yep.' We look at each other directly. I do this hard-blinking thing I do when I'm feeling self-conscious.

'Sure?'

'Yes, fine. I'm fine. Just . . . '

'Not so sure you like the look of me any more in full daylight, now you're sober?' he suggests.

'Don't be daft.'

'So, what's up?' he persists.

'Nothing. No, I'm okay. Just feels a bit . . . I'm feeling a bit *awkward teenager,*' I admit, feeling silly and immature even as I'm saying it.

'Don't think I could've quite managed to go

there myself when I was a teenager. Though I'm sure you were probably a much wilder one than I was?'

'Actually, I was pretty sensible as teenagers go. Well, maybe not so much sensible. I just preferred to keep the boys at arm's length. Think I was quite cruel at times,' I tell him.

'Can't imagine you would be.' He slips his arm round me.

'Oh yes. I liked to take the high moral ground. I did for myself what fathers often have to do for their daughters. The lads were allowed just so far and no further. No one was quite good enough. A walk, holding hands, a few kisses maybe. But only if they were lucky.'

'A girl of ice and steel. Why not? They probably craved you even more for it. Nothing like a look of disdain from a beautiful girl to fuel a teenage lad's lust. Though still glad I managed to coincide with you later. Don't know that I would've had the courage or confidence needed when I was that age. I was quite prepared to be used. I had to rely on girls taking pity on me.'

'I'm sure that's not true,' I say, feeling less self-conscious now.

'No joke! I was a real softie in those days, wet behind the ears when it came to the ways of women.'

'And now you're all tough, street-wise cop?'

'Of course. Though now and then I do still get the odd awkward, teenage feeling when I find myself in a new and quite unexpected situation, however pleasant. And I start wondering.'

'Wondering what?'

'Well, if for example, what I said and did last night when we were . . . that I wasn't in any way out of order? Being as I was, well on my way with . . .' His voice is lower, less jokey, more hesitant.

'You didn't have that much wine. I had a lot more than you did.'

'I wasn't talking about the wine. I meant I was well on my way with *lust*,' he kisses the top of my head.

'So, what's wrong with that? You weren't the only one. We were having a good time.'

'We certainly were. So, as long as it felt okay for you, maybe we can both let ourselves feel a bit less *awkward teenagers,* being as we're not?'

His tentative way of talking and his upfront logic makes me smile and feel safe.

'Yes. I know. You're right. Though I suppose the awkwardness isn't just about the sex. Maybe more about, you know, what we do next? Know what I mean?'

'Course I do.' His hand slips down to stroke the front of my thigh under my dressing gown, giving me goose pimples. 'Although I . . . '

'You think I talk and think too much?' I suggest.

'Yes and no. I do get what you mean. Though I think perhaps some of it can just happen, can't it? You have go with it, just see, don't you? Even when easier said than done.'

We've only just met and slept with each other. After what I told myself down in the kitchen earlier, about trying to stay with a simple feeling of contentment, I do have this annoying tendency to want things settled mentally in advance.

'You're right. I should just go with it more. I suppose it's more about . . . what with us each coming here separately for our own reasons . . . Suddenly neighbours . . . And now . . .'

'I think it'll be okay, you know? We can still carry on doing our own stuff. We can do things together too, just play it by ear?'

I love him for being so straightforwardly patient, holding onto his sense of humour and unlocking me. He starts kissing me, while undoing the belt on my dressing gown.

It's a quarter to twelve by the time we eventually get out of bed. David offers to cook us brunch. He'll go to his cottage to get us some more eggs and bread.

I get into the shower. At first, I feel a slight pang, a reluctance for a moment to wash the lingering traces of David from my body. But then I stand and enjoy the jet of hot water against my back, going over our conversation, smiling to myself as I remember the details of our sober and intoxicating morning sex, that had the same persisting feeling of connectedness as last night's.

I'm still there when I hear the door opening downstairs.

'It'll be ready in about ten minutes!' David shouts up. 'It's a good day. Feel like going for a drive somewhere? You could do some work as well?'

'Yes!' I call back. 'Won't be long.' I turn off the shower, grab a towel, dry myself off quickly. I want to just go with what feels a natural direction, steer clear of cul-de-sac thinking. After the time I've had with Laura and Tony and Claire recently, I'm determined to have some uninterrupted happiness. Isn't giving yourself up to someone or something that makes you happy as much an owned decision as it is an act of compliance or surrender?

Chapter Nineteen

David

After they've eaten, he leaves Gillian getting her stuff together for the day and goes back to his cottage to take a quick shower. He changes into some fresh shorts and a T-shirt, throws a few things into his rucksack. He doesn't know if she'll want him to take his car or not. He'll maybe suggest they drive down and cross the mouth of the lough on the ferry. He's feeling good, physically and mentally. Clearer, much less tense. He's having a great time with her. It's what he needs, on all kinds of levels. The conversations, the physical and emotional closeness, simply sharing cooking, food and drink, have taken away that sense of unrelenting isolation.

There's no denying something else is still there in his mind, like a piece of grit or a lash in his eye. Something that needs dealing with, that isn't going to go away on its own. And sooner or later, he'll have to give it his full attention. Unless he decides of course to keep on being tormented indefinitely, or to try to numb that part of himself in order to live with it. *So then, what would've been the point of you coming here in the first place? C'mon! Wise up, Davie!* In Skinny Kev's voice.

But for the moment, he wants to expand,

not contract. Go forwards, not forever back. He just wants to take his chance to be with her, this woman who makes him feel upbeat and appreciated for who he is. For the moment he's choosing to push back those encroaching thoughts and images. Forcing them into his mind's far-reaching crevices, making them retreat, like barnacled old crabs, thrown into reverse. Temporarily out of sight. But still as obstinate. Lurking, simmering, bubbling. Resting for another day.

She's happy for him to drive. She's sure he's more of natural, she says, which he laughs about. He doesn't mind, just feels a bit aware of how his car's in its usual unkempt, untidy state, the boot smelling of fish and worms, his sweaty trainers. There are empty Coke cans and screwed up sandwich cartons, sweet wrappers in the back seats and foot wells. She says it doesn't matter – as long as she doesn't have to clean up, she's okay with any amount of mess in other people's cars.

'So, where do you fancy going?' he asks. 'I was wondering if we might go down and get the ferry? The harbour's really nice over there. Probably plenty of scope for you – if you want to get some ideas and do some drawing?'

'Yes. That'd be good. Don't know how much I'll be able to concentrate with *you* there. But I can try.'

'I won't hover, promise. I can always head

off for a walk myself if you want to work.'

It's a beautiful, mild Saturday afternoon. There's a fair amount of weekend traffic in both directions on the lough-side road. They drive with the windows down, buffeted by the briny wind which smells of kelp and green summer fields. In places the road closely skirts the lough's shore. In others it runs back inland, losing sight of the water, with a varying border of wooded and high-hedged ground in between.

'We used to go in there quite often with Mum and Dad in the summer,' she tells him, as they pass the end of a rough track in a hedge gap on the lough side of the road. 'There was hardly ever anyone else around. You have to walk for quite a while to get to the place. It's a bit marshy and jungly, but when you get to the little narrow beach, it's really sheltered, like a sort of hidden warm sleepy lagoon in summer.'

'No sign of Brooke Shields?' he asks, enjoying the way she describes things.

'Not that I noticed. Unless Dad was keeping her hidden somewhere round the corner. He always took himself off for a longer walk. Mum and Claire and Laura and I would only go so far. We just wanted to play in the water and picnic. We collected sand eels sometimes. Couldn't believe it the first time I saw them. We were raking around in the sand with our hands and suddenly the place was hiving with these little leaping flecks of silver bodies.'

'Great fishing bait. Didn't mind eating them myself either, dipped in a bit of flour and fried.'

'So, were you along this way a lot when you were a child with your family?' she asks him.

'Sometimes. It was a real treat if we got to go across on the ferry. But my dad worked on farms without a lot of holidays. When I was younger, I used to play with my mates more round the village on the fields and about the town. After my friend Kev started driving, we'd hang out quite a bit on the other side of the peninsula.'

'So, when was it your family moved over to England? You said you'd lived across the water most of your life?'

'I went to live in Manchester at my aunt and uncle's when I was fourteen. My Dad was ill and died. Mum took her own life not long after. My brother Mark was already established out in the States, so my aunt and uncle adopted me.'

'Sounds like you had a pretty hard time, putting it mildly,' Gillian says quietly.

'It wasn't easy, but sure, sometimes these things happen.' He doesn't mind telling her, but doesn't want to dwell on it. Today he wants to stay in the present as far as possible. 'How about you? Been over there a long time yourself?'

'Since I was eighteen. I went to art college in London straight from school, then worked there in a couple of graphic design jobs. I met my ex-husband Matt and we lived in Manchester around fifteen years. I moved to Liverpool to work for myself after we got divorced.'

'Fifteen years. Long time.' He's thinking out loud. But he doesn't want her to think he's probing for more details of her marriage. 'Sorry. You probably don't want to go there?'

'It's okay. Yep, Matt and I were together quite a while. Strange to think about it sometimes. Water under the bridge, as they say. Not that acrimonious, as it happened. He went to live in London. We still exchange Christmas and birthday cards, but that's about it. I don't bear any grudges. I always felt it was more my fault than his anyway.' She sums things up quickly and factually. He senses she'd rather not dwell on some parts of the past either. 'You said you were divorced too?'

'Yes. Sophie and I were only married for literally a couple of years, though. Not that acrimonious in our case either. It helped that she got a fairly good deal out of me financially, including the house, which pleased her. Mind you, she's got a bigger, grander place, now she's remarried. Always liked her *things*, Sophie.'

'A lot of people do. It's a way of life. Things are a big part of who they think they are.' Gillian looks ahead, her elbow still propped on the edge of the open window.

'Yes. That's Sophie. She's the sort of person who lives through stuff and owning it. She feels, you know ... *at one* with things?' He's feeling more amused than irritated as he's telling Gillian about it now. 'Sophie could get so much out of a new table or a properly *dressed* bed. Used to drive me mad. *I* drove her mad, the way I couldn't quite get it. Don't get me wrong – I've nothing against living in a comfortable home. But all the fiddling and fussing over the details left me cold. I could never see the point in it. Felt a bit sorry for her sometimes too, all the same. One thing, living with a grumpy fella doing a nasty, gruesome job. But he could at least share your passion for lampshades.'

'And get passionate about dressing the bed? Even if you no longer feel the passion when you're in it?' she says, coming straight out with it, then checking herself. 'Sorry. Not my business to say how it was for the two of you. I'm probably fairly biased, you know, after last night?'

'I'll not argue with that! Actually, that's how it was with Sophie and me. Splitting up was the best thing for both of us. It was as well it wasn't prolonged. Anyway, as you said yourself, water under the old bridge. And we're here now. Quite a nice wee church there, isn't it? Not as drab and plain-looking as some.' On the left they're passing an old neat village church with arched windows in well-kept grounds fronted by a rendered white wall with a wooden gate.

'Know what you mean. Some of them look so colourless and mournful,' she agrees. He gets the feeling she wouldn't miss much. Even as they're talking, she's turning her head, looking out, taking it all in. 'That one looks a bit like a beached shell. As if the landscape is beginning to take it over.'

'Artist and old pagan that you are?'

'Oh yes. That's me. If I was going to be any kind of evangelist, I'd have to have long naked retreats out in the wilderness. I'd need that, to keep me balanced. I'd be less dangerously zealous,' she says.

'Good idea. As long as you told me where exactly you were going. I'd offer to carry your food and water. It'd be a waste otherwise. All that time and unappreciated nakedness?'

'Though I'd definitely have to pray for guidance first!' She rummages in her bag at her feet. 'Thought I'd brought a bottle of water.'

'You'll find a couple of cans of Coke. On the floor, behind my seat? Open me one while you're at it.'

They're not far away now from where the ferry leaves. It's less than half an hour's journey, including the time to drive on and wait to be let off on the other side of the mouth of the lough. He remembers the harbour town over there, although it's been a long time since he's been. Only small, with a few shops, more than its fair quota of bars for its size. There was a grocer's, probably long closed down, where he'd occasionally stopped off with his parents. As a special treat, he'd been allowed to go in and get himself one of his favourite pineapple or pear ice lollies, or a whipped ice cream cone 'lemon top'. His mum would ask him to get a family brick of raspberry ripple at the same time, which she'd wrap in a newspaper to keep cold until she got it home to put in the fridge.

As they drive off the ferry on the other side the town doesn't look that different. He parks on the front, just a couple of minutes from the pier and they walk back down to explore. It's a bit more spic and span if anything, inevitably geared towards visitors. The town square is smarter, with clean stone paving, strimmed grass, flower beds and new wooden benches. There's a small supermarket instead of the grocer. What used to be a basic chippy has been developed into a pub restaurant.

It's too early for the bigger fishing boats to return, but there's the odd small boat and dinghy coming and going. The simple unwalled rectangular pier is short as piers go, but still busy enough. There are mooring rings and posts with lengths of low hanging chain in places, but you can get right up to the edges.

It used to make his mum feel giddy and frightened, but he'd always liked sitting on pier edges, throwing stones or letting down a crab line. Sometimes it'd been so clear, it seemed as if he'd had a sharp gull's eye view of the oblivious creeping crabs and exposed quiet fish on the sandy bed far below, between his feet. At other times, as you peered down into the opaque blue-green depths, you could only imagine the nature of what you'd find if you fell in.

Today there's plenty of people taking a stroll, a few men with rods, others just looking out to sea or eating fish and chips from papers on the benches. The babble of talk mixes with the ever-present backing track of wailing and squawking gulls and other sea birds fearlessly swooping in to feed.

There's a big bobbing boat like the coastguard would use moored on one side of the pier, down a flight of stone steps with a metal handrail. It's already quite loaded with people, sitting two abreast, facing forward on the saddle-like seat columns with chrome hand bars, all wearing the same waterproofs and life jackets. A guy of around his own age is at the top of the steps offering information about trips out on the lough.

'How about we go on one of your man's trips? Good day for it – quite calm out there at the moment?' David suggests, nodding towards the steps.

The boat is on the point of leaving, the organiser tells them, although he's more than happy to take a couple of extra passengers.

Gillian

I'm increasingly wary of speed, especially on the road, but it feels thrilling to be fast forwarding into the fresh rushing wind and glinting light. The boat runs out, riding high, skimming the surface of the water, mostly horizontal, sometimes tilting on its side, getting the children on board shrieking and squealing with surprise and excitement. We're hearing the running commentary behind us in snatches carried by the wind, 'You get some of the fastest flowing tides in Europe here.'

David obviously thrives on acceleration and on the sway and tipping of the boat. 'Look over there!' he shouts, putting an arm over my shoulders, pointing towards a stretch of rocks with splashes of bright green weed on our right. 'Grey seals!'

It always makes me think of humans doing sack races when seals move on land. The grey-brown lumps of their bodies start to shift towards the water's edge. As soon as they're there they become immediately more agile and graceful. A couple of them pop up only a stone's throw away from us, rising and falling in the boat's wake, their dark, shiny turning heads like black olives in brine.

'Cute, aren't they?' I shout back to David.

'Not half so cute if you're a fish!'

We race up towards the mouth of the lough, then we make a wide turn back. Our guide explains how the whirlpools and boils we're starting to see are caused by pinnacles of rock below the surface. Together with the strong currents and state of the tide, you can get some very spectacular effects.

David looks almost mesmerised. I can't hear everything the man's saying so clearly, but the features he's describing speak for themselves. To one side of us the water churns and boils around many different centres. In places it spins into gurgling vortices as if constantly emptying into unseen plugholes. It's one of those nudges you get from Nature. The parallels are there all along but sometimes it feels as if she grabs your attention with something more dramatic, reminding you that you're made from the same chaotic stuff as everything else. In the wider scheme of things, nothing about you is particularly peculiar or original. Even the most intense churning and knotting of your mind has a reflection here. While things may appear smooth and dependably calm, there's always something else below the surface, restless, on another axis, on the turn. Nothing in the flow stays still or is ever permanently fixed.

We return to the harbour and climb off the boat. I'm feeling excited about being able to translate the textures and movement of the water's surface out there into works in glass.

'Mind if I do a bit of sketching before we drive on, David? I'm thinking about those whirlpools. It'd be good to do some quick drawings and notes while it's all still fresh.'

'No problem. I'll go down and have another potter round the pier.' He seems happy for me that I'm inspired, content enough to wander off for a while on his own. That was one of the aspects of living with me that Matt found particularly trying. He'd look gloomy and hard done by whenever I needed to work in his company. It was especially inconvenient if I got inspired on holiday.

I sit on one of the benches on the small town square, visualising a big abstract stained glass textured panel, subtle whorls and more intense centres of colour. I imagine myself out in the water, becoming a part of it. Still, churned, going with the forces of the tide.

David

He wanders back down to the edge of the pier and stands looking out, close to the men fishing. He likes the way Gillian's so motivated. You can tell she's getting immersed by the way she's unselfconsciously closing her eyes to think and then keeps her pencil moving, totally absorbed in what she's doing.

He was never much good at art himself. He'd cringed when people'd laughed at his spidery, tentative attempts at drawing figures and animals. Not that his first teacher at secondary level had been very encouraging. She'd been the limited type who'd quickly favoured those ready to emulate her own safe, derivative style. Her people and landscapes had been meticulously drafted, but in wishy-washy colours drained of any hint of feelings or personality. She'd not so much criticised him and the other unchosen ones, as ignored them, implying that it was her prerogative to know from the beginning who'd had the talent for what. At least he'd had the message elsewhere that he wasn't bad at numbers and remembering facts, which he'd clung onto. *She's a Cyberwoman, Davie. There's nothing behind those poky wee eyes,* Skinny Kev used to tell him, to try and help him laugh it off. He'd grown to accept that was just how things had to be. But he still thought what a shame it was that such an unimaginative, narrow-minded person had been in a position to prematurely shut down an avenue of possibility in someone else's life.

It'd always puzzled him the way that some people chose to work with the young when they didn't seem to care or believe in them enough to give them chances and encouragement. Especially if they showed some interest. Not that Mrs Hunter had been the only one, of course. He'd known his fair share of them— those self-appointed arbiters of youth who'd found it came more easily to spit on the glimmerings of a child's spark than to fan it into flames.

He does his best to stop his thinking there, knowing where the train of thought is bound to take him. It's uncanny how, when you're trying your best not to go somewhere, every mental track, however apparently unconnected at first, wends back in a particular direction. He needs to bring himself back to simply being in this place with her, to the view of the lough in front of him. He makes himself observe the colours and other details of the boats, the lighthouse in the distance. Then tunes in to some of the words around him.

'I've not a single bit of bait left,' one of the lads fishing beside him is complaining, in a tone of heavy disappointment. The men are probably somewhere in their thirties, one thin, the other stoutish, both pale-skinned and rough-shaven. In spite of the weather, they're bundled up in khaki outdoor jackets and camouflage trousers, wearing similar peaked caps. 'Give us a bit of yours, will you?'

'Go on then,' the other guy agrees, obviously feeling twitchy and reluctant.

'Or I'll have to go home . . .' the offender carries on, sidling up closer, trying to get some sympathy.

'Jesus, what are you waiting for? I said to take some, didn't I?' his friend snarls back. Nothing more annoying than someone sponging bait off you.

To the other side of him there's a crowd of kids, sitting on top of the low rusty bollards. They've finished eating their fish and chips and they're jumping around competing with each other to feed particular gulls, daring one of the lads to catch and stroke them right up on the pier's edge. Kids just being kids. The lad reminds him of a fatter version of Skinny Kev. He's the same kind of crazy energetic front man, has a similar wired, whinnying laugh.

From where he's standing now, it seems all good-natured, at peace. You wouldn't think you'd have problems getting along there in a small boat. Easy to forget there's that potential for turbulence at depth, that doesn't go away. The thought of it is starting to lever up the edge of something in his mind. What was it now? Some words he'd been read so long ago at school from the Bible come bubbling up suddenly, circulating now, swirling in his head, from Jeremiah? *'For they have healed the hurt of the daughter of my people slightly, saying, Peace, peace; when there is no peace.'*

Gillian

David has come back from the pier. 'Bloody good,' he says, looking over my shoulder. 'More abstract than I'd usually go for myself, but have to say, I'm jealous. You know, the way you can just *do* that? It's like you've taken what's there and made something quite new and different out of it. When you've known the original you can still make a connection. You know it's that thing transformed, even if you can't quite analyse exactly how one maps onto the other. You didn't think I could be so profound now, did you?' He sits beside me on the bench and puts his arm round me.

'Oh I did!' I correct him, flipping my

281

sketchbook closed. 'I knew as soon as I saw you coming round that shore that you were the strong profound type.'

'And when you saw the way I despatched that gull, you knew I had troubled, murderous depths as well?' he jokes.

'No more troubled than mine, probably.'

'That could be true,' he agrees. 'Under that cool exterior lurks a wicked sister Grimm?'

I buy some chips for us and we eat them, staying on the same bench. He pretends to disapprove when I throw my scraps to the gulls instead of giving them to him.

'Well, would you just look at *that?*' he follows on, pointing at one of the moulting, scraggier-looking birds. 'That's just an excuse for a life, isn't it?'

'No, don't be so cruel. The poor wee thing can't help it,' I play at arguing back, throwing the bird another chip.

'Of course it can! Will you look at the state of it! You're not telling me that happens all by itself. It has let itself go, hasn't it? It's an eyesore. Needs to be put out of its misery, once and for all. Don't worry, Gillian. There won't be any waste. *You* might be vegetarian, but as you once wisely said yourself, I'm not *picky!*'

'Och, stop it! Stop it! You're making a teenager out of me again.' We fall in against each other laughing and he puts his arms round me.

'We could go for a drive towards Audley's

Castle, if you like? Although, I don't mind. We could just . . . Feel like going back sooner rather than later?' he whispers.

'Yes. How about we go there another day?'

We take the next ferry returning and drive back.

We rush into my cottage and go upstairs, undressing each other, doing the things we've been anticipating doing again all day.

Later on, we run a deep bath and get in together. Tired, full of the sun and sea air.

'I think we should get out before we both fall asleep in the water,' I say.

We take turns to dry each other. Then stumble into my bed like dazed animals, wanting nothing more than to lie close and drift to sleep.

Chapter Twenty

Gillian

I'm suddenly awake. David's on his side facing away from me, eyes still closed, hand against his forehead. He starts making a sort of wailing sound in his sleep, getting louder and louder.

He's twitching about, breathing faster, 'No! No!' he shouts. 'No! Leave her alone! No, you can't do that!'

'David, it's okay,' I tell him, putting my hand on his shoulder. 'It's just a dream.'

His eyes are still closed, his hand clamped over his face. 'Rapist bastard! You sick bastard,' he mutters, only just coming to.

'You're okay, David.' I stroke the top of his arm, wanting to gently bring him round. He jerks suddenly at my touch, opens his eyes wide, startled, blinking hard, then turns over sharply. 'What did . . .? Oh . . . it's *you*. Sorry, I . . .' he says, awake now, sitting up.

'You were dreaming. Talking out loud. Sounded like a nightmare. Are you alright?'

'Yes, yes I'm fine,' he says in an automatic way. 'What was I saying?'

'Sounded like you were talking to somebody. You were telling them they couldn't do something. "Leave her alone", you were shouting.

You called whoever it was a rapist. A sick bastard. Something to do with work maybe?' I suggest.

He screws up his face, rubs his eyes, clearly still feeling the disturbing effects. 'No, it's not work. If it was work, then I might be able to ... But it doesn't matter. It's my problem. My fault for bloody procrastinating.'

'You can tell me if it would help. You sounded really upset. You can talk to me, David. I've hardly held back from telling you about my problems, have I?'

'I'd rather not talk about this one,' he says quite abruptly, getting out of bed, pulling on his boxers and shorts. 'Sunday, isn't it? What's the time?'

'It's only ten. Will I make us a drink and bring it up?' I offer. He seems in such a different mood from last night, suddenly preoccupied, disconnected. He hasn't been so blunt with me before. I understand how gutting nightmares can be and how their mood can take hold of you, but I can't help feeling hurt too that he won't open up and confide in me.

'Thanks. But no, no thanks. I need to be getting on with something today.' He slips on his T-shirt, pats the pockets of his shorts. 'See where I left my keys?'

'With your wallet – there, on the floor. You left everything else downstairs. Want to get together later on?' I want to know what's on his mind, what's had such an impact on him.

'I don't know. I'm going to have to just play things by ear. Do what you need to do yourself. Don't wait around for me, okay?' he finishes curtly, stuffing his wallet into his pocket, holding his keys in a tight fist.

'Meaning don't wait around for you this afternoon? Or actually, don't wait around at all, Gillian, from now on? As in, maybe all this wasn't such a good idea?' I ask him directly, reflecting back his abruptness.

'Bloody hell! I didn't say that, did I?' he snaps, in exasperation.

'So, what is it about then? Why can't you just talk to me properly, upfront? Doesn't have to be games and mystery all the time, does it? I might be just as capable of keeping confidences as you are,' I persist.

'It's not like that. This stuff . . . It isn't about you, Gillian.'

'Right,' I state coldly, sitting up on the edge of the bed staring at him stonily. He's standing outside the bedroom door at the top of the stairs.

'Och, c'mon, Gillian! We don't have to do this. Trust me, please? You don't need *this*,' he says, pointing to his head. 'And I haven't got the energy at the moment to . . . '

'Right. Hold on. Okay, I know. Tell you what, Gillian? Let's trust each other to get up close and personal enough so we can have some really good sex and intelligent conversation. And feel free, won't you, to trust me with all your own stuff and your family problem too. But sorry, *my* information is actually in a bit of different category. And being as this is just a wee holiday couple of nights' thing anyway, I need to remember where to draw the line?' I'm raw and angry now, dramatically antagonistic. Part of me knows I'm being unreasonable and bloody-minded. But his unexplained tightness and unwillingness to share with me feels like a complete contrast to what I believed was a real depth of mutual intimacy. I get out of bed, start getting dressed briskly as well.

He runs his hand through his hair, rubs hard against his scalp. 'No, Gillian. No, it's not like that. Fuck!'

I can tell that he's frustrated and struggling for words. Something's bothering him. But I'm on my own way now, working myself up, letting myself be carried in a strong current of my own making. However much I criticise my sisters for it, we're not without our similarities. I'm not going to slow up or negotiate. After all I've had to put up with recently from Laura, Claire and Tony, I've had enough of other people's tangles and game-playing. Why can't he just tell it as it is?

'No worries, David. It's fine. We're both free agents, aren't we? We came here independently to do our own thing. So, no need for strings.' I don't even like my own voice as it's coming out – so detached, stagey, false.

'Gillian, look. The thing is . . .' he presses his

forehead, as if he's got a headache. For moment he seems on the brink of explaining, but then he shifts direction, makes another decision. 'I'm sorry. I can't have the conversation you want right now. I need to go. See you later on?'

'No need to feel obliged,' I reply brusquely, lifting my hand, waving him off. 'I don't know exactly what I'm doing yet. And I need to get on with some work. As you said yourself, have to just play things by ear. Hope you get things sorted,' I finish. *Sorted.* It's not a word I'm fond of usually, especially as I associate it with Claire. I'm on the point of welling up and determined not to cry in front of him. I need to just say something, no matter how detached I am from the words.

David

There's nothing more he can say to her at the moment. The beginnings of tears flash in her eyes and he hates himself for doing that to her. In spite of her spiky front, she's obviously upset with him, for not telling her about the dream and especially for not explaining what's caused the sudden shift in his mood· and behaviour. The last thing he wants to do is hurt her, although he also feels annoyed and frustrated she didn't just leave him alone and has pushed him to talk when it isn't what he can do. It isn't about a lack of trust. At the moment he just hasn't got the mental space it will take to properly explain and summarise.

The dream was such a disturbing, visceral one; he felt as if he was really in it. Part of him still does. Nauseous, in a sweat, crouching behind that hedge, hearing those unbearable sounds from the hen house where Santie trapped Linda. The man's laugh, hard as unrelenting gunfire. The crash on the wooden floor inside. Linda's cries, Santie grunting and huffing like some unstoppable, merciless, grotesque monster. None of it really goes away. It just keeps rearing up, each time more forcefully. Never weakening. Strengthening, if anything, over time. Thriving perversely on his attempts to ignore it. Demanding to be met and fought, once and for all, outright, head on.

David turns and heads off down the stairs. Slams the front door behind him. His whole body feels hard, keyed up. He wants to scream, unrestrainedly. He's fucking had enough. As he goes inside his own cottage, it seems empty, cold and dismal compared to hers. He goes straight upstairs, sits down on the edge of his own unmade bed, doubles over, puts his head on his knees. *So, what are you going to do now, Davie? Do something!* 'Christ!' He's on his feet again, pacing up and down, not knowing what to do with himself. He can't go on like this anymore, endlessly tormented by the past. You start to think the stuff's gone, that there's a chance your life could be carried away in a fresh, new direction. You want to just go with it. But it's just a temporary lull, a cruel false sense of security. The old current still has the strength and abiding power to take you over, to hold you captive in its centrifuge. It's time for him to take control, do something to still the force. *C'mon! Be a man, will you, Davie? Do something?*

The only way is to go back to the source of it all. Back to Santie. What exactly he's going to do when he comes face to face with the man, he still doesn't know. But he can put himself there, can't he? And hope that when the time comes, he'll have the courage to be guided by his instincts.

He goes to the wardrobe. Chooses a black shirt, a dark green tie, a pair of black chinos, his black shoes. He takes out the only smarter jacket he has with him. It's one he wears at work sometimes - dark navy, fine wool, thinnish lapels, quite low-key. Before he puts it on, he'll have a shower and a shave. If he gets himself looking sharper, it'll help him feel he's mentally sharper too. For what's coming up, he needs every keen edge about him he can find.

Before he leaves the cottage, David takes Trevor's pearly handled fishing knife from his rucksack and slips it into the pocket of his jacket. It's just after 12.30p.m. when he drives off. Gillian's car is still there. However hard it feels, he tells himself he can't think about her and what happened between them now. He'll lose it if he starts to soften. For now, he needs to concentrate, stay with the drive of his decisive anger, in touch with the urge to act and not be dissuaded. He can't allow himself to be deterred or delayed any longer.

He drives through the town in the direction of The Hill. Below it, there's an older housing estate. It used to be entirely owned by the council, with the tenants gradually becoming owners of their properties. Santie could easily have afforded to move into a much bigger house elsewhere, but he'd carried on living there. A community man needed to be at the hub, didn't he? Sharing in the trials and tribulations of his people.

Instead of parking outside the house itself, David parks round the corner, in one of the small estate car parks, and walks there. As he expected and after his conversation with Linda, the pavement alongside is lined with vehicles. It reminds him of how it was on all those Sundays when he was a boy. When the streets outside Santie's church were lined with cars. Santie is now housebound, no longer able to get to his church. But his church will faithfully come to him. *For Thine is the Kingdom, the power and the glory.*

The house itself doesn't look so different. Still a cut above the rest. Bearing witness to its owner's intentions – to be a part of his community and yet at the same time over and above them, in a custodial, supervisory role. With the constant support and homage of his network of tradesmen, the place had been meticulously repaired and significantly extended. David and Skinny Kev and Sammy had often walked the streets around it, casting apparently careless glances, hoping to observe something, imagining what might've been happening in its rooms.

The exterior of the house was dependably well-appointed and maintained, rather than beautiful. The small garden lawn and privet hedges always looked to have been just cut, the windows recently cleaned. The property was guarded by a sturdy, quality wrought-iron black gate. It was one of the first to have a small conservatory and white PVC window frames, doors and guttering. At Easter, there was a line of daffodils like a parade, either side of the path to Santie's door. In summer, his standard rose bushes, heads and shoulders above the front hedges, were literally the talk of the town. 'You won't get good rose bushes like that without plenty of pruning and spraying,' David's dad had said every year, in admiration. 'You'll never see a black spot on Santie's roses.' As his mum had said, although Santie had been given the credit, the success of his flowers was probably due to the work of his wife and other helpers. 'I'm sure it's Ruth or the family doing the gardening. Sure, you never see *him* outside in the garden. He's got more important things to do than pruning roses or planting up geraniums.'

Today, by the front step, there's a pot overspilling with bizzy lizzies and a show of bright trumpeted petunias. Below the doorbell, there's a neat polished gold plaque, engraved with a text: *Knock and it shall be opened unto you.*

David presses hard on the bell. His heart's racing. He makes himself breathe slowly, tells himself he must stay calm. The heat of the anger inside him is only just keeping at bay the cold churning undercurrents of fear. How could he ever have anticipated this moment? He'd only ever called once at that door before. On the day when he'd returned Ruth's forgotten gloves. Even then, he'd had to take his courage in his hands, but that was nothing compared to what he's dealing with now.

'How are you doing?' A man, probably in his late 50s, answers the door. He's wearing a brown suit, shirt and tie, the remains of his grey hair close-cut. The lenses of his steel-framed glasses magnify his blue-green eyes with dilated pupils. Even after all this time, there's such a resemblance that David knows it has to be Santie's son, Stuart. 'Mum?' the man immediately confirms the fact for him, calling back into the house.

'Give us a minute, Stuart,' a woman's voice calls back.

Behind Stuart, the hall is milling with people, in and out of the downstairs rooms, talking in hushed voices. There's a few older women but those gathered are mainly men, most of them also wearing suits, shirts and ties, holding cups and saucers. Who knows what violent, twisted histories are assembled here, behind tidy shop fronts of apparent reverence and respectability?

'I was just passing. Thought I'd call in and pay my respects to your father. Sorry, probably should've phoned first?' David explains quietly, trying his best to sound casual.

'No problem at all,' Stuart says, moving to one side as his mother makes her way through to join him in the doorway. Ruth's older of course - Santie himself will be in his late seventies now and David guesses Ruth is two or three years younger - although instantly recognisable and remarkably well-preserved. She still has the same carefully groomed appearance, a modest and self-assured air about her. She's wearing a pale pink, three quarter-sleeved jumper, a knee-length navy skirt and low-heeled patent shoes. Her neat, permed hair is surprisingly dark, with only a few white hairs.

'The man's calling to see Dad,' Stuart explains, looking David up and down, taking him in as he speaks to his mother. 'And you'll be . . .?'

'Just one of the many children who visited your father, at Christmas, in his shop. Although I wonder if your mother'll remember me too?' David says, looking at Ruth, directing his words mainly to her. 'It's a very long time ago now, but I was the boy who brought you back your gloves after you'd left them behind on the church wall one Sunday. Remember, you rewarded me, with one of your own lovely fairy cakes?'

'Och, yes! For goodness' sake, you've grown-up, haven't you? Remind me, son. What's your name again?' Ruth asks. He'd never told her his name before, but she was clearly wanting to show that she remembered him personally.

'John,' he replied quickly. It wasn't a lie, given that John was his second name, after his father, although he'd never been known by it.

'Och, yes. C'mon in, John. You're very welcome now. Very thoughtful of you. Will you take a cup of tea or something to eat? There's plenty of sandwiches and pastries in the kitchen,' she offers. 'The nurses have just been in to change his bed and make him more comfortable,' she informs him.

David steps into the hall smelling of fresh baking mixed with aftershave and men's oiled hair. It feels as if the radiators are on full, in spite of the weather. He nods and lifts his hand in greeting to the rest of the company. Those in the hall stop talking for a moment, some lifting hands to briefly acknowledge him, studying him fleetingly, then resuming their conversations. He can imagine there's probably been so many comings and goings. It'll be to his advantage to blend in with the crowd.

'I'm sorry, I can't stop. Appreciate the offer of the tea, but . . . '

'Not a problem, son. Are you wanting to go

up and say hello? He's always happy to have a visitor. Even if he's not able to talk these days himself, since the stroke. Want me to come up with you?' Ruth offers. There's something poignant about her David can't deny. He can't afford to dwell on that too much. He can't let himself be distracted. She's a kind, ordinary woman, trying her best to cope with stressful circumstances, preparing herself for the imminent death of her husband. She'll be consoling herself with memories of the years of their Christian marriage and joint service to the community. It could well be that over the years, she's known some things and has had to turn a blind eye, but he's pretty sure the woman's oblivious to her man's other side – his cruelty, violence and perversity, so contrary to her own uncomplicated nature, probably far beyond the scope of her imagination.

'Och no, don't trouble yourself. I'll introduce myself. I'm sure you've enough of running up and down the stairs. Anyone else with him at the moment?' If he's lucky, the man'll be on his own.

Stuart's nodding, looking thoughtfully at David, obviously needing to weigh him up. His father knew so many people. The son is more likely to be less trusting than his mother, more likely to be aware of some of the reasons why Santie has gained as many enemies as friends.

'Want me to go up with him, Mum?' Stuart

wants to check with Ruth. 'With it being so long since Dad's seen him . . .'

'Och no, son. He'll be fine with John going up by himself. And maybe it was a long time ago, but this boy had a heart of gold. There weren't many boys who would've thought to bring a woman back her gloves the way he did. Your dad wouldn't want us keeping good people away from him.'

Stuart nods again, puts his hands in his pockets and rocks forward in his shoes. He doesn't seem entirely convinced. But will he challenge his mother further? Ruth carries on talking to David. 'I know a kind man when I meet one, John. There's no one with him at the moment. You'll have him to yourself. First room on the left, at the top of the stairs.'

There's no time for him to hesitate. As he climbs the narrow staircase with the same thick beige carpet and shiny heavily glossed white woodwork of the rest of the hall, David feels at the same time triumphant and anxious.

The door at the top on the left is slightly ajar. There's the sound of a continuous babble of voices on the radio. He can hardly believe where he is and the relative ease with which he's got himself in. It seems dream-like somehow, but the way his heart's thumping leaves him in no doubt that what's happening is very real. He knocks, hears a dry cough but nothing else. Even if he knows Santie can't answer, he still needs permission somehow to enter.

'Just go on in, son,' Ruth shouts up.

Inside the room is decorated in cosy tones of peach and cream. It has a slightly retro feel about it but everything has been done and maintained to a high standard. It's been turned into what looks like an upmarket private hospital room, the bedside cabinets stocked with tissues and fruit, a water jug and radio. In the corner there's a draped table laden with extravagant flower arrangements, some with those waxen highly perfumed lilies you get in a church at a summer service, or a wedding. There's a strange, slightly sickly smell hanging in the air too, badly masked by cloying floral air freshener. A smell of something going off, like sour milk or fermenting fruit. The floor-length curtains are drawn back, Venetian blinds at the window tilted for privacy and to allow some light. On his right, as David comes through the door, there's a wall of built-in wardrobes, running round to a mirror-backed dressing table in the same style, with drawers and cupboards either side. The bed is on his left, lit with wall lights under cream shades. It's a double divan with a cushioned, buttoned headboard.

'Hello,' David says as he enters the room. 'I did knock, but . . .'

He's aged a lot, has lost most of his hair and shed a few stone, but it's still Santie alright. He's sitting propped up, ensconced in an armchair shaped arrangement of fat ivory-coloured pillows, covered with a thick puffy peach duvet. Whatever drugs he's on are probably making him more drowsy and beaded with sweat. He looks well-groomed for a sick man, recently shaved by the nurses, his lips shiny with lip balm. He turns his head slowly in David's direction, his puffy shadowed eyes just opening as his visitor speaks. He parts his lips, makes a basic grunting sound, then flushes up with the effort of a coughing spasm which forces his tongue forward out of his mouth.

'Need me to get you a tissue or something there?' David offers, going towards the box on the cabinet, but Santie shakes his head as he coughs, indicating it isn't what he wants. Who'd have thought back in those days the man would come to this? Speechless, immobile, no power in his hands. Dependent on others to wet his lips.

It's such a strange thing. In spite of everything, all the years of his resolve hardening, something in David is still telling him that, if he's got a shred of humanity, he should pity the old man and his people and have mercy in the hour of his illness and suffering. Perhaps the time for revenge has long passed? What good will it do anyone now? Isn't the man only a sad, gurgling shell of his former self?

But then as his fit of coughing passes, Santie turns his head slowly again. His eyes, no longer hidden behind glasses, prise themselves open, narrow to focus, then fix beadily on David, taking him in. One side of Santie's lip and nose lifts, as if tugged by an invisible hook and line. Santie may not be able to speak, but his eyes show that he's still in there, on the alert. Though his body may be weak, his mind's still calculating. If he was able, would he shrink from rape or punishment if he saw fit? Is it not less of a mark of David's humanity to give in to a general mindless habit of taking pity? What was it the good book said? *And thine eye shall not pity; but life shall go for life, eye for eye, tooth for tooth, hand for hand, foot for foot.*

On the far side of Santie's bed there's an upholstered plush beige chair, clearly intended for the use of visitors. Santie gestures with his head in its direction, grunting again.

'Alright if I take a seat?' David acknowledges, going round the foot of the bed and sitting down, all the time aware of the man's eyes following him. He wants to stay as far as possible with simple observation now, keeping himself clear of the temptations of sentimentality, pity or guilt. Constantly reminding himself of why he's here, of everything that's been said and done. The things that will go on and on festering and tormenting him, spoiling what's left of his own life. And that's the least of it. He knows he's not here just for himself. He's here for all of them.

'I'll not stay long. Don't want to tire you out, do we? You'll not be short of visitors. A man who's made Christmas so special for so many children is never going to be short of friends. It's a long time ago now, and you may not remember me, Santie, but I'll never forget the first time I sat on your knee by the present tub in your shop.'

A look of recognition gleams in Santie's eyes. Not recognition of David personally, but recognition of his own importance and achievements. He's happier now he knows which category to put his visitor in. He motions with his head towards the bedside cabinet.

'Want a glass of water?' David guesses.

The water in the jug's a little warm but he pours half a glass, stands up and brings the drink to Santie's lips. The man flushes up again as he strains to bend his head over, puts his mouth to the rim and allows David to tilt up the glass. He manages only enough to wet his mouth before he starts coughing and spluttering. His swallowing's obviously not so good. David takes the glass away and stands back.

An image suddenly comes into his head. Of him keeping the glass at Santie's mouth, continuing to pour the water in, pouring and pouring until Santie is choking, helpless to push David away. He pictures the man going redder, then bluer in the face, gasping, his head thrashing about to no avail. Part of him reels at the dark, graphic cruelty of his own thoughts. At the same time, he wants them to be there, to remind him of the punishments Santie has given to others. And has so long deserved himself. *C'mon, Davie! Be a fucking man!*

'Alright Santie? Terrible cough you've got there.' Something darkly amusing occurs to him as he says it. When he first entered the room, the way Santie was lying up there in his bed reminded him of something. There was an element of a big tom Tabby cat about him but that wasn't quite it. Now he has the persistent feeling they're both characters in a sinister fairy tale. What he was searching for before clicks in his mind. Santie's less of a cat and more of a wolf, even if he is in perfectly ironed, brushed cotton night clothing. And even if David's still as fearful as Little Red Riding Hood, he has to have the presence of mind to call upon the decisive skill and attitude of a wood-cutter.

He sits back down on the bedside chair as Santie's coughing settles and slips a hand into his jacket pocket, feeling the smooth surface of the knife's pearly handle, holding it tightly, thinking about the sharp shining blade tucked inside it. He recalls Trevor's calm voice for a moment, his quiet strength. *Boys, that's a big fish you've got there, Davie. Careful. Keep your hair on. Get him well in, now. Get him properly hooked. Easy does it, son.*

'All these years I've never forgotten you, Santie,' David says, in a low, tempered voice. 'Must feel so good, thinking about all those children who'll always remember you and everything you did for them?' David notices the smug gleam return to the tyrant's eyes. 'All those lovely wee gifts. You never knew what you'd find when you tore off Santie's special paper. There are not many people who have such a knack of being able to guess what a person wants and being able to give it to them.'

Santie keeps nodding, his eyes closing slightly with the enjoyment of an animal lapping up strokes and praise, waiting for more. David's hand stays closed around the knife as he speaks. He's past pity now. And growing clearer about the kind of damage that needs to be inflicted. To punish Santie by drowning, stabbing or suffocation would never be enough. What would that do but send the man more quickly to oblivion? He might suffer for a moment in his body, but in his mind he would rest unchallenged, never doubting that, while his Lord might judge him for whatever secrets he had on his conscience, He would finally grant him absolution and the peace of His everlasting arms in Heaven.

'Although the thing is, Santie . . . ' David edges forward now and turns up the volume on the radio. There's a farming programme on. They're discussing some kind of disease in sheep. He touches Trevor's knife again in his pocket then stands up and goes close up to Santie, leans in and puts his mouth just a fraction away from the man's thick-lobed red ear. David lowers his voice to a whisper. 'The thing is, in spite of all those thoughtful wee gifts of yours, Santie, I can't help remembering those other things you did as well.

You know? Like those terrible beatings you organised and your lads gave to all those people, when you thought nobody else was watching.'

Santie's starting to get agitated. He tries to lift his arms but there's no power in them. He squirms and tries to move away from David, but David puts a hand on the other side of his head and holds his face firmly in position. 'And you know, Santie, I was *there* when something else happened too. Remember that day when you had to have that wee private word with Linda? In the hen shed, at the back of that old derelict house? I know what you really did to her in there. Are you listening there, Santie? Because, in spite of how a lot of people round here think you're the big community man and you can do no wrong, some of us know the real truth, don't we? We know that your life was about nothing but your fucking ego. You raped that wee girl in there, didn't you? After you'd got your mates to knock her and her friend about first? The way you'd raped her poor mother and her auntie too.'

David's hissing hard into Santie's ear, trying not to raise his voice. Saying the things he's wanted to say for so long, feeling free, no guilt. He pulls back slightly for a moment so that he can take in the look of shock in the old man's widening eyes, feeling the heat and greasy sweat from Santie's head gathering under his hand. He moves back in against Santie's ear.

'I've got to be honest with you. I'm no

believer myself, Santie. But we all saw you there, at your church, didn't we? Every Sunday saying your prayers, bowing your head, making sure everybody was paying their dues and that they were all kept on the straight and narrow. So I'm just struggling now, Santie. I'm struggling to work out . . . how is such an evil sadistic bastard as yourself going to square all this up with God? I'm not a one for needless suffering myself, but if I were him, I'd be thinking that the kinds of things you've done deserve *never* to be forgiven. I think we both know it'll not be long before you'll be on your way to *Hell*, Santie.'

Now Santie's grunting, drooling, pushing his head ineffectually against David's firm, restraining hand.

'I wonder what Ruth and some of those nice ladies downstairs would think if they found out? And maybe I'll never need to tell them. But who knows, maybe one day I'll have to. I'm still thinking about it, Santie. You've given me a tricky wee dilemma.'

He suddenly moves away, letting Santie's head fall back. For a moment Santie just looks up at his accuser, breathing fast through his mouth, stunned into silence. Santie had brought so much fear to others, but never before had David seen fear piercing the man's own eyes.

'Anyway, there you go. I suppose I should be getting on now,' David says quietly. He turns the volume down again on the radio, then moves away and stands down at the end of the bed, crossing his arms. 'I promised your kind wife not to tire you out. We all need our personal space. We've probably both got a wee bit of thinking to be getting on with now, haven't we?' He pauses and nods, begins to walk towards the door then stops and returns to the head of the bed, turning up the radio again.

Santie stares up at him, rearing his head backwards into the pillows, bracing himself, his face twitching.

'So . . . reconciliation my arse!' David hisses hard into his ear, feeling Santie start with the blast of his voice. As soon as he's said it, he quickly moves away, cutting round the bottom of the bed and heading for the door.

Santie begins grunting again, triggering another bout of coughing.

'Everything alright up there?' Ruth's voice calls up.

David reaches the bedroom door as Ruth appears.

'That cough starting up again? He probably just needs a wee drop of water, son,' she tells him.

'Want me to . . .?' David offers gently, feeling sorry for the woman, the look of concern and strain on her face. As they're speaking Santie's eyes are flitting erratically between them. He makes an attempt to gesture and grunt in David's direction with his head, only succeeding in making himself splutter again.

'Och, no. But thanks for asking, John. I was coming up to stop with him for a bit anyway. Why don't you help yourself to a plate of sandwiches downstairs and a cup of tea? There's a big fresh pot just made in the kitchen. I'll be back down soon.' She goes to the other side of the bed, pours some water and brings it up to her husband.

'Very good of you to offer. Although I'm afraid I have to be going. I'm just glad to have seen Santie. You're obviously doing a great job of looking after him. I'll see myself out, no problem. And sure, I can always call back on you another time in future when the house is less busy and you've got more time to talk.'

David looks at Santie as he says it. He sees the haunted look in his eyes again. The wolf's feeling the fear, unable to howl or run.

'Good to see you,' David tells him. 'Relax yourself, now. It's not everybody that can rest knowing they've done so much for others, is it?' he adds, looking at Ruth. She brings the glass of water up to Santie's lips but he turns his head away from it.

'You're right there, son,' Ruth agrees. 'And that'd be lovely to see you another time. We could talk about other things from the past, couldn't we? I'm sure your memory's a lot better than mine is, all the same.'

David leaves the room quickly and cuts down the stairs. He wants to shout and explode with the feeling of exhilarating release, but for the moment he has to contain it. He needs to leave as quickly and quietly as he came, avoiding interaction. At the bottom of the stairs he turns and stops for just a moment, signals to those still in the hall that he's leaving.

'Right you be, son,' one of the suited men acknowledges in return, lifting his cup. 'Good of you to call in. Ruth's awful touched by the gesture, son.'

He's a slightly built elderly man, his hair shorn back to white bristles. The loose skin of his jowls and the way his suit hangs from his shoulders and around his legs suggests that he's lost weight from when the suit was first bought. Something about him is familiar to David, the tortoise-like beak shape of the man's upper lip, the ruddiness of his now sunken face. After all these years thinking of him, he realises that he's looking into the wizening face of Santie's chief Helper. A cold draught wafts up through him. Will the man know him?

'No problem,' David replies, trying not to flinch, doing his best to hold his own course. You can never be certain of anything when you're looking into such eyes, but everything he knows tells him nothing's registering, that he's safe.

He opens the door and steps outside, clicking it closed. Strides along the pavement in the direction of his car, without turning back.

Chapter Twenty-one

Gillian

The same place can seem so suddenly different, depending on what's happening in it. Within a day, even an hour. This time yesterday, I was getting into the shower while David went off to get things for breakfast. I felt happy, full of the buzz of sex, excited about what the day ahead would bring. Everything seemed inviting, vibrant.

Now in the shower, I'm shivering though the water's hot. The light seems dingy and unforgiving. I notice a long crack in the plaster above my head I never saw before, a dark wavering line with creeping tributaries, a faded brownish stain on the pale blue cotton bathmat. The thought that I'm seeing Claire, Laura and Tony tomorrow evening for tea makes me feel even more sapped of energy. I can be resilient, though also fragile when faced with uncertainty. People can tell me I look happy when actually I feel cracked open, sad, on the point of spiralling downwards. In retrospect, it can be a creative state of mind as far as my work goes, although at the time I feel so frustrated by who I am.

I wish David and I hadn't argued the way we did. I overreacted. I knew that I was going that way at the time and gave up to the mood impulsively, carelessly. As if what happened didn't matter to me. I can be stupid and lose balance sometimes. Let myself get snagged up in details. I should have just accepted that he didn't feel like talking and kept things just moving ahead. Why didn't I allow him to do what he needed to do, without being so demanding and childishly dramatic? If our situations had been reversed, I'd have expected that of him. We've only just met. Couldn't I have just cut the poor man some slack?

I try to steer away from superstition, but at the moment I'm wondering if there's something inherent in me, doomed to fail in close relationships? I don't seem to be much good at working at untying knots. When things get difficult, my immediate instinct is to distance myself. To be convinced that at least in that way I can hold on to my sense of self, to a degree of certainty and freedom. What makes me believe I'm so different from my sister's? I'm set in my own ways too, so inflexible, predictable. Maybe it's better that I just stay as I am, detached, living on my own? Finally, I decide – instead of trying to attempt any further analysis – to retreat into my familiar, self-absorbed, dependable artist's world.

I take my sketchbook and pencils and go outside. It's duller than yesterday with more cloud cover, though warm. I noticed when David and I were sitting that evening in the field close to the cottages, that there was an ancient looking gorse bush in the opposite corner, with a patch of trodden soil underneath it – a natural sheep shelter, I guessed. I cross the field. I'm right – the dried mud has been trampled and compacted by sheep's hooves.

There are wisps of wool on the floor and caught like cobwebs across the dark green mass of merging spikes above. I get down, crawl into the shelter and put my head back, looking up at the dry, wind-twisted old trunks supporting the dense gorse thatch. I concentrate only on sketching the branching, cross-hatching lines above my head.

Later in the afternoon, at the cottage, after a slice of toast and a cup of coffee, I look at my map and remember another place we used to go when I was younger. You drive through Stewartsford, then round to the shore at the top end of the other side of the lough. It's not as far as the wildlife reserve where I met Laura. You can park on a quiet, small lane and get down to the shore for a walk along a sheltered concrete path, below a steep grassy bank. After a while you come to a place where at low tide you can walk over a short strip of causeway, with barnacled weeded rocks either side, onto the tiny mound of an uninhabited island.

I sit on the low concrete wall, by the path, facing an island in the lough. The sun is starting to break the cover of the cloud. I close my eyes, remembering how our family used to walk around the island. This time I decide to sketch more abstractly, imagining how the forms of land and the little island could look in aerial view. I visualise the colours of glass I'll use: lively greens for the land, textured clear glass for the surrounding water, the causeway opalescent.

By the time I get back to the cottage, it's after six.

David's car's there. The curtains are half drawn upstairs. He could be out somewhere on foot. As I go to open my door, I hesitate. Shouldn't I just swallow my pride and apologise for how I was earlier? On the other hand, he said he'd got things he needed to get on with. It could be that he's still involved and won't thank me for turning up. I'm not in the mood for getting it wrong and risking making a move, only to be turned away. He told me just to carry on with my own plans. Probably I should take my cue from that.

The prospect of spending all tomorrow evening at Laura's makes me want to get outside again as soon as I get into the cottage. I butter the end of a baguette and get some cheese and a bottle of water from the fridge. I'll take a few recent sketches with me to look over, drive down to the car park and have a bit of a walk on the shore.

The sky is clear now. You can almost hear the banks of weed baking in the sun on the shore, like drying strips of tagliatelle. I'm not sure of the exact state of the tide. The water's well out, the calling birds taking their chance to settle and pick over the sand's pocked bare back before the sea's return.

I leave most of my things in the car. I can come back once I've had a stroll. There's a mild breeze, although I'm happy in short sleeves as I make my way over the rocky shore, stopping now and then to pick up a piece of driftwood or a particular stone that interests me.

As I round the curve and walk back into another small bay, I suddenly see David not far ahead of me. He's in bare feet, standing where the stones meet the edge of the flat expanse of sand, wearing his usual shorts and T-shirt, holding his trainers in one hand. He's standing still and straight-backed as a heron, looking out towards the water. For a moment it occurs to me that perhaps it may be best for me to retreat and let him be there, alone. But before I can act on the thought he turns, sees me and waves. 'Gillian!' he calls, gesturing for me to come over.

I'm not sure what to think. I just let my feet take me there.

'Hello,' I say, feeling a bit awkward as I reach him and stand alongside, looking at the horizon too. 'Shame the sea's too far out for a paddle.' It sounds more than a bit pathetic. There are so many other things I probably should say instead, connected with what happened when we were last together. But he grins. His face looks much more relaxed. Everything about him seems looser.

'Never mind. She's always on her way back, isn't she? When she's so far out, you think she might not. But if you wait, she will. That's how she is.'

'Yes,' I reply. 'And she's lucky. When she can just come and go, no questions asked. She does what she does.'

'No choice but to be herself, has she? We just have to try and go with that, don't we?'

He's still smiling, wryly, then looks away, down at his bare feet and up, out again to the lough. He turns and looks straight at me, biting his lip. It's a look I can't ignore. It hooks me in, keeps me looking back at him. It's offering an apology, understanding, an invitation to begin again. He rubs his eye. 'Sorry, Gillian, I . . . '

'No. I'm sorry, David. I was well out of order,' I tell him. 'I can be really bloody-minded. I shouldn't have tried to force you to talk when you didn't want to.'

He lets his trainers fall onto the sand and takes my hand. 'It's okay. It doesn't matter now. Not your fault. It was fair enough. I should've tried to explain myself better. Even if I couldn't help it, you must've wondered why I changed so quickly. I was pretty abrupt. And I was lucky, you know, that it mattered to you – what was on my mind, what was getting me so worked up.'

'I'm fine if you want to talk about it now?' I offer tentatively.

He squeezes my hand hard for a moment,

turning to face out to the lough again.

'Let's just say I've been living with things from the past in my head for a long time. Things that happened not far from here. Maybe at some point, if you want, I'll tell you more about that. But today I've finally let myself off a really big hook. And I'm determined to let myself run free. I need to just face forward again. Before it's too late and I'm too old to enjoy it.'

'You know, I think that sounds like a good idea. You don't need to tell me anything at all. It's as I said before. We're both here for ourselves, no strings, free agents.'

I'm repeating the words, though I sense I'm using them to pull away from my real feelings for the sake of certainty. 'I mean, don't get me wrong, it's been really good. But we've only just met and the holiday's not going to last much longer.' I'm upsetting myself as I speak – I can feel my eyes pricking. I'm trying to sound brief and in control, which isn't how I feel.

He puts his arm round my shoulders, still keeping his eyes on the horizon. 'It's been really good for me too, Gillian. And actually, I'm sure it could be for a lot longer, for both of us. Doesn't really feel like just a holiday thing to me.'

'Oh, no. I'm sorry, that must've sounded horrible.' I'm cringing at the memory of my stupid words. 'It didn't . . . It *doesn't* feel like that to me either.'

'I mean, we hardly live at opposite ends of

the universe, do we? It's not that far from Manchester to Liverpool is it, if we have a mind to keep on seeing each other? Although, as this is a day for letting people off hooks . . . If you need me to, I'll let you off this one?'

'I think you know that's not what I want, David.'

He pulls me towards him and kisses me. His mouth tastes sugary.

'What've you been eating? Your mouth tastes sort of sweet.'

'Just chewing a bit of grass. We'll get you some too if you want? Nothing wrong with a bit of good local grass to help you go native.'

'If we were cows, maybe. And the way I've behaved recently, I'd forgive you for calling me one,' I tell him. 'But then I couldn't offer you a lift back in my car.'

David

'I could come along, if you want? Turn the garden hose on the lot of you, if things get too dangerously heated,' he suggests.

It's just before 4 o'clock on Monday afternoon. Since they got back to his cottage from the shore last night, they've been sleeping, eating and drinking. In and out of bed. Making up for lost time.

They're lying in bed now, her head on his chest, one leg crooked over his, laughing, observing the contrast between their skins. Hers smooth, always so pale. A good Northern Irish girl's complexion, she'd joked. His more tanned, darkened by what she describes as his 'forestry'. She's been telling him more about her sisters. And the long-suffering brother-in-law, Robbie. How she's going to handle the evening meal and especially speaking to Tony.

'No!' she says, highly amused by his offer of coming along. 'You'd hate it!'

'I wouldn't. I'm sure I'd cope. I've met girls' families before, you know.'

'Yes, I'm sure you have, but not mine. Mine are in a league of their own.'

'Although they're probably lovely towards strangers, aren't they? On their best behaviour?'

'Oh yes, they can be. They'd make the effort with you, without holding back on pointing out my flaws. Though I'm not being made to look the bad one this time. It's Tony's turn to take the flack tonight.'

'Do you think he really will? I'm not convinced. I think excuses might well be found. The show of married and sisterly strength must go on. Even if your sisters don't like him for it, he'll still be needed. *Please* let me come? I'll be on your side?' He's being daft and they both know it. She moves her leg off his, lightly kicks his foot.

'Sometime, maybe. But not tonight. It won't be nice. And I don't want you to have to put up with the family feuds.'

'Always easier to cope with family feuds as an outsider. But fair play. I think after yesterday morning, you're more than entitled to go off and do something on your own. And be as blunt with me as you like,' he says still reflecting on how sharp he was with her.

'Och, don't be going back to that,' she tells him, stroking the side of his face before disengaging herself and getting up. 'Better go and get myself ready. Lucky for some, having a whole evening to themselves.'

He lies on in bed, listening to the sound of her in the shower, the thud of her feet as she gets out. He feels like a different man. There'll always be some mental debris you'd rather be rid of and you will never quite sieve out − like small persistent floating drifts of weed, swaying in and out of the flow of your mind − but everything seems so much clearer for him than it was. He was careful and left no physical evidence of the extent of his impact on Santie. The taunting psychological card was, no doubt in his mind, the strongest he could have played. It's unlikely there'll be any come-back for him, although of course he knows in such things there can never be watertight guarantees and he'll have to be forever watchful. Last night was the first for as long as he can remember when he'd not had those dreams.

You're never a hundred per cent sure who might've seen something and put pieces together. But Santie himself would never be able to repeat the words David whispered into his ear. He couldn't speak, he no longer had enough power in his hand to hold, let alone write with a pen. No one appeared to recognise him, apart from Ruth and actually, she didn't really know him. She'd wanted to be reminded of a perfect boy with a pure and simple heart of gold. She'd gratefully remembered a past kindness and gently spoken to him. Such a lovely wee boy, who'd been so good and honest, and had personally returned her best Sunday gloves.

He's mostly beyond worrying. He had to do what he had to do. There was no getting away from it. And he'd seen with his own eyes the effect his reminders had had. He'd not laid a finger on him, but he'd offered Santie food for indefinite, tormenting thought. He'd pinpointed experiences for the man to contemplate alone, without the support of his helpers. Immobile, in the silence, preparing to meet his Lord.

Chapter Twenty-two

Gillian

I arrive at Laura's house just after a quarter to six, drive through her painted white metal gates and park on the spacious uncluttered tarmac area, at the front. Most of her front garden is wall-to-wall tarmac. There's a small corner of concrete-edged shorn grass, and two nicely clipped cone-shaped box bushes in modern metal containers either side of the front door, but otherwise you get the feeling that Nature, and especially soil, isn't quite welcome at Laura's home, unless it's strictly controlled and in small, manageable quantities.

The house itself, not surprisingly, is quite similar to Claire's. On the same kind of modern, moneyed middle-class development. If anything, Claire's place is a touch more interesting and colourful, Laura's being a more subdued, toned-down sibling property. Virtually everything inside and out is clean-stone coloured, in bland shades of white, grey and cream, which, as Laura and Claire agree, conveniently 'go with absolutely anything and everything'.

As I get out of the car and go towards the front door, I notice a slight flickering in the white vertical, office-type blinds in the front window. My arrival has been noted. I'm just on the point of pressing the rubber encased door buzzer when the door opens.

It's Tony. Who else? 'Hi Gillian.' He acknowledges me solemnly, immediately stepping outside, closing the inner door, pulling the front door almost to behind him. He narrows his eyes slightly. His tone's flat. There's no buoyant, flirty 'Hi Gillie' for me tonight.

'Oh, hi, Tony,' I say, as neutrally as I can, passing him the bottle of wine. 'Bit late, as usual, sorry. Another bottle of rosé. I wasn't sure what to bring this time, but seeing as Claire's favourite is the rosé at the moment, I thought Laura wouldn't mind it either. Being as they can be quite similar?'

He takes the bottle from me quickly, almost snatches it.

'What the *fuck* do you think you were doing, telling Laura about me and Kelly like that?' Tony hisses, under his breath. He brings his face up close to me. He's reeking of whiskey, already. 'And Claire knows all about it too now, you got Laura so worked up. I tell you, I'm only just hanging in here, Gillian. I'm fucking struggling to try and rescue this marriage. And it's no thanks to yourself. I thought we'd had an understanding? I mean, I owned up to you, didn't I? I thought that was the end of it? It never crossed my mind you'd have to go on and tell Laura as well.'

'Laura knew there was something up before I said anything, Tony. She was worked up already. She wanted to know what was happening, so I told her. And I told you I was still thinking about what I was going to do. No, actually it wasn't the end of it for me. We didn't have any *understanding*, Tony. We've never really understood each other, have we? And yes, eventually you *owned up*. But if you could've got away with it, we both know you'd have lied through your back teeth to save yourself. Stand back a bit? I'm hearing you well enough, from where you are.' I put my hand out, indicate to Tony I want him to move away from me. He backs off. Physically, at least. I'm clear and clean with it, not holding back. *Let's bloody finish this thing, once and for all, Tony.*

'But I thought you and me were *family,* Gillian? Isn't family about looking after each other? Supporting each other's lives, marriages, the kids?' My sly little weasel brother-in-law, Tony. Though to be fair, a weasel, or any other animal, has a lot more integrity.

There's a noise suddenly, from inside the house. Someone else is coming out, working at the inner door handle. It's Robbie. He opens the front door, beer can snug in hand. It seems incongruous, seeing Robbie at a front door instead of in an armchair facing the TV.

'Hello, Gillian! How's about you? You're taking your time coming in. How's the holiday been going?' There something reassuring about seeing Robbie. Like the sight of a steady lighthouse or a simple familiar guiding rock on an otherwise unmarked stretch of coast.

'Alright, thanks, Robbie,' I reply. 'I've been enjoying myself. Getting some work done too.'

Tony gives me a dark glowering look then turns back into the house with my bottle.

'Glad to hear it,' Robbie says. He steps outside, closing the front door behind him, just as Tony did. He stays at his usual distance, hand in trouser pocket, taking a swig from his can, lowers his deep voice. 'And good for you too, Gillian. I mean about keeping us all right. Your man's only had what's been coming to him.'

'Yes, I think so too, Robbie, although . . .' I don't quite know where it's all going to go from here. I cross my arms, look down for a minute. How it's going to be when I go inside and meet Laura and Claire.

'C'mon in, Gillian. We'll get you a nice wee glass of wine. They're still in the kitchen doing the tea, like, but it'll not be long. Chilli con mince, apparently. But what do *I* know? We'll be alright.' There's something touching and dependably genuine about Robbie. He tries his best to tell it as it is, as he finds it, with and without prejudice.

'Yes, we will, Robbie,' I tell him, as he turns back into the house. I follow him inside, into the warm hall smelling of cooking, fresh paint and new carpet.

For the first time in his life, as long as I've known him, Robbie goes straight ahead, instead of into the lounge, and knocks on the door of Laura's kitchen. I follow him. He opens the door, not waiting to be answered. 'Gillian's here,' he says. 'Just getting a glass of wine from the fridge.'

As soon as the door's open, I hear the whirr of the extractor fan, see Laura and Claire, standing with their glasses talking, in flowery summer dresses, their backs to the sink.

'We're almost ready,' Claire answers Robbie. Then notices me looking through, standing behind him. 'We'll be there in a minute, Gillian, okay? The chilli's done, the rice isn't too far off. Have a seat in the lounge and Robbie'll be through with your drink.' She speaks like a dental receptionist. Whatever happens, some things must stay the same, must never give. We could simply say hello, acknowledge each other with something spontaneous, start anew. But we don't.

'Okay, Claire,' I agree, giving up, taking her cue and going with it. 'See you in a minute.'

I go into the lounge while Robbie's getting my drink. The news is on the TV. Tony's sitting at one end of the settee, nursing an empty whiskey tumbler. I sit down on the other end, saying nothing, and stare at the screen too. Out of the corner of my eye, I see him turn in my direction, look at me, shake his head and return to the news.

'Here you go, Gillian,' Robbie says as he comes in, a wine glass in one hand, another beer can in the other. He hands me my drink, then goes to his armchair and tends to filling his beer glass with the concentration of a squirrel on a rediscovered prize hazelnut. He relaxes back. There's an inane staged family quiz on. The three of us stare at it without a word. Tony gets himself another glass of whiskey.

It's not before Laura appears at the door. 'Tea's ready,' she says. 'Want to come through?'

We gather in Laura's dining room with the polished smoked glass-topped table and high-backed black basket-weave chairs. In spite of her carefully handwritten place cards, Laura makes sure we sit in the right seats, then disappears to help Claire dish up in the kitchen.

The starter's a tepid glass of grapefruit and orange segments, from a tin. There's a dull, mottled whiteness about them that reminds me of calcium-deficient, speckled nails. Robbie lifts them up whole, tosses them into his mouth, swallows them down with a shake of his neck like a guzzling herring gull. Tony looks sullen, eats without a word, as does Laura. She looks pale, weary and older in spite of her heavy full make-up.

'So, you've been having a good holiday then, Gillian?' Claire starts up, as she works away at her starter, diligently cutting her fruit into smaller, more polite pieces.

'Yes, great,' I reply briefly, just eating, not supplying the further details she's after. 'Where are the kids? Haven't seen them for ages.'

'Another wee sleepover,' Laura explains. 'We thought it'd be just as well. We can all eat in peace and we'll not have the hassle of getting everybody into bed. You'll not have to cope with our usual routine.'

'It wouldn't be a problem. I wouldn't have minded. And I'm not staying that late anyway.'

'Somewhere better than here to be going later on?' Tony inquires snidely, briskly. Needing to blame, desperate to deflect negative attention away from himself onto me. He searches for affirming eye contact with Laura, wanting her on board.

'Sure, we're only *family*, aren't we, Gillian?' she says, acknowledging him apparently graciously, giving me the critical eye. She's starting to replace the cement, repointing their marriage, even if she has to sell her soul to get the job done.

'Just going back to the cottage,' I tell him, impassively. 'Hoping to get plenty done again tomorrow. I'm not so good with late nights anymore, generally.'

'So, you've not managed to pull that fella next door yet then?' Tony strikes again, in a mocking tone. 'I'd have thought someone with your feminine wiles . . .? Being as it's only the two of you staying there, no competition.' He pushes his empty starter plate forward, puts an elbow on the table, rests his chin on his hand and stares at me.

Robbie frowns slightly in Tony's direction and reaches for his beer. Laura gives Tony a forced smile then looks towards Claire for support. Claire laughs along, in collusion with Tony. He may have offended, but things need to be getting back on track. They both look to me to join in and laugh it off to show Tony he's amusing and accepted, still loved.

'Not really your business, is it, Tony?' I answer tersely, instead. 'And *pulling*'s not so much my personal style, these days. Though, seeing as you're asking, for what it's worth, David's lovely. We've been having a great time.'

I set down my spoon, lift my wine glass and toast Tony with it before taking a mouthful, then continue staring back at him. Tony's clearly trying to keep his face straight, although his mouth twitches with tension and embarrassment. He blinks hard as if his eyes are smarting. He shifts self-consciously in his chair.

'Och for crying out loud, spare us the bloody details, will you, Gillian?' Laura slams in.

'Tony was only having a bit of fun, pulling your leg!' Claire follows on. 'Too much information, Gillian. We don't need to know the details of your love life, do we?'

'Well, maybe he shouldn't have asked her then?' It's Robbie, coming back at Claire, nodding over in Tony's direction. He's holding onto his pint glass on the table, just keeping it there, for moral support. His voice sounds bolder than it's sounded in all the years I've known him. Good old Robbie. Coming through, cutting the crap.

'What was that, Robbie?' Claire answers, taken aback.

'Tony was asking her, wasn't he? Sticking his nose in. Good for you, Gillian! You deserve to have a bit of a life. Get on and enjoy yourself now and think yourself lucky you're not tied up here like the rest of us, boring ourselves fucking stupid. Cheating, flaming bickering.' Robbie sits more upright in his chair, his voice clear, uncontrite. He sounds more alive, proud of himself.

'That's more than enough now, Robbie. Don't be forgetting, we're in Laura and Tony's house,' Claire warns him, lifting her finger. 'Don't be stirring things up. We'd agreed we weren't going to mention . . . '

'What, Claire?' Robbie asks, straight out.

'You know!' Claire motions awkwardly towards Tony with her head. She's in a state of bewilderment. Robbie's new-found defiance was never even pencilled into her script.

'Tony messing with Kelly, you mean?'

Laura's eyes well up, her mouth starts trembling, she covers it with her hand. She pushes back her chair, gets up, leaves the dining room, slamming the door behind her.

'Christ, Robbie! Look what you've done now, will you?' Tony tells him, bitterly screwing up his serviette, getting up and throwing it in a dramatic gesture down onto his chair. 'You couldn't just leave things be, could you? And what do you think you're doing, taking sides with *her?*'

'I'm not taking sides. Just telling the truth. You'd better go and see to your wife. She'll be needing your attention,' Robbie suggests evenly. 'I rest my case,' he adds, in my direction, widening his eyes and seeming pleased with how he's acquitted himself.

I smile back at him in acknowledgement. Claire eyes him with contempt.

'Whatever you were thinking of there, I've no idea, Robbie. But whatever it was, I'll have to go and see Laura. Why couldn't you just leave them in peace to have their tea? They're certainly not going to be able to manage anything now. Feeling proud of yourself, are you?'

Robbie and I exchange glances and begin to laugh.

Claire gives an exasperated snort, getting up. 'You and I'll be having words later, Robbie. Don't think you'll be getting away with this. I'll not be getting you any more cans for a while, I can tell you. And there's a whole pot of good chilli wasted now. It's a crying shame.'

'Don't worry about that, Claire. We'll make sure it's not wasted. Fancy some chilli, Gillian? How about I put a couple of bowls of it out for us and we'll bring it through and eat in front of the telly? Might be more relaxing in the other room. Feels a bit like a bus station after midnight in here.'

'Don't you dare!' Claire snaps back at him, as she reaches the door. 'Laura'll not want her lounge smelling of food. You never get the smell of garlic out of curtains and carpets.' She gives Robbie a final look of disapproval and leaves the room. We can hear the pounding of her footsteps as she hurries up the stairs to comfort Laura and rescue Tony.

In spite of Claire's prohibition, Robbie brings us each a large bowl of Laura's chilli mince with a soup spoon, to eat in the lounge conspiratorially. 'Laura's still crying her eyes out by the sounds of it. They'll probably be a while up there,' he says, as he hands over my bowl. 'Though better not hang about with eating it. Get that down you. Once it's down, it's down. There'll be no taking it off us then.'

We watch a wildlife programme, freed up from the imperative to make small talk for the sake of it. I can't remember eating with such a feeling of relaxation before at Laura's home. Something, no doubt, to do with the fact that neither of my sisters are actually in the room.

'Thanks, Robbie,' I tell him. 'I hope you're not going to get into too much trouble over this?'

'Sure, it'll pass over, Gillian. It all passes, doesn't it? And if I do, I do. Wee bit of dangerous living for a change. Closest to a thrill I'm likely to get. And with any luck, I'll have my cans back within a week,' he says, winking, enjoying himself. 'Don't know about you, but I'm starving! They didn't build the Titanic on a tin of orange and grapefruit segments, did they? We'll be doing them a favour anyway - Claire and Laura hate wasting food.'

'Though the smell won't go unnoticed.' I can't get over how different Robbie suddenly is.

'Och sure, Laura's not short of air freshener, is she? Your sisters buy the stuff in like they're needing to fumigate a factory,' Robbie returns. He's got a taste of revolution and he's not giving up. Probably tomorrow he'll have to go back to the old regime, but tonight he's making the most of his moment of freedom.

When Claire reappears about half an hour later, her expression is suitably solemn and composed. In spite of the air freshener, the lounge is bound to be smelling of food, but she doesn't comment.

'I think we should all be making a move,' she tells us. It's not a suggestion. 'Laura's calmed down a bit, but she's exhausted herself. And I think we should give them the time they need as a couple to talk.' I'm sure Claire's concerned about Laura, but you can also tell there's a part of her that feels pleased to be in charge and in her long-standing role as indomitable saviour and knowledgeable agony sister.

'Right you be,' Robbie agrees, getting up, keeping his head down, no doubt thankful he's been spared his usual immediate ticking-off.

'And you'll be taking those glasses through to the kitchen for us, Robbie?' Claire adds, still reminding him of his place. 'I'm not sure we'll be able to see you again before you go back, Gillian. Although it sounds like you've got plenty of company anyway. You'll need to mind and be discreet in front of the owner. And I hope to God you're being . . . careful?'

'Sorry, Claire? *Careful?*'

'As in, if you can't be good, be *careful*,' Robbie puts in, smiling as he leaves the room with our glasses.

'Oh right. Thanks for that, Claire. Although I think by now, being as I'm in my forties, I might've managed to work that one out. Or not?' I tell her, getting up.

'As long as you know what you're doing, Gillian. I mean, I thought you'd as good as made up your mind at this stage in your life to concentrate on your career,' Claire says grimly. 'Nothing worse than a woman in her forties making a fool of herself.'

And you would know that, wouldn't you, Claire? I can't stand the way she assumes the right to view me within the same restrictive framework of fixed 'stages' as she views herself. It's as if she wants you to accept that most of your life is a totally foregone conclusion, and once you're at a certain 'stage', there's no going back, let alone forward.

'Right, Claire. So, will we help Laura clear up?'

'No. Robbie and I'll do it quickly before we go. You may as well get yourself home. Give them a shout up the stairs, so they know you're going. And phone us on Saturday before you leave,' Claire says, her parting words a list of instructions.

'I will. I hope ... Look after yourself, Claire?' I go to hug her goodbye. She'll always be my one and only older sister, but I know already she'll be as stiff and unrelenting in her body with me as she is in her mind. She allows the hug for a few seconds and gives me a glancing kiss on the cheek.

'Goodbye for now, Gillian. We'll be in touch,' she briefly acknowledges, moving towards the door. 'Gillian's going, Robbie,' she calls through to him, as I make my way into the hall.

'I'm off now,' I shout upstairs to Laura and Tony, not really expecting a reply. Robbie comes out with a tea towel over his arm to say goodbye.

'Enjoy yourself, Gillian,' he says, warmly, as he opens the front door for me. 'Make sure you do everything I'd do, if I got the chance,' he adds, with a wink.

'Thanks, Robbie. Tell all the kids I'm asking after them, won't you?'

I'm on my way through the door when I hear Laura's voice behind me and turn back. She's standing looking down from the top of the stairs, her face pale, eyes shadowy with rubbed mascara, hair dishevelled.

'Bye, Gillian,' she says, in a fragile voice, her nose and throat congested from crying. 'Give us a ring before you're leaving? Tony says to pass on his goodbye.'

I feel sorry for her, she looks so empty and shattered. Whatever's happened in the past, I genuinely wish there was something I could do to help her.

'I will. And pass the same on to Tony, won't you? Hope you get things sorted out.'

It's a relief to be outside again in the cool summer evening air, such a sane contrast to the claustrophobic, pent-up atmosphere of Laura and Tony's centrally heated house, overcast by the gloom of their rocky relationship.

When I get back to the cottages, I find David standing, cup in hand, in the doorway of his cottage, looking out on the yard.

'Your turn for yard gazing and gathering gossip?' I suggest, as I get out of my car.

'Yep. Just been speaking to Derek and the dog. They were asking for you. Left us each some carrots and spuds. Have a good evening? Want a drink? Hospitality's not as good as the standard next door. But if you'll take a chance?'

I put my arm round his waist, slip underneath his shoulder. Face out with him onto the yard. For a moment, I have an image in my head of that weathered old gorse bush shelter with the trodden mud floor, with just enough room for two sheep. I'm thinking of how much more at home I feel here with this man who I've met only just a week ago than I did at my sisters' houses. Perhaps, even at my 'stage' in life, as Claire puts it, there might be other possibilities?

'Tea would be good,' I tell him. 'I'll take a chance with the hospitality. Different from next door's maybe, but I'm sure it'll pass the inspection.'

Chapter Twenty-three

Gillian

It's Wednesday morning, just after eleven. David and I have been sitting out in the corner of the field where we drank the whiskey together. The sun's hot already and he's dozing while I'm sketching, concentrating on the stone wall in front of us edging the field and the horizontal layers of hedge and sky beyond.

When my mobile buzzes, David jerks slightly but doesn't wake. I get up and answer it, heading further across the field so as not to disturb him.

'Gillian?'

'Laura? I hadn't expected to hear from you so soon. Are you alright?'

'No. No, Gillian, I'm not alright. I'm fucking not alright,' she repeats, crying, her voice breaking up.

'What's happening? Is it about Tony or something else?' I can't help sighing. Part of me feels weary. Aren't we just going to go over the same things again and end up in the usual cul-de-sac? At the same time, I notice something different and less managed in the way she speaks that makes me keep listening.

'Yes, it's still about Tony. But this time . . .

This time it's about me too. I won't, I can't do this anymore. I've had enough. It's making me feel so crap.'

'I'm really sorry, Laura. I can only imagine... It is crap. You must feel awful. Do you want me to come over? I mean I know you're probably busy there, but...' I offer, anticipating her response.

'I'll come to you. I need to talk,' she replies unexpectedly, her voice suddenly firmer. 'Why don't we meet on the shore? At that first spot along the lough where we used to swim and have picnics when we were younger? Unless you've made other plans already?'

'No, that's fine, Laura. As long as you feel alright to drive. Meet you there in three quarters of an hour?'

David looks quizzically at me when I tell him that Laura has been in touch and asked me to meet her down by the lough. No one is more surprised than I am.

In spite of the heat, I shiver as I stand close to our old picnic place, waiting for Laura.

Parts of your world can be the same for a long time. No matter how uncomfortable, you accept that you have to adjust and live with things you never imagined you'd put up with. You start to assume things will remain that way. But then, occasionally, without warning, everything changes. It's like swimming over small wave after small wave, taking for granted that your body can stay at exactly the same angle. But then you get that bigger breaker, reminding you that change, however unexpected sometimes, is always possible.

I don't know why Laura wants to meet me now and especially why she's offered to come my way to a place outdoors that she herself has connected with our childhood. What would she need to talk to me about so desperately that she's prepared to abandon her home routine? *It's about me too. I've had enough. It's making me feel so crap.* The way she was crying, her words, and her tone especially, seemed quite out of kilter with her usual scripted style.

Whatever's on her mind, Laura's timekeeping isn't affected. Exactly forty-five minutes on from our phone call, she has parked her car and is walking towards me on the shore. Her pale legs are bare, she's wearing a strange combination of a smart navy skirt, flat summer sandals, a flowery cagoule and a pair of sunglasses on her head. She's carrying a woven straw beach bag and has two rugs, including what looks very like our old family tartan rug tucked under her arm.

'Where do you want to sit? Up here okay?' she shouts over, stopping some distance away from me, setting down her bag and pointing up to the long grass.

'Yes, fine,' I answer, going back to join her where she's spreading the tartan rug. 'Didn't know you'd kept that rug. It's the one Mum and

Dad had when we were children, isn't it? Looking a bit threadbare now. But still thick with memories. And isn't that their old thermos and cups?'

'Yes. Tony kept saying we should get rid of them, but I never wanted to. You change, but some things about you never do. Giving those things up would've broken my heart.'

She was pale and stiffly composed at first, but her eyes are filling up now, her voice is faltering again. She takes her sunglasses off her head and puts them on. We sit down side by side on the rug.

'Appreciate you coming at such short notice, Gillian. I'm sure you've other things to be getting on with. Want a cup of coffee? I've got sweeteners, but sorry there's no milk. I just needed to get out as soon as I could.' She's already unscrewing the flask, setting the plastic mugs on the rug. No matter how upset she is, Laura has to be *doing* something.

'You didn't have to think about bringing anything, Laura. But thanks, black coffee, no sweetener would be good. So, what's going on with you and Tony now? You were obviously upset when I was round for tea, but I thought you were talking, trying to work things out?'

Laura doesn't say anything for a while. She takes a sip of coffee and sets the mug down, off the rug, making a hollow in the grass so that it stays upright. Then puts her hands on her knees and closes her eyes, making herself breathe more slowly and deliberately, obviously in an attempt to calm herself before starting to speak.

'You and I haven't talked properly for a long time, Gillian. What with you being away and us living very different lives,' she begins, putting her sunglasses back up on her head, looking directly at me now. Her eyes are bloodshot, heavily shadowed underneath. 'I know you think most of what I do is pretty humdrum and conventional. You've always been the exciting, glamorous one.'

'On my own most of the time, working with glass in a basic studio in scruffy jeans and T-shirts? No, Laura. You've always had this thing about me being more talented, somehow better at things than you. It's just not true. I could never take on the responsibility of looking after all those sick people the way you do.'

'Och, I'm sure you could. You're clever, you're got plenty of confidence in yourself. Which is more than can be said for . . .' She sighs, shakes her head. 'Sure, I'm just nothing these days compared to how I was. I'm pathetic. I'm such a pathetic, stupid cow.' Her tone is sneering, sneering at herself. She's on the edge of crying again, covers her mouth with her hand. In spite of, because of, her distress, I feel she's finally talking just as herself, stripped of her social veneer.

'What's going on, Laura? Tell me what's really going on?'

'You see, the thing is, Tony's not the only

person who's been lying, Gillian,' she says quickly, spikily, shifting gear, folding her arms over her chest.

'What do you mean?'

'I've been putting on this act for such a long time, Gillian. This isn't the only time Tony's been unfaithful. He's been messing around with loads of girls over the years. He has this addictive thing for girls in their late teens – he never goes for women of his own age. I've never been able to tell anyone before.'

'Och, no.' After all the years of thinking I knew Laura to the point where I could have almost written her side of a conversation in advance, I'm lost for words. I didn't see this coming at all. What made me assume that I could forever second-guess her? 'I'm so sorry, Laura. How horrible for you. You should've . . . '

She's started now. No matter how painful it is, she needs to pour out her story. 'I've caught him at it a few times myself. The first time it was this wee girl they had doing work experience. I was on days at the hospital and hadn't been well, so they'd sent me home early from work. I thought I'd call quickly into his office on my way back. The two of them were all over each other in the front of his car round the back of the building. They didn't see me, they were so engrossed. I drove away. I only just managed to get home before I vomited. It seemed surreal, like I must've dreamt it. Then there was the time at his friend's wedding.

I could tell from the start of the reception that he had his eye on one of the young waitresses. He'd had a lot to drink and started putting his arm round her waist and whispering in her ear at the bar. She didn't seem to mind. Later in the evening, he told me that he was taking a walk in the hotel grounds to try and sober up a bit. "You might want to go and see what your man's up to outside, pet," one of his colleagues' wives told me about fifteen minutes later. I felt sick to my stomach.' Laura lets her head fall forward and closes her eyes as she relives the grief and humiliation.

'Laura, you don't have to tell me. Don't go over it if it's too much,' I say.

'It is, but I have to, Gillian. I want to. When I went outside, the same waitress was on the bonnet of one of the cars with her legs wrapped round Tony and he was fiddling with the buttons of her blouse. I screamed his name. He left her there and rushed over to me, all stupid, pissed apologies. It was just a wee bit of silly fun, he told me. I started hitting him hysterically, but as soon as he held me, I just dissolved into tears. I was so exhausted with work and the kids at the time. In the end I decided not to make a meal of it, however hurt I was. He would never do it to me again, he assured me. But as time went by, he couldn't give up carrying on. There were lots of other times after that – I didn't witness them, but there were all the obvious signs – dinner and hotel receipts, last-minute urgent work arrangements.

Sometimes I've tried to convince myself I had to be imagining it and I've not said anything. At other times I've confronted him. We've argued, and he's kept telling me I'm insecure and it's all in my mind. I've been feeling worse and worse, but I couldn't bring myself to tell anyone. I needed to hang on to the front of a happy marriage. And other people's respect and admiration for us. Apart from the children, it seemed like all I had left.'

'Och, Laura, what a nightmare. I mean, you know I've never really got on with Tony, but . . . He's such a self-centred stupid bastard. And you didn't even feel you could confide in Claire?' I ask almost automatically, struggling to take in what she's saying.

'No, I didn't. Claire and I have been through a lot together over the years. Nothing against her, but I knew telling her would make it all the more real and painful for me to live with. Marriage is so important to her. She enjoys the fact we have that in common. And it's helped me to feel more on a par with her, even if she's so much better and in charge of her life than I am. It's like even now, she just wants me to persevere and make it work.'

'Though when it matters, she usually on your side, isn't she? And to be fair, she doesn't know yet what's really happened and everything you've had to put up with, does she?'

'That's true. Probably if she did, she'd be sympathetic. And understand that all I feel like doing now is . . .' Laura wipes her nose on the cuff of her cagoule.

'Is . . .?'

'Leaving Tony. Stopping pretending I'm still in love with him. Starting a new life with just me and the kids. Being honest again. Getting back my self-respect. Doing what Mum and Dad would tell me to do. Sounds pathetic, but I just wish they were still here, Gillian, so wish they were here. I miss them so much.' She holds her face in both hands and sobs, rocking to and fro.

'I know. It's not pathetic. So do I,' I tell her quietly. 'It's going to be alright, Laura. You'll be alright.'

I lift the other picnic rug, drape us both with it and put my arm round her. She rests her head on my shoulder. 'I know we don't always get on and it's not the same as when Mum and Dad were here, but we're still sisters, aren't we? We can still talk to each other if we need to. The future's not set in stone. Things can always be different if we want them to be, can't they?'

'Yes. I really hope so,' Laura replies. 'I'm not sure what I'm going to do, but . . . '

I don't know what to say. I simply keep my arm around her and we sit in silence, nodding as a seemingly smiling, breezy woman with an obedient Highland terrier walks past.

'Who knows? You could always take the ferry and come and stay with me sometime if you wanted to,' I offer gently, after a while.

We sit on together, looking forward, out to the lough. The tide is further out now and a new untouched surface of sand is emerging, free again of footprints.

David and I spend our last two days on holiday together. I decide not to do any more work – I don't want to feel divided or as if I'm juggling as usual. There are times when you have to let yourself have some unscripted moments of pure joy.

On the Thursday we drive up to the north coast, explore the beaches at Portrush and Portstewart, then go to the Giant's Causeway. On the Friday we leave the peninsula, head round and down towards the Mourne mountains, get sandwiches in Newcastle and walk along the beach by Murlough Nature Reserve. Looking out to sea, perched up in a Marram grass 'nest' in the dunes, there's part of me feels like a child again.

'It's a shame, isn't it? So many people across the water are still putting off coming here. Even so many years on after the Troubles,' I say.

'You're right,' David agrees. 'They can't get away from thinking it'll never change. There's still the chance old fires will reignite. But Northern Ireland's not the only part of the world where there's that risk.'

'It certainly isn't. When this is where you come from, in spite of everything that's happened, you know how beautiful the place itself is. No human in-fighting can taint it.'

The power of the landscape can take you over, in the same way that the sun does sometimes. It brings you back into your body, the reality of your senses. There's nothing like being able to stand alone or with someone you trust, facing the sea. Allowing yourself to know that you can simply exist, you don't have to justify yourself. You naturally belong with everything else. You're as much a part of Nature as a rock or an oyster-catcher is. Bare as you were born. As you were and will be. The tangles and politics of human society go on, but here, facing the sea, you'll always have a place.

Chapter Twenty-four

Manchester, late August.

David

It's been a pig of a day. He's been working a lot of late nights through into the early hours, so it hardly feels as if he's ever away from the job. Two of the team are still off sick. So much to weigh up and hold in his mind. A lot ongoing, new things coming to light, starting to really kick off.

It's already seven, thankfully a good bit cooler. He doesn't mind heat when he can get outdoors, by the sea, but this hot spell's dragging on, adding to the oppressive burden of his workload and being back in a city.

He nips back home for a break, to get a bite to eat and put his feet up for a while, although he'll not really be able to relax knowing he's going to have to go back out again, expecting his mobile to ring at any minute. His flat's like a tip, the way it always is when he's working like this. Unwashed dishes and pots in the kitchen sink, glasses and cups all over the place, laundry piling up, wads of unchecked bills, letters and junk mail lying on the table in the hall. He'll have to do something with it all by tomorrow. Gillian's coming over from Liverpool to stay with him at the weekend. She'll hardly thank him if he leaves it like this.

347

After he's had a sandwich, David takes his cup of coffee through to his small home office and turns on his computer. It relaxes him sometimes to look at this and that online, just idly surfing, following what takes his interest at the time. Although recently, he's been keeping an eye on two particular newspaper websites, looking out for something quite specific. News of Santie's funeral.

At the beginning of the week, while searching the Death Notices, he read the final confirmation of the man's demise, couched in the conventional words he'd read so often, to apply to the passing of the good and the bad alike. Anodyne, impartial acknowledgements, saying nothing really about the deceased. Respectful, yet at the same time denying the individual's identity, noting the facts, recording some of the connections within a life. Using soft, 'appropriate' words with the intention of dignifying the beloved and soothing those in mourning, undermining those words' original value and meaning, by pasting them in, attaching them unconditionally to all, irrespective of whether or not they'd earned or deserved them. An earthly version of an anticipated, mass heavenly pardon?

Can the fact of your death really atone for what you've said and done? But sure, they're always someone's husband, or parent or son? Bless them. R.I.P? Santie, the twisted, merciless tormentor. But still the 'beloved husband', the 'ever loving father', the one 'deeply missed' by his 'sorrowing family and community.'

David gets the newspaper home webpage up on screen. On the left side of the page there's a heading for Local News. Below it, a section with some of the main stories, with the beginnings of the articles you can read in full, by clicking on a heading to take you to another screen.

'Bloody hell!' he says out loud, as he begins to read the excerpt from the second listed story. 'Car defaced before funeral', he reads first. Then, 'Police are making inquiries in connection with the defacement of a car belonging to a late respected champion of the community.' He clicks quickly on 'Read more,' switching to the page with the short full article.

Family, friends and community were devastated to learn that on the morning of the funeral of a man known affectionately in his home town as 'Santie', his car had been spray-painted with a highly offensive, defamatory message, which included the word 'rapist'. Family friend and community spokesman, Rob Brown, said, 'I'm sure I speak for us all, in expressing my profound shock that such mindless disrespect has been shown to a man who has spent his days doing his utmost to help the people of his beloved community. Whoever has done this knows who they are. They will have to carry it on their conscience for the rest of their days. They fully deserve to be punished by the law. However, we will not allow this disgusting incident to cast any shadows over the memory of our dear brother in Christ. We will continue to grieve for his loss and always thank the Lord for the example of his loving and giving life.' The woman arrested is thought to be local. Otherwise no further information about her has been disclosed at this time.

'*Yes!*' David brings his fist down on the desk, hard. That such news fills him only with a sense of triumph and vindication is a mark of the depth of his hatred of the man, and clarity about his rare perversity. In all his years in the police, there are few people who have left him quite so cold and emptied of compassion. He may or may not find out who the woman was. Who knows how many other women were raped by Santie? But he'd still be very surprised if it wasn't Linda.

Liverpool, late August.

Gillian

I get out of bed and head to the bathroom. It's already 9.30 a.m. I'd put the alarm on snooze and overslept. These mornings, I feel as if I could sleep for years. I've been late finishing in the studio most nights since I came back from Northern Ireland, pushing myself on, almost manically developing different pieces of glass work from my collection of sketches. I'm pleased with what I've achieved and also fairly confident I'll not have a problem selling the work. The quality is consistent, strong and lively. The wind is sweeping through it, the light, the colours shifting. It's full of the water's movement, a sense of the particular place and its authentic, natural voice. The piece I'm most pleased with so far is propped up by the window of my living room. It's one I developed from the drawing I did, sitting on the low concrete wall, thinking about how that narrow strip of causeway, connected to that small tear-shaped island, would look as on a map, from the air. All the memories are still very much with me, of being alone with the landscape and also of being with David.

I've continued to wonder what had affected David so deeply, what those things were in the past he couldn't speak of. What he'd meant when he'd said he'd let himself off that 'really big hook'. I still don't know. Maybe at some point I'll ask him about it again, or he might tell me in his own time.

I have an abiding memory of Derek, in the yard with the dog, waving us off as we each left in our own cars to drive home, his long blade of an arm raised, the way he'd greeted me when I'd first arrived. I've no doubt he'd picked up that something had happened between David and me. He kept giving us wry smiles. There was a touch of pride there. Perhaps because he'd known there might've been the possibility of us getting on, even before we could've known it ourselves. 'Make sure it's not long until you are coming back over, now,' he'd said, as we'd stood by my car. He'd carefully folded my cheque, slipped it into the back of his worn leather wallet and returned it to his jeans' pocket.

Laura and I have been in touch a few times since I got back. We don't usually spend a long time on the phone and neither of us pretends that we're suddenly completely on each other's wavelength, but something in us has reconnected and we can talk more honestly about what's happening and what we feel.

Soon after we spoke by the lough, Laura decided to confide in Claire as well. Claire is still 'reeling' from the information Laura says, 'disgusted' with Tony's behaviour and 'gutted' that Laura and Tony's marriage wasn't as happy as she believed it to be for so long. As I predicted however, she's firmly on Laura's side. Claire and I haven't yet spoken, though apparently she's glad that Laura was able to talk to me 'to get the ball rolling'. Since Tony moved out to live with one of his brothers, Claire and especially Robbie have been brilliant with her and the kids, Laura says. There's no doubt that the unthinkable has happened, but there are the makings of the foundations of a new life beyond.

Yesterday morning I discovered that I'm pregnant. I felt a sense of time suspended. In a state different from disbelief, somehow insulated from question or thought. The start of a life. Some stories begin so softly.

Before, when I'd tried to anticipate how I would be at such a time, I'd imagined much more extreme reactions. Surprise, excitement, apprehension – panic, even. Now, however, I feel just a quickening warmth. Something more like a quiet, simple nod of agreement. A feeling of hope that the course of life can be happily unpredictable, different from the past, not a foregone conclusion. Sometimes, there may be chinks of light. You may not have to spin in whirlpools or be carried in the currents you always believed were irresistible and inevitable.

I'll tell David when I see him in Manchester. It's not something I want to do over the phone. I can't begin to think about what this will mean for us, but what I know about him makes me trust and be hopeful he'll be glad; that however things unfold, we'll work it out.

Later, after I've checked my emails, I spend some time searching on the internet for inspiring images, as I often do. Before I go to the studio, I can't resist looking for pictures of developing embryos. Tiny pink curling projections. Semitranslucent; more or less symmetrical. The beginnings of human life. Presents, futures, embedding into pasts. Brave new peninsulas of flesh and blood.

*****

Acknowledgements

Susan and Paul Feldstein of The Feldstein Agency and Dalzell Press, my publishers and literary agents. For their belief in my writing. For all their work on *Peninsula,* for helping me to make it happen.

Jon Clayton, artist. For his beautiful cover painting. Jon's moving evocations of landscape both communicate and inspire a love of nature. They're breaths of fresh air.

All my family and friends. For their abiding encouragement. For all the conversations that fuel creativity and further understanding of the multiplicity of human experience.

.

Printed in Poland
by Amazon Fulfillment
Poland Sp. z o.o., Wrocław

64027022R10211